PRAISE FOR *THE WARNING*

FINALIST FOR THE PHILIP K. DICK SCIENCE FICTION AWARD

**WINNER OF THE PEN NEW ENGLAND SUSAN P.
BLOOM CHILDREN'S BOOK DISCOVERY AWARD**

★ "A fast-paced adventure that will keep readers compulsively turning pages to see what will happen next."

—*School Library Journal,* starred review

"An engrossing exploration of *what if…*"

—*VOYA Magazine*

"Measured pacing, captivating relationships, and unexpected plot… The breathtaking conclusion will leave you yearning for the second book."

—*The South Coast Almanac*

ALSO BY KRISTY ACEVEDO

The Fallout

THE WARNING

CONTENT WARNING

This book contains depictions of mental illness, including but not limited to anxiety, depression, PTSD, and suicidal ideation. In addition, it includes moments of physical abuse and violence.

If you or someone you know are in crisis, dial 988 or call the SAMHSA's National Helpline at 1-800-273-8255, or contact the NAMI Helpline by texting HOME to 741741.

THE WARNING

KRISTY ACEVEDO

sourcebooks
fire

Copyright © 2023 by Kristy Acevedo
Cover and internal design © 2023 by Sourcebooks
Cover design by Andrew Davis
Cover image © Magdalena Russocka/Trevillion Images
Internal design by Laura Boren/Sourcebooks

Sourcebooks and the colophon are registered trademarks of Sourcebooks.

Published by Sourcebooks Fire, an imprint of Sourcebooks
P.O. Box 4410, Naperville, Illinois 60567-4410
(630) 961-3900
sourcebooks.com

Originally published as *Consider* in 2016 in the United States by Jolly Fish Press, an imprint of North Star Editions, Inc.

Cataloging-in-Publication Data is on file with the Library of Congress.

Printed and bound in the United States of America.
WOZ 10 9 8 7 6 5 4 3 2 1

TO ELADIO, KYLEE, AND CHLOE

PART 1

MESSAGE ONE

Affliction comes to us, not to make us sad
but sober; not to make us sorry but wise.

—H. G. WELLS

CHAPTER 1

DAY 1: AUGUST

When the Boston outbound T screeches to a stop, I lose my grip on the silver pole and slam into Dominick. His black-rimmed glasses twist on his face, but he retrieves my purse from the floor before straightening them.

"You okay?" he asks and hands me my bag.

I nod and try to act nonchalant as I glance out the windows at the distant headlights of highway traffic. The train has stopped somewhere after the North Quincy station. My mind begins to spiral through possibilities. *Could be a suicide. Or a terrorist attack. Maybe a car exploded. With babies inside. Decapitated. And one survivor, the driver, left screaming on the side of the road. Little bloody hands and feet scattered on the tracks. Tiny severed toes.*

I fish in my purse for my anxiety meds and pop one little white savior.

"Seriously?" Dominick asks. "You already took one at the concert."

"It wore off." I swallow before he makes me feel guilty. Other passengers mutter about the delay, and each complaint seeps into my skin and mingles with my fears. "I knew we shouldn't have taken the train."

"Cheaper than parking at The Garden. Plus, no traffic."

"Except we're stuck." Dad wanted me home by 11:00, and my phone says it's already 9:45. If we don't get moving soon, I'm never going to make it home in time.

The image of tiny severed toes repeats in my brain.

"Why do you think the train stopped?" I ask. "You think someone pancaked on the tracks?"

"No, no. Probably something electrical. Happens all the time."

Pancaked. Brain oozing on the tracks. A mother with a spatula and tears.

I swallow hard and cross my arms over my chest. "I bet it's a suicide. Or a terrorist attack."

"No, it's nothing. It'll be fine." He moves in closer and brushes my neck with his fingertips. "Plus, I love being stuck with you. Tonight was so much fun. I wish you would stop worrying."

Like being with him should be a magical cure since he cares. But telling me not to worry is like telling me not to breathe. It's like tickling someone to cure depression.

To escape the gruesome images in my head, I trace the pale scar on Dominick's middle knuckle with my pointer finger, the scar he got trying to gut a striped bass for the first time with his father. He tucks one of my golden-brown curls behind my ear. His thumb slides down my neck and runs along the strap of my sundress, sending shivers across my shoulders even though the air conditioner is malfunctioning as usual. His touch brings me out of my head and back into my body. I wish we were alone.

"I can't believe we only have a few weeks left of summer," he whispers.

I peck his cheek. "I know. It went by so fast."

We both know what we're not saying. Senior year. The pressure's on. We started dating in April of our junior year, and only four months later, we already have to make major college decisions that could pull us apart. It's time to start my slow transformation into Alexandra Lucas, Kick-Ass Lawyer, and I'm afraid to let anything distract me from that future. Even him. It's hard enough for me to stay focused.

A sweaty man to my left bumps me with his shoulder and apologizes. His body odor absorbs my oxygen and makes my stomach twist. I lose focus on Dominick. To ground myself, I stare at the rainbow swirl pattern on the seats, the fake marbled black-and-white floor. The air becomes too heavy to breathe, too thick for my lungs to process. *What if I'm being poisoned by everyone's carbon dioxide?* The intense urge to pry the doors open or claw my way out of the tinted windows for fresh air builds inside me.

Ativan, please don't fail me now.

It usually takes ten minutes or so to kick in, so until it does, I need to focus on anything other than the fact that I'm trapped in a hot, crowded train. Think positive: at least we're not stuck underground. Maybe I should pick a fight with Dominick. Arguing helps me feel more in control. That's why I'll make an amazing defense lawyer, arguing my way to mental health while helping the underdogs of the world get a break for once.

My cell phone blares the *Stranger Things* theme song, snapping me into the moment. A shriveled woman sitting behind me jumps and mutters, "Jesus," so I silence my phone before answering. Rita Bernardino's name appears on the screen under a picture of Dominick, Rita, and me at our annual beach bonfire.

My best friend never calls. Only texts. She doesn't wait for hello. "Alexandra?" She only ever calls me Alex.

"What's going on?" I ask, then mouth Rita's name to Dominick. He raises one eyebrow behind his glasses and makes a goofy face by touching his tongue to his nostril. Wish I had time to take a photo so I could remember him like that.

"Did you see the news?" she continues in rapid speech.

"No, I'm stuck on the train with Dominick. What's wrong?"

Rita starts screaming facts that don't register in my brain. "In the last ten minutes—over three hundred so far—"

"Wait, slow down. What are you talking about?"

Sitting across from me, an elderly man wearing a corduroy coat much too heavy for early August rises from his seat. He points his arthritic finger at something beyond the window glass ahead of the train.

"God have mercy on us." His voice cracks.

People jump from their seats and crowd the windows. Dominick pulls me closer as we fight for a view. Rita continues yelling nonsense into my ear.

And then I see it. The train didn't stop for a suicide. Or a terrorist attack. It's something. Else.

———

If I could take the idea of technology and somehow turn it into a living thing, it would look like this thing. The size of a doorway, it glows a deep electric blue, the center shimmering like a metallic, moving liquid.

Like something has punched a hole into the fabric of the universe.

"No one knows what's going on," Rita says on the phone. I hadn't realized she was still talking, and she's not an easy person to ignore. "Eyewitness reports are rolling in. They've appeared all over the world."

"We're near one now," I manage to say. "I think the train stopped"—I take a breath—"since this thing's close to the tracks."

"No way." She pauses. "Take a picture."

"I'll call you back." I hang up without listening for her response.

My heart and lungs compete in a death match for my attention. I relay the jumbled information to Dominick and other passengers. Most people aren't bothering to listen; faces are glued to phones, and thumbs are doing the communicating.

The train conductor's voice booms over the crackling loud-speaker: "We've been advised to stop travel at this time. Please remain calm and exit the train when the doors open. Alternative transportation will be provided shortly."

One lady weeps. Another blesses herself with the sign of the cross and kisses a gold crucifix dangling from her necklace. She grips it so hard I'm afraid it's going to puncture her palm. Others stare out the window at the oval phenomenon hovering near the tracks in front of the train. Some hold up their phones to capture it on video.

My stomach churns like an angry ocean. I step away from the windows and take in a deep breath for a count of five, hold it for a count of two, and let it out slowly in six like I've been trained to do when my anxiety escalates. I repeat the ritual, but it's not designed for actual moments of terror. Dominick notices and squeezes my hand. My prescription beckons me from my purse, but two pills in one night is already pushing it.

A woman around my mother's age bursts into a fit of angry tears. Her traveling companion rubs her shoulders. I try not to stare.

Police officers, firefighters, and ambulances arrive and form a barrier around the supernatural occurrence. An army of city buses charges over the dark horizon and lines up in an abandoned lot to carry us to our destinations—my escape route from the mass of bodies surrounding me.

"Holy crap," another teenager says, holding the visor of his Red Sox hat. "Holy crap."

"Open the goddamn door," the old man in the corduroy coat yells. "Let us out of here!"

My feelings exactly. I focus on breathing again and visualize my safe space. *Island. Hammock. Book to read.* Dominick catches me rocking back and forth. I stop and feign coolness even though I'm ready to ignite.

"Are we gonna die?" a little boy asks his dad. The father lifts him onto his shoulders and says firmly, "Not on my watch."

I catch Dominick staring at the boy and the father. It must be hard for him. I squeeze his hand again, and my own worries sink below the surface.

Two high-pitched beeps fill the train before the automatic doors open. People file out in clusters. I'm not sure if we are being rescued or trading one bad situation for something worse. It seems wrong to leave the train in the middle of the tracks.

We have to pass the thing in order to cross the tracks and reach the buses. As we approach, no one talks. The perceived danger creates a reverent silence.

What if I accidentally fall inside? What if it's a black hole and it swallows us all? What if it's an alien-powered vacuum cleaner and we're the dirt?

Up close, other colors swirl inside of it, embers of green, silver, and a bright darkness. My eyes can't seem to focus on the depth. It's like watching a 3D movie without the glasses. Except instead of the 3D images projecting forward, the colors are falling inward.

Like an enormous, ridiculous, technological belly button.

The crowd fades into the periphery, and I forget about my own safety. The blue glow illuminates Dominick and me. Maybe it's the medication talking, but it's like I've walked onto the set of a great sci-fi movie, and my brain can't figure out if this is supposed to be scary or amazing.

It's both.

"This is like something outta Stephen King," Dominick says.

"*Doctor Who*. It has a happier ending," I joke back nervously. My pill has definitely kicked in. A warm invisible blanket has wrapped around my organs.

The crowd inches forward since no one wants to pass it. People continue to hold up their cell phones and take videos. The cops try to herd us over to the buses, and Dominick squeezes my hand tighter. It keeps me grounded.

Then something pushes through the blue fire in the oval.

The cops draw their weapons. Some people scream and run. I don't. Dominick pulls my hand to move, but I pull back. I'd like to credit my compulsion to stay on curiosity or stubbornness, but more likely it's the result of my meds dulling my reaction time.

The Something looks like a transparent human in a gray uniform. I can't take my eyes off it. "Hello," it announces to the crowd. "We've come to save you."

First contact. Binge-watching thousands of hours of sci-fi shows has trained me for this moment. I want to say, "Greetings from Earth. Live long and prosper," or stick my pointer finger out at it and ask, "Phone home?" but my stomach has swallowed my voice—a first for me.

"Freeze!" yell several cops at once. "Hands up!"

It reaches into its translucent coat pocket.

And they open fire.

Dominick forces me to the ground and lays his body on mine. I watch over his shoulder as the bullets pass right through the ghostly figure. The transparency gradually fills in, gaining weight and dimension, yet the bullets still have no effect on its now opaque body. It's the most advanced holographic image I have ever seen. More like an actual person than a projection of light.

The cops realize their error and cease fire. They shout at everyone to evacuate to the buses immediately for our own safety. Dominick pulls me up from the ground and straightens his glasses. I know I should leave, but my brain still wants to know what's going on. Ambiguity breeds anxiety.

The androgynous hologram holds out one hand like a mime and reveals a slip of paper the size of a sticky note. Everyone stops to watch. It's not a trick; we aren't under a type of mind control or magical spell. We simply recognize the moment as one for history, regardless of the consequences. The paper unfolds to form a three-dimensional image of Earth. The hologram sets it on its palm, and the paper Earth begins to rotate. Then in a calm, emotionless voice, it speaks.

"We are humans from a parallel future in the year 2359. We are here to save you. In six of your calendar months, a comet will destroy your planet. This is your known destruction; there is no way to prevent it."

The paper Earth silently ignites into a fireball, and then all traces of it vanish before our eyes.

"We have opened five hundred vertexes across your planet to send you to our time and dimension. We have enough space to accommodate all who wish to join us. Simply walk through one person at a time. It is your individual choice. Please bring minimal personal items. You will be given all the resources needed to live here.

"We apologize for using images as representatives, but we can only carry physical beings in one direction. Our images are equipped to answer your questions using our standard database responses available in multiple human languages.

"This automatic message will repeat once a day at each vertex location. You have approximately four thousand three hundred ninety-three hours to decide. The vertexes will remain open until then.

"Consider. Save your people. Save yourself before it is too late."

The crowd stands like a dangling participle, confused, pointless.

Sweat beads down my spine, and my pulse pounds behind my eardrums. Everything around me seems muffled, slow.

A bearded man from the horde breaks the silence and shouts at the hologram, "Who are you?"

I can't believe he asked that question. Wasn't he paying attention?

The hologram responds, "We are humans like you."

"Humans, my ass. This is alien invasion shit."

The hologram responds, "We do not understand."

The crowd laughs uneasily.

"They're not as smart as they think," a woman whispers to Dominick and me.

I can't laugh with them. A question burns inside my head, but my mouth battles with my mind for freedom and words. I take a deep breath and let loose.

"Why should we believe you?" I yell out over the crowd.

The hologram responds, "You have no other options."

CHAPTER 2

We crowd onto the buses. Dominick sits near the window, giving me the aisle seat. It's an automatic accommodation between us—like most of the decisions in our relationship. He knows that aisle seats make me feel more in control. Easier escape route. Rita calls us an old married couple because we are too easy together. She thinks peaceful is boring and that fighting would spice things up. She doesn't understand. She comes from a religious family, not a military one like mine.

As soon as I sit, the whirling thoughts resume in my head. *Alien invasion*—War of the Worlds. *Government conspiracy to hide the apocalypse from us.* At least with meds in my system, I shouldn't lose it. Dominick has never seen me in full-blown anxiety mode.

No one can take their eyes off the vertex and the hologram

outside the bus windows. Like rubbernecking a car accident. As the bus leaves, I strain to capture one last glimpse. I remember Rita's request and pull out my phone to take a picture. To show her. To show myself. Physical evidence that I'm not losing my mind.

My phone has three missed calls on the screen: Dad, Mom, and Benji. Only Mom left a message. The call from Benji surprises me the most. We don't usually talk. At least, not like that. Not since we were little.

"Benji called," I say to Dominick.

Dominick checks his glasses for damage. "Call him back. Maybe he knows something."

My older brother, Benjamin Lucas Jr., joined the military two years ago after he graduated from high school. Dad convinced him to follow in his footsteps since he served in the army during the Gulf War and appreciated every minute of it. Said it taught him how to be a man, how to serve his country, how to protect a nation. I think it taught him how to be strong, distant, and paranoid. Now that I think about it, Dad was probably all those things beforehand. Maybe the military heightens the personality traits that already exist in people. Benji joined the army, completed basic training, and has been on active duty, stationed in various overseas locations ever since. Last I knew, he was in Germany. He only calls my parents once a month, if that.

While I return Benji's call, Dominick calls his mother. He lets out a silent sigh and slides his phone back into his pocket. She never answers him—even when he stays late at my house, even when technology from another planet announces the possible apocalypse. Since his father died last year, she spends long days working and longer nights mourning.

Benji's phone rings once before going to voicemail. I almost leave him a message, but I'm not sure what to say. I'm not sure about anything right now.

Holograms have just descended and announced the end of the world. It has to be a scam.

Dominick's leg shakes up and down, making me more nervous. I place my hand on his knee to stop him.

"Sorry," he says. "The gunfire freaked me out."

Growing up with a military dad and brother, gunfire doesn't bother me. Dad used to bring me to the shooting range with him, believing every person should utilize their right to bear arms. Even me, his bookish daughter. He wants me to enroll in the military after graduation and use the GI Bill for college, but I want to go straight to college and major in pre-law. I can't wait to get away from the testosterone in my house and be around strong women for a change.

I pat Dominick's knee. Dad and Dominick have nothing in common except me. Maybe that's why I like him. Dominick thinks my father thinks that he's not man enough. What he doesn't understand is that my dad has antiquated ideas of what being a man is.

From a distance, the vertex glows on the dark horizon. It carries with it so many unanswered questions. I pick at a piece of Blue My Mind nail polish, peeling a whole section off my nail. Mom always nags me that nails matter—first impressions and everything, sign of good grooming. I wonder if she'll think they matter after this.

Dominick touches my elbow. "Alex, you're bleeding. Are you okay?"

I examine the back of my arm. A quarter-sized wound mixed with specks of dirt marks where I hit the ground. A stream of maroon blood trickles to my wrist. My first battle scar with the aliens.

"It's fine," I say. "It doesn't hurt." I search through my purse for a tissue.

His eyes tell me he's not convinced. He's probably thinking that it's his fault since he pushed me to the ground. He's always worrying about me, trying to protect me. Sometimes I like it. Sometimes it makes me feel small.

I press a tissue against my elbow to stop the bleeding. After a minute of silence, I ask him, "Do you think it's telling the truth?"

He deliberates longer than I expect. He runs both hands around the back of his neck and holds them there like a hammock for his thoughts.

"I think it's too soon to decide. It said we have six months. It's the beginning of August, so that would bring us to the end of January. That would mean"—he mentally calculates— "one hundred eighty-four days counting today."

In another hour or so, one hundred eighty-three days.

"It could be lying," he continues. "If there was really a comet capable of destroying the planet, we'd already know about it."

"You think the government would tell us this soon?" I chip at another piece of polish.

"I don't know. Maybe not. Depends if they thought they could do something about it. They wouldn't want us to panic early."

Panic: from Pan in Greek mythology, a satyr—half goat, half man—who was known to create irrational, sudden fear in people for fun. Something that happens to me when I feel trapped.

"What do you think happens now?" I ask.

Dominick looks at me, into me, like he'd really like to give me a clear answer because he knows that I overanalyze everything. He replies, "We wait."

When the bus pulls up to Beth Israel Deaconess Hospital instead of the train station where Dominick parked his car, passengers bombard the driver with questions.

"Just following orders," he announces. "They want to check everyone for radiation exposure."

"I don't like this," Dominick whispers to me. He hasn't been back in a hospital since his father died. At the time we were only friends, but his father's death bonded us together more than we expected. We spent every free moment texting and calling each other, and a few months ago he suddenly kissed me in my backyard. It's not a good idea starting a relationship in the spring of junior year, but no one ever said love was convenient.

Outside the bus windows, the hospital parking lot brims with activity. Officials covered in white hazmat suits with hooded masks usher passengers off the buses ahead of us.

Hazmat team. Oh shit, we've been poisoned by aliens. I touch my head to check my temperature.

"I'm calling my dad," I say to Dominick, almost as an apology. I take a deep breath and wait for the ring. Dad answers immediately.

"Alexandra, where are you?" he yells through the phone.

I go back to picking at my nails. "I'm fine. Just freaked out." I let my breath leak out like deflating a balloon.

"We've been calling you. Did you hear the news? Or are you too busy screwing around with Nick to care about what's happening in the world?"

I take another breath. "Dad, I'm at Beth Israel Deaconess Hospital in Milton. It's chaos here. They want to run tests on us since we came close to one of those...things."

"What the hell were you doing near one of them?"

"It was near the tracks. The train had to stop."

He goes silent for a few seconds. "You have your medication with you?"

"Yes," I mumble, turning away from Dominick. "But I'm still freaking out. They're wearing hazmat gear."

"I'm coming to get you." He hangs up before I can argue. His words sounded strong. Clear. The events haven't triggered him. Yet.

The hazmat team reaches our bus. I wonder if there are scientists or doctors underneath those suits. Or both. *Or neither.* They round us up, including the bus driver. I don't think he saw that coming by the look in his eyes, like an innocent man being arrested for treason.

As we enter the hospital, one worker shouts, "Women to the right, men to the left. Children under twelve years old remain with a parent."

I give Dominick a quick, hard kiss on the lips. For the first time in years, I can't tell what he's thinking—if he's more concerned with leaving me or being alone himself. Those are two very different things, and the distinction makes all the difference in the world to me. One means he's afraid that I can't handle the situation. The other means he's afraid. *And that my fear is justified.*

As I am sorted according to my gender, my mind recalls horrific events in history when this happened. *The Holocaust. The Titanic. When do you know that an event is the beginning of what will become a tragic end? Is it only at the end?*

The herd of women and some children quietly move down a tented hallway lined with plastic and brown butcher paper. A person in a hazmat suit approaches me with a clipboard. The only facial features visible through the front of the hood are a pair of cold blue eyes.

"Name?" a female voice asks. She clicks a pen with a gloved thumb.

Stay strong. I clear my throat. "Alexandra Lucas."

"Age?"

"Seventeen. Almost eighteen," I add.

"Address? Phone number?"

Her bedside manner needs work. Maybe she is a scientist after all. Or a really bad doctor. "Why are we here?" I ask.

The woman ignores me. "Address? Phone number?"

"I'm not going to answer your question until you answer mine." My voice cracks. My dad taught me to know my rights. Respect leaders, but don't be afraid to ask them tough questions. That's how the world stays strong.

"She's right," another female passenger from the bus pipes in. A young boy, maybe three years old, clings to her leg. "Why are we here?"

The blue eyes behind the hooded plastic stare through me. I stare back. I am my father's daughter. I can be a real pain in the ass when it's necessary, even if my heartbeat dulls my hearing the whole time, even if I need a pill to help calm down later.

"This is for national security. The protection of the country." She points the tip of the pen at the clipboard and addresses everyone in earshot. "You were all exposed to something that we don't understand yet. For all we know, those things reek of radiation or something worse. We need to run some tests before allowing you to mingle back in with the public. Don't want to end up with an epidemic on our hands. Do you understand?"

We nod. I tell her my address and phone number. The female passenger who spoke earlier hugs her child and then holds the back of her wrist to his forehead to check his temperature. I look down and examine the exposed skin on my arms and legs. The wound on my elbow glows redder and angrier under the hospital lights. The rest of my skin still looks the same: golden, freckled in some spots. *Could be skin cancer. Especially if I've been exposed to some cosmic radiation. Has to be worse than the sun's radiation, right? Wonder how fast you die.*

"All standard protocol," she adds. "There's no need for alarm."

"Yet," I say.

The breathing mask blocks her mouth, but the corners of her blue eyes wrinkle as if she smirked. Makes me wonder if she'd be happier finding nothing wrong with us or finding something dreadful. It doesn't reassure me.

She explains the next procedure: We must remove all clothing and shoes. Even bras and underwear.

With all these people watching? What if someone takes a picture and texts it to everyone?

"I'm underage. You need my parent or guardian's permission before subjecting me to medical treatment, never mind asking me to remove my clothes in public. I could sue you."

I hope I sounded like I meant it. Bravery doesn't always strike at the right time. Sometimes it's an afterthought. Sometimes it's medically induced once my pill works.

"We will be calling any parents or guardians momentarily. However, due to the nature of radiation, the longer you are exposed, the more you and those around you are at risk. Decontamination cannot wait for consent. We have provided curtained areas for privacy. As for suing us, young lady, go right ahead. Now, we can do this the easy way or the hard way. Your choice."

The hard way. Police holding me down. Taser. Needles. Straitjacket. I beg my cheeks and ears not to turn red.

"Good choice. Let's move."

I watch the process ahead of me. Clothes are being bagged and tagged, personal items confiscated. My phone and purse will be taken and locked up somewhere. I feel withdrawals from my pills already, but that can't be right. My medication usually lasts in my system for eight hours. Well, on a good day.

As much as I hate to admit it, I wish Dad were here right now. He'd never let this happen to me.

For the concert with Dominick today, I wore my favorite summer outfit, a brown sundress with a tiny yellow, white, and red floral pattern, paired with red bangle bracelets and strappy sandals. In a curtained area, I unbuckle my sandals and remove the bracelets. *Run out of the building. Get out while you still can.* Instead, I slip off the straps of my dress and let it fall to the floor. Unhook my bra, pull down panties. Naked, I pass my belongings outside the curtain for bagging. I want to cry over the loss of my clothes. It's like they've died and been placed in a body bag.

"Will I get my clothes back?" I ask from behind the curtain. No one responds.

One at a time, we must move to the shower area. When it's my turn, a hazmat worker gives instructions from outside the curtain. "You must scrub using the special disinfectant soap. Make sure to do your entire body. Even your hair."

The lukewarm water hits my body like spittle. The soap smells like chemicals used to scrub a toilet, not a person. The wound on my elbow screams when the soap hits it. *What if the soap travels through my bloodstream? What if it's toxic?* When I rub it into my hair, my curls mat into a sticky, knotted nest. As I rinse, a dry film covers every pore of my skin, every strand on my head. It won't rinse off. *Get it off me! Get it off me!* I scrub and scrub and scrub without breathing until my skin turns a livid pink.

Outside the shower area a towel waits for me. After I cover up, a hazmat woman hands me two paper hospital gowns, one to put on facing backward, one to put on facing forward, so I'm not exposed as I walk. As soon as I'm ready, I must turn in my towel for bagging just in case I'm still leaking alien radiation after the shower.

Next, another worker points me toward a sectioned-off area labeled with a paper printout that reads CLEAN. The sign makes me wonder what they considered us before. My body shivers uncontrollably as I shuffle barefoot down the corridor. Cardboard and plastic cover the floor. A worker assigns me a hospital cot and tells me to leave the curtains open. My file is clipped to the end of my bed. I am a disinfected patient with a serial number.

Time passes. More women and children join the CLEAN area. I touch my hair. It's drying wrong and curling in weird directions. I need the extra hair tie that's in my purse. Then I think of the vertexes. The holograms. My hair shouldn't be important during a world crisis, but it still is. If I'm going to die, I'd rather not die wearing a paper hospital gown with my hair sticking up like a ball of brown cotton candy.

My hands start to shake. I need to talk to Dominick or Rita or my parents, but they confiscated my cell phone with everything else. I refuse to cry. If I do, I'll crumble.

Another hazmat worker appears at my side. She reads my name and birth date from the file, then asks a billion questions:

"How much do you weigh?"

"Approximately how long were you exposed to the phenomenon?"

"How close were you standing to it?"

"Do you feel any itching, burning, tingling, or swelling?"

"Any nausea?"

"Vomiting?"

"Diarrhea?"

"Headache?"

I try my best to answer all her questions truthfully, but the whole experience is becoming a blur. I have no idea how close I was to it. I can hardly believe I was there at all. That it was there at all.

She proceeds to take my temperature, blood, and a urine sample. When she discovers the wound on my elbow, she asks, "When did you get this?"

I'm not about to tell her that I froze in a line of police fire, so my boyfriend had to throw me to the ground. She might send me for a psych evaluation. "I fell getting on the bus."

"Are you sure?" I hear the urgency in her voice. *She wants to turn me into a lab rat. Her alien lab rat.*

"Yes, I'm sure. I fell. There was even dirt in it earlier. Before the shower."

She jots down notes into my file. *Probably writing crap about me. About my nervous behavior being a possible sign of exposure to extraterrestrial energy. Further evaluation needed.* Wonder what she'll think of my dad when he gets here.

She cleans my wound, applies a clear antibiotic cream, and bandages my arm. I feel like a science project. She's lucky I'm not a hypochondriac. Medical things don't scare me since science is technical. It uses data and provides clear answers. In fact, the whole time she's working on me, I watch her every step. I swear if I ever have to have surgery, I'll ask to stay conscious. No ambiguity, no anxiety.

A commotion begins down the hallway as a team of hazmat workers struggle with an unruly patient. The hazmat woman finishes my medical interrogation and moves to help. They bring the female patient over to our area but avoid placing her near any children. She's around my mother's age with long brown hair that's dripping wet from the forced shower. When they carry her through the unit, the smell of burnt rubber follows her body, even after being cleaned. As she struggles with them, her paper dress rips and exposes her ribcage.

I want to cover her with a blanket and force feed her oatmeal.

She puts up a valiant fight against invisible demons, her eyes focusing on inanimate objects instead of people.

"Between the idea and the reality," she screams at a wall.

"Relax," I hear a male voice command from a hazmat suit. She kicks and bites at his uniform. One person preps a syringe. They lay her on a bed and hold her down.

"Falls the shadow," she yells at a monitor.

Someone pulls the curtain closed. "She'll be out in a second," I hear one hazmat suit say. The curtain opens, and most of the hazmat team leaves her private cocoon.

As they pass by me, I hear one of them say to the other, "This is only the beginning."

———

As I sit on my hospital cot waiting for the next round of testing, I can just make out the unruly patient through a crack in the curtain. Her chest rises and falls like a robot on a schedule. I'm not sure what they gave her, but whatever it was, it worked. Something about her stirs a deep fear in me, and I think about my dad. After returning from active duty, he suffered from post-traumatic stress disorder and Gulf War syndrome. When Benji and I were little, we used to watch Dad secretly as he unraveled at night. Seeing the patient spout nonsense reminds me of Dad back then. I hated watching him self-destruct, yet I couldn't stop being the ever-vigilant daughter. Still can't.

Hours tick by. If it takes any longer, I might need some of the unruly patient's medication when mine runs out. I wish I had my journal to keep track of everything. Plus it would give me something to do rather than just sit and think in circles.

The hazmat worker with the cold blue eyes returns. "Your parents are here. They have to wait in a separate area apart from vertex patients, but I'll let them know you're okay."

"Thanks," I say. I almost ask how my dad seemed, but I stop myself. "How much longer?"

"I have no idea. It's up to the CDC."

CDC. Centers for Disease Control. My anxiety antenna spikes at the thought of having an alien disease.

Another staff member turns on television sets and plays *Encanto* on all screens.

I close my eyes and visualize my safe place. It's a scene I remember from a screen saver. *Bright blue island sky. White rope hammock tied to palm trees. A book waiting for me. Pages flipping in the wind.* I wonder how Dominick is doing. If they called his mother. If she actually showed up. If he's as afraid as I am.

The staff brings cheese or peanut butter and jelly sandwiches with milk or juice. It's weird to accept food from people wearing head-to-toe protective gear. All I can think about is the *Doctor Who* episode where people's faces turn into gas masks. Makes the food much less appetizing.

An hour later, my legs can't sit still anymore. I need information. As soon as the workers move out of our section, I scramble off the cot, patter across the plasticized floor for the remote, and change the screen to the news. I run back to my cot before anyone can blame me.

I watch as the media replays a hologram's message for the public. It's identical to the one I witnessed in Quincy, but the bottom of the screen says it's located in Springfield, Massachusetts. The newscaster returns to the screen with a microphone in her hand.

"As of the hour, scientists claim that no comet of this magnitude and trajectory has been detected anywhere in our vicinity. Scientists across the globe are rushing to verify the information. Governments warn everyone to stay away from the phenomena until further testing can be done to determine their origin and safety. They are asking people to remain calm and wait for more information."

One worker returns and stops short when she sees the television screen. "Who put the news on?" she asks.

No one tells on me. She clicks it back to *Encanto* and moves to the next bay, taking the remote with her.

So they're telling us the truth. Well, the truth as far as anyone knows it. As far as they can tell, there's no comet. That's good news. *But then why are the holograms here?*

After *Encanto*, the workers play *Cinderella*, and then start *Mulan*. I try to pay attention to the talking dragon and the battle scenes, but I can't get past the musical numbers. After what must be more than five agonizing hours, they reevaluate us with the same checklist of questions and tests. The little boy nearby has fallen asleep on his mother. I watch as they try to examine him. When he wakes, he screams like his brain is being probed with an electrode. My hands start to shake again, so I hold onto my thighs through the paper gown. There's only so long I can live in an outfit that crinkles like a potato chip bag.

Another hazmat worker approaches me for reevaluation. "How long is this going to take?" I ask for the umpteenth time.

She answers with the same response as every other time I've asked. "Depends on the CDC findings."

"But I feel fine."

"So far. Radiation symptoms show up within the first six to twelve hours. Depending on the tests, doctors will make a call whether they want more tests at the twelfth hour."

"What?" I complain. "Six more hours?" I lie back on the cot. They will need to strap me down soon if they think I can stay here much longer.

I focus back on *Mulan,* trying to ignore how strange and terrible my date night has gone, when exhaustion hits. I wake up to a woman handing me a black T-shirt, jean shorts, and flip flops. They aren't the clothes that I arrived in, but they are clothes that I recognize from my wardrobe at home.

"What's going on?" I ask, groggy.

"Everyone's been cleared. All testing came out negative so far— on people and at the sites."

She hands me a cup of water. As I drink, I realize she's the same woman from before without the hazmat suit. She watches me with the same cold blue eyes, but now I can see her cropped black hair. She is younger and prettier than I expected. Tormentors should be hideous.

"So they aren't afraid we're contagious anymore?"

"No," she answers. "The government released a statement. Scientists have tested several vertex sites, and all of them are completely sterile and benign. Cell phones have worse radiation emanating from them. It took a while because the data kept scrambling. Some sort of incompatibility with our technology. Speaking of cell phones"—she returns my cell phone and purse—"I believe these are yours."

I hold on to my phone like she's handing me a newborn. "So this was all for nothing?"

"If that's how you want to look at it. I'm just happy to go home like you."

"Where are my other clothes?" I ask.

"They were sent for decontamination. If anything had been found, the CDC would've burned everything. You can pick them up at the front desk."

The attendant hands me discharge papers that explain the warning signs of exposure to radiation. If I experience vomiting, diarrhea, hair loss, dizziness, weakness, or end up with a fever, I must return immediately. Apparently, there's also the chance of death at any point in the next two weeks if there was actual exposure that our primitive earthly machines cannot measure.

Stuff to look forward to. Worry about. Overanalyze. Thanks a lot for supplying my brain with dire side effects and possibilities.

She closes the curtain and leaves me to get dressed. As I pull the T-shirt on, my brain replays everything she just said, everything I just experienced. Something inside me finally breaks and releases an avalanche of tears. I pull tissues from the box on the counter and try to piece myself together. Hands shaking, I hunt through my purse for my pills. My bag slips and goes into a nosedive, contents scattering everywhere. I crawl on the plastic lining the area and collect the items. Lipstick. Tampons. Loose change. Hair tie. Pill bottle. Gum. Wallet. Tears blur my vision. I check to see if my money, license, and debit card are all still there. Everything seems intact. Normal. On my phone a string of texts wait to be answered, mostly from Rita.

Dominick texted a few minutes ago:

Are you okay? I'm waiting for clothes. Meet outside?

My hands shake so out of control they don't feel like mine. I text back:

I'm fine. Just tired. Do you need a ride?

He doesn't respond. I wipe more tears with a tissue and pop a pill before leaving the bay.

Everyone in my unit is allowed to leave, everyone except the unruly patient. As I walk past her curtained area, I can't help but peek inside. She's alert and makes eye contact with me.

"Mississippi?" she says and climbs out of bed. I pull back from the curtain.

Her IV stand crashes to the ground. She gets a weird look in her eyes and starts patting at her paper gown and frantically searching the floor around her bed.

"No!" she screams. I back farther away. Thankfully, the nurses arrive, pulling her back into bed. She flails, about to fight them, but keeps focused on me. I turn and run.

I need to go home. The world is not safe. The world has gone mad.

The moment I hit the waiting area, Mom runs and hugs me. Dad stands and waits. "Thank God," she breathes into my hair. "Are you okay?"

"Yeah, just tired. I can't believe they kept us so long."

"Let's get out of here," Dad mutters, looking everywhere else but at me. *First sign.* My heart drops lower in my chest.

I look around at the crowd of people waiting for loved ones. Dominick's mother and little brother are nowhere in sight.

"Did you see Dominick?"

"No, honey," Mom says, taking a cursory look around.

"Wait, I need to see if he needs a ride back to his car." I pull my phone back out. Dominick has texted back:

Probably. Be right there.

"Doesn't that boy have a family of his own?" Dad complains. Mom touches his shoulder. It's a love warning. It means, "I know you are annoyed, but you are crossing the line."

While we wait for him, I head to the front desk to pick up my clothes.

"Last name?" the attendant asks.

"Lucas. Alexandra Lucas."

"One moment."

She disappears behind another door and returns shortly with my clothes and shoes neatly folded in a plastic bag.

"Thanks," I say. As I turn to leave, I catch a glimpse of my reflection in a door window. My curly hair is flattened on one side, sticking up on the other. I grab the hair tie in my purse and pull my frizzy, brown hair into a quick bun. Just in time—Dominick appears around the corner.

His face perks up when he sees me. He's dressed up in his clothes from our date, the same dark jeans and striped button-down shirt. His shirt is wrinkled and must be misbuttoned since it doesn't meet evenly at the bottom. It's not fair that he looks sexier disheveled while I look like the bride of Frankenstein. He walks over and hugs me. The stress in my shoulders releases, but I push away sooner than usual since I feel Dad's eyes staring at us. Dominick's back straightens to full attention. He notices the difference.

"Sorry," he announces, and I think it's because of the hug. "It took me a little longer since I didn't have another change of clothes. I had to wait for them to find mine."

"Nick, stop with the excuses," Dad comments. "Guys like you in the military—always behind, always an excuse—didn't last long."

Dominick cringes at the nickname. His father's name was Nicholas. I've reminded my dad a million times.

"Dad, not now. Please." My medication kicks in faster since I haven't had much food, filling my body with warmth and laziness.

"He put you in danger," Dad mutters, "and I'm the bad guy."

"He didn't know we were gonna have a freaking hologram invasion," I argue in exhaustion.

"Enough," Mom says. "Let's go home. It's been a long night."

Dad grunts his disapproval as we walk to the car. Mom rubs his lower back. Like taming a lion.

Outside, the August morning air soothes my aching skin. I breathe in for an easy five counts, hold for two, and let it out in six more. The early sky holds the sun in one corner, the moon still visible in another. Neither look the same anymore.

CHAPTER 3

ABC 6, Boston 7 news, and every other news media outlet I flip through broadcast the same loop of information. Five hundred vertexes. The hologram's message playing in different languages depending on the country. Maps of vertex sightings across the globe with clusters of them spotted in China, India, and the U.S. Some small countries without any sightings.

They're guessing that the placement of the vertexes is connected with population percentages. Officials are still asking everyone to stay away from the vertexes for their own safety. They have no way of knowing how many people may have been exposed before they set up perimeters and emergency medical protocols, but all tests show no ill readings as of this point.

That means no radiation poisoning for me or Dominick. *Give it two weeks, then I'll believe it.* Doctor's orders.

I grab my navy blue journal with the hot pink polka dots that Grandma Penelope sent me for Christmas last year. Not my style, but if there were ever a time to chronicle something, now would qualify. I scribble details about my ordeal last night and list all the facts I can glean from the news. My hand can't write fast enough.

President Lee appears in front of the White House for a press conference. She repeats again that "there is no credibility in the holographic message. No such comet has been located at the present time."

At the present time. So there's still a possibility.

NASA is all over the news explaining the importance of "planetary protection" and warning about "interplanetary contamination." They are "deeply concerned" that the arrival of these vertexes may have "contaminated our biosphere with extraterrestrial bacteria." The CDC is running every test imaginable at various sites, but so far "nothing of interest" has been uncovered.

Nothing of interest. They can't be serious.

Newscasters report live from various locations across the world, and despite the warnings, throngs of people have flocked to see the phenomena for themselves. How can they not? It's a spectacle— something so extraordinary and overwhelming that you have to see it to believe it.

Even though I saw the one in Quincy, I already want to see another one. If I hadn't seen it with my own eyes, I wouldn't believe it.

Why would the holograms come to rescue us from nothing? Did they get the date wrong?

What are they hiding?

Maybe it's all a lie, and our very own scientists created the vertexes by accident. The holograms could be an elaborate cover-up for their mistake. Weren't they trying to make their own black holes, their own Big Bang in some large underground collider machine? I bet they screwed up an experiment and cracked the universe.

The whole thing is just unreal. My mind won't stop spinning.

My phone rings, and Benji's name and face appear on the screen. I'm surprised he's called me twice and not Mom or Dad. Whenever we talk, either it's awkward or we get into a fight. I set my journal aside and click off the TV to shut out the media before answering the phone.

"Hey," I say, "What's up? Where are you?"

"Doesn't matter. They're sending me home."

"Home home?" I grab one of the striped side pillows from the sofa and hug it.

"Yes, but not off duty. They're stationing me at one of the vertexes. Not sure which one yet, but they're supposed to assign us to one close to our families."

"Lucky us," I comment. "You'll be back."

"You would think that, wouldn't you?"

We both allow seconds of silence to tick between us.

"I can't really talk details," he continues, "but from where I sit, none of it looks good. Every country is having a different reaction. It's bad."

I think about what he's saying and what he's not saying. He's usually a die-hard patriot, like Dad, a rare creature to find these days. For him to say something is bad in our country, it must be catastrophic.

"Why didn't you call Mom and Dad?" I ask. I pull on a tiny string on the corner of the pillow, and it starts to unravel the seam.

"Because Mom will be emotional, and Dad will be Dad. What does it matter? Can you just tell them that I should be back in a week?"

"Sure," I say, annoyed. "They'll love having you back."

He sighs into the phone, and I get the impression that he'd rather be overseas in a foreign land dealing with foreign wars than be on the home front dealing with the new unknown. Or maybe his real problem has less to do with the holograms and more to do with the family.

"One week. Tell them."

———

Curly hair is a punishment in August humidity. Rita's coming over around three o'clock to hear all about the hologram and the vertex firsthand, and then Dominick's coming after dinner. I have an hour to shower and tame my hair into submission. I step into the tub, careful not to get the bandage on my elbow wet. The smell of disinfectant from last night burns into my memory. I grab a loofah and lather half the bottle of berry vanilla body wash on every inch of my skin. The water rinses over me as I let the wall hold me up.

Stepping out of the shower, I wrap myself with a huge mint green towel and dry off. It's a struggle to put on my clothes, a Billie Eilish T-shirt and jean shorts. As I lift my hands to slick my wet curls into a ponytail, a dull pain shoots through my heart and takes my breath away. My heart spasms into a million little unnatural beats. If I didn't know better, I'd think I was having a heart attack. But I know better.

During middle school, my parents brought me to the emergency room three times for supposed heart attack symptoms. By the third time, the diagnosis was panic attacks caused by generalized anxiety disorder. The doctor recommended counseling, which I tried for a while but found medication more effective than talking about my physical symptoms to a stranger.

The bathroom walls close in on me. My body rebels and screams, *Get out! Can't breathe. Get out!*

I grab the knob and fight with the door at first, pushing instead of pulling. I flee to my bedroom to get my anxiety pills, but it's going to be bad regardless. The attacks that sneak up out of nowhere for no apparent reason, those are the ones that get you. I pop a pill, sit on my bedroom floor, and hug my knees. My brain continues to short-circuit, reacting as if I am under imminent threat of death when I was just doing my hair. The explosion inside of me feels so real I want to scream. Sweat pools down my back, and hives break out on my arms. I peel my T-shirt off my body to escape the heat, but nothing helps.

What if it's not a panic attack? What if it's related to the vertexes? Maybe it's radiation poisoning. Oh God, what if I really am dying this time? I need to go back to the hospital before my skin starts melting off my body.

"Mom," I yell from the floor. "Mom? Mom!" I don't think she can hear me from here. She's the only one home, and the last time I saw her she was in the backyard gardening.

Oh, God, they're going to find my corpse, and Dad will flip into PTSD mode, Mom will never stop crying and have a nervous break-down, and Benji will blame it all on me and refuse to come to my funeral.

"Honey?" Mom's voice calls. It takes her a second to find me huddled in the corner wearing only a bra and shorts. "Alex, are you okay?"

"I need to go to the hospital. I think I have radiation poisoning." I begin to sob and rock back and forth.

"Honey, they said the vertexes are fine. No radiation. Did you take your medication?"

"Yes, but it's not working. It's from the radiation, I know it. Are you just going to stand there and watch me die?"

"Honey, no." She wraps her arms around the back of me. "I know you're scared, but we've been through this before. If you don't feel better soon, then I promise I will bring you to the hospital. We just have to wait it through."

Waiting is the absolute worst. "Fine, but if I die, you're going to feel really guilty."

She nods and slips the hair tie from my wrist.

"Can you call Rita? Tell her not to come over?" I beg as she smooths my hair back. I almost tell her to cancel on Dominick too, but I need to see him tonight to talk about yesterday. We couldn't exactly talk about it on the ride home with my parents listening.

"Absolutely. Climb into bed and I'll sit with you."

She pulls the crisp, purple and blue patterned sheet up to my chin. A cocoon. I pray that when I wake it will be over.

Two hours later, I open my eyes and feel exhausted. My chest still has phantom pain, like soreness after a muscle spasm, but nothing like before. Mom was right—I didn't need to go to the hospital. But I'll never admit it to her, and she'll never bring it up again. It's a silent code we have in our house, a code we use to cover up a lot of things.

———

At dinner I inform my parents that their precious Benji is returning. Mom practically leaps from her seat at the dinner table while Dad starts bombarding me with questions. Now I understand why Benji called me to deliver the news. Jerk.

Dad badgers me for information that I don't have. Stuff about "world security versus national security" and "pulling out of volatile regions too soon without the right reinforcement and protection of our interests." I push salad around my plate, take a bite of my cheeseburger. At least once Benji returns, he'll be stuck in the hot seat.

"Regardless of what happens, we're staying put," Dad finally states.

I speak up. "No matter what? Even if a comet comes?"

"Ben, we need to discuss it as a family," my mother says.

"We're staying put," Dad repeats.

Mom places a hand on his forearm. She's not going to fight him, though, as usual. I roll my eyes. Dad catches me.

"You mean you'd go?" He holds his fork over his salad and waits for my response.

Or maybe to poke my eyes out.

"Well, no," I say, "I don't have enough information." I pick at the remains of my dinner. "According to the news, there's no comet in our vicinity." I feel like a newscaster spewing regurgitated facts stored in my journal.

"Exactly," Mom says. "There's not enough information."

"True," Dad concedes, "but regardless, we're staying put. A captain goes down with the ship. People go down with the planet."

"What?" I argue. "That's ridiculous."

"Why is it ridiculous? We were born here, and we should stay here. Humans weren't meant to time travel to other universes. It's unnatural. If time is up, time is up."

I can't eat. "You mean to tell me that if there was a comet, you'd expect us to sit here and die?"

Dad slams down his fork. "No, I expect the UN to get involved and stop the damn thing. I expect us to wait as a family while the government does what it does best."

As a family. Mom and I look at each other. I can't tell what she's thinking. Does she think we should wait and die together too? Bullshit. I'll be gone. They can kumbaya together all they want.

At the sound of the doorbell, I escape the conversation to let Dominick into the house. He embraces me in a soft hug and follows with a long kiss. How we were ever just friends for so long is beyond me.

"You okay?" he asks. "You look tired."

"I'm fine." If he had seen my condition hours ago, he would've called an ambulance.

"Strange date last night," he says.

"That's an understatement," I add, swinging my ponytail off my shoulder. "It's even stranger in here."

"What do you mean?"

"You'll see. Don't say I didn't warn you."

We pass into the dining room, and Mom smiles at Dominick. Dad stabs at his salad. "Nick, let's settle something," Dad begins.

"Shoot," Dominick says, holding the back of a dining room chair for support.

"What do you think about the whole vortex thing?"

"Vertex thing," Mom corrects him, clearing her plate.

"Vortex, vertex, same thing," he adds. "You staying or going?"

"Dad, leave Dominick alone," I say.

"Let the man speak," Dad comments. "I want to hear what he has to say for himself."

Dominick laughs uncomfortably. He rocks the chair back and forth. "I have no idea. I think the whole thing is surreal."

"You got that right. It's goddamn lunacy."

Dominick grins, but I see him stick his hands in both pockets. He does that when he's uncomfortable but wants to seem nonchalant. Like when he talks about his father.

"A vertex and a vortex are not the same," Mom interrupts. "Didn't you see the explanation on the news?"

Dad blows her off and goes into the kitchen with his empty plate. Dominick turns to my mother instead. "No, what'd they say?"

Mom's eyes light up since she actually has the stage. "Well, a hologram explained it to some scientists, and the scientists tried to explain it to us. They even drew a diagram, but I didn't understand that part. Maybe you will since you like math."

"That's an understatement," I say. "He wants to major in math at college."

My mother's face glows. "Really? That's wonderful. Well, the holograms explained that traveling to parallel universes and through time both work on the... It sounded important, so I wrote it down. Where did I put it?"

She searches through a pile of papers on the side table and grabs a yellow sticky note.

"Here we go—the 'parabolic principle.' It sounded fascinating, but I couldn't really follow it. Part of it involves something called a vertex."

Dominick rubs the stubble on his chin. "It must work on parabolas then." I can see his brain turning. "Do you know what a parabola is?"

"No," she says.

So Dominick draws one.

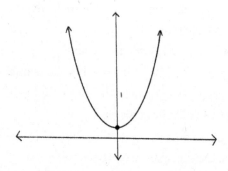

"That's a parabola. It works on, like, a mirroring philosophy. See the dot I drew? That's a vertex. It's the point of intersection where the two sides meet."

"So that must be why they call it a vertex. It's where our two worlds meet. See, Ben. Vertex, not vortex," she shouts into the kitchen.

Dominick studies the shape for a few minutes. I can tell his head is spinning with possibilities. If only parallel universe time travel were a language-based phenomenon and not a mathematical one, maybe I'd follow along.

Dad returns, and Dominick pockets the paper before there's an opportunity for criticism. Dad judges what he doesn't understand.

"I don't trust it," Dad preaches, ignoring Mom's clarification. "Nobody gives something for nothing. Everyone has an agenda. It says we have a choice. Yeah, wait 'til that thing starts collecting us against our will. Mark my words: it's gonna get violent."

I nudge Dominick to follow me and escape for some alone time. On our way out of the room, I hear Dad say to Mom, "Those holograms sound like fucking communists."

His words are something I understand even if it makes me cringe; it's language at its finest. And I know there are probably many other people out there uttering the same thing in their homes, trying to understand the impossible and putting a label on it.

In my backyard, Dominick and I sit in our usual spots on the warped tan and peach striped patio furniture that Mom found on clearance. The ominous stars blink innocently in the sky, holding secrets in the universe I never even considered before yesterday. For years I've sat in the same spot plotting my escape by becoming a lawyer. To be seen as strong. Capable. Determined.

I still want that, but I can't escape the fact that a part of me wants to stay where I am. Change is harder than I thought it would be. How these vertex things fall into my life equation I have no clue.

Dominick's typing and scrolling frantically on his phone. Why did he come here if he just wants to stare at his phone? I bite my tongue. I understand the need for information with everything going on. I check my phone and see a string of texts from Rita over the past hour. She's freaking out. I had invited her to sleep over tonight since I canceled on her earlier, but her parents said no. They are strict Seventh-day Adventists, and their congregation is having an emergency meeting to warn against the holographic prophets. Reading her texts makes my stomach turn. I don't know what to write back to her to make it better.

"Sorry," Dominick apologizes while still typing. "I'm looking up the math involved with the vertexes. It's awesome stuff, except it gets way too advanced for me."

"It's okay. I don't even understand what a parabola has to do with traveling through time and space."

"The basic principle is like this." He walks over to a basketball in my driveway, leftovers from when Benji used to play. Sometimes I shoot around to pretend the house is still the same. Dominick lets the ball bounce on its own. "Did you see that?"

"See what?" I was too busy watching him look athletic. It's not a normal look for him.

"How it bounces. Watch again."

I watch. The ball bounces in a series of hills, slowly getting smaller the more it bounces.

"Did you see it? It moves in a series of parabolas, like the drawing. Energy travels in parabolas all the time. It's even how microwaves and satellites work."

While I still don't completely understand what he's telling me, I totally appreciate how adorable he looks when he's inspired.

"The fact that they can keep five hundred vertexes open for six months is mind-boggling. Scientists asked the holograms how they harness enough energy to create a vertex and how they calculate the angle needed to reach a fixed coordinate." Dominick notices my blank gaze. "How they control the bounce, so to speak. But the holograms said the technology is beyond our current level of understanding."

I love hearing him passionate about something. Even if that something scares me. I walk over and pull him by his shirt, pressing my lips against his.

When we finally come up for air, he asks, "What were we talking about?"

"The vertexes." I grin.

"Screw it. The vertexes can wait."

CHAPTER 4

Two days later, the same news stories play on the same loop. No new evidence has surfaced. Each day, holograms at five hundred vertex sites across the world have repeated the same recorded message. The only thing that changes is the amount of time they say we have left. Scientists have dismissed their prophecy as "pure fallacy."

All vertexes are currently under guard, and citizens are being kept at a "safe" distance until the governments across the world decide what to do next, which makes me think they're still worried about radiation. I store the information in my journal and check my skin for signs of mutation every few hours. Okay, maybe every hour. My temperature too.

They've asked everyone to continue "business as usual." I don't know if that's possible. It's asking a lot of people to pretend there aren't giant blue circles glowing all around us with weird holographic people not only from the future, but from a whole other dimension telling us the world is ending and expect that we can continue as if nothing is going on.

Other than that, my life has been pretty normal, or as normal as things can be when the world feels like it's in a temporary holding pattern.

———————

I'm in the kitchen, deciding on a quick snack before dinner, when Dad returns from his work as the manager at Stop & Shop carrying a huge cardboard box. Mom holds the door for him as he struggles to bring it inside. As soon as I see it, I know he's up to something. Major changes always start with minor things.

He heaves it onto the kitchen countertop. "I come prepared," he announces.

Mom smiles until she flips open the cardboard flaps and pulls out a can of peaches. "Cans?" she questions. "Why did you bring groceries? Our pantry's full."

"Canned food, toilet paper, and other nonperishables are flying off the shelves. Looks like people are stocking up, just in case. At this rate, the supermarket will be wiped out in no time."

"But we're on a budget," Mom reminds him. "Alex is headed to college next year. I'm only working summer hours."

Mom works as a secretary at my old elementary school. I can still feel the burning humiliation of the days when I had my mom at school with me. Whenever I'd pass by the main office, she'd wave frantically at me until I waved back. The only times I appreciated it were when I forgot my lunch money or felt sick.

Thinking about school reminds me that my senior year starts in a few weeks. *Do schools stay open while the world's dealing with a supernatural event?* I mean, nothing's actually happening.

Maybe the vertex phenomenon will postpone my future. It's a good stall tactic. I wouldn't have to make any crucial, life-altering decisions. *What am I thinking?* I've been dying to start my adult life. Alexandra Lucas for the Defense, Your Honor.

"Survival is more important than our budget," Dad explains to Mom. "Even if it all blows over, the panic alone will cause crisis in supply and demand. We need to be prepared."

She places her hand on his shoulder. It's not a love tap or a warning. I can tell by the way her fingers curl around his shoulder. She's holding on instead of patting or touching. There's a difference, and the difference matters.

"We don't have space on the shelves," she says. "You'll have to keep them in the basement." Her hand relaxes on his shoulder.

I hate when she compromises with him, acting like he's listened to her needs even though it's clear to me that he's about to spiral out of control. Which makes me feel out of control. How can she not see it?

"Good idea." He lifts the box, gives her a quick peck on the cheek, and heads toward the basement door. My inner alarm blares with warning, like ants biting me from the inside. Someone has to watch him, make sure he doesn't jump overboard, and that someone is me.

Mom shrugs and gives me a half smile. "Can't live with him, can't live without him."

Over the next five days I notice Dad sneaking more and more boxes of food and supplies into the house when Mom isn't home. I find them stacked in a corner of the basement covered with blankets and sheets. Soon, an entire side of the basement becomes a ghastly landscape of hidden contraband. I know he's doing it as a precaution, but planning for the worst makes me expect the worst. The possibilities are harder to ignore.

———

My parents receive a call, text, email, and letter from my school advising all students to return to school in the fall and continue business as usual per the government's request. They're probably afraid of poor attendance rates lowering their funding.

Like Dominick said, the holograms' warning gives us until the end of January to leave or perish. If I stay home and it's all a hoax, then I will have wasted those months instead of finishing the first half of my senior year. I didn't plan out the course of my life only to have strange beings from a parallel future lie to the world and prevent me from graduating on time.

But what if they're telling the truth? I didn't want to think about it yet, and here it is, staring me in the face. *How do I plan if the world might end? How do I plan for the unknown?*

I run to the bathroom and spend the next fifteen minutes sitting on the toilet. Another side effect. When life turns, so does my stomach.

———

The next day, the United Nations makes a decision: citizens will be allowed access to the holograms to ask questions. Knowing that the decision may create mob scenes at vertex sites, the UN has built a website to provide a constantly updated list of all the questions asked, along with the holograms' answers. They're hoping people will search for answers online rather than seek out a crowded vertex site.

If they are letting people near it, it's probably safe. I can stop checking and double-checking my body for symptoms of death.

I want to ask more questions. Lots of them. I need to see it again, wrap my mind around its existence so my experience doesn't feel like a bizarre dream.

Even though my parents and Rita's parents have forbidden it, Dominick, Rita, and I decide to go see the vertex in Quincy anyway. Dominick can pretty much do whatever he wants since his mother is so busy between work and taking care of Dominick's younger brother, Austin. She's lucky Dominick's such a good kid.

Rita arrives at my house and comes inside to change. Her parents don't let her wear jewelry or makeup or real clothes, so throughout high school she's developed the habit of changing clothes in bathrooms. She steps out of my bathroom wearing a black blouse, black shorts, and black flats. What makes the outfit pop is her neon green beaded necklace and matching earrings.

"Check me out. Alien chic." She poses in the doorway while I snap a photo of us.

My clothes are anything but chic. Purple cotton tee and jean shorts, gray Converse sneakers. Typical American chic, if that's a thing. I'd rather blend in than stick out.

We pick up Dominick and start our journey to the site. Rita drives so she can have full rights to the music selection. She brings along a playlist to set the right mood. I have to give her credit—she did her research. We're jamming to Five Man Electrical Band's "I'm a Stranger Here." I've never heard the song before, but it's hilarious with everything that's happening in the world. A minute ago it was Radiohead's "Subterranean Homesick Alien" and before that, Katy Perry's "E.T." and Kesha's "Spaceship." Next up on her list is Will Smith's "Men in Black," Blink-182's "Aliens Exist," and the Killers' "Spaceman."

Rita sings obnoxiously out the driver's side window. I look at Dominick stuck in the back seat. He's grinning and looking at his phone. It's nice to have one loud friend and one quiet one. Balances things out. It's even nicer that they get along.

Rita screams lyrics at a family crawling past us in a Jeep while her jet black hair swirls in the wind. The mother in the Jeep gives Rita the another-wasted-teenager-on-drugs look. Little does she know Rita's stone-cold sober. Drunk, she's actually less fun and usually vomits and falls asleep.

"Alex," Rita says, "remember that night when we slept in the tent in your backyard and told stories with flashlights?"

I laugh. Good times. "Yeah, remember Benji scaring the crap out of us?"

"Yes, that's what I was going to say! He kept insisting that some flashing lights in the sky were a spaceship, and we totally believed him."

"He said they would come down and suck our brains out. Then he kept making freaky suction noises all night. Typical Benji, trying to drive me nuts. I had nightmares for weeks."

Dominick chuckles in the back seat.

"Leave your brother alone," Rita says. "I'm gonna marry that boy someday."

"Yeah, in another dimension maybe," I say. Benji thinks everything that comes out of Rita's mouth is petty and gossipy and loud. It's funny that what makes him dislike her is exactly why I like her.

"Weird that we are actually dealing with something extraterrestrial," she says. "I just want to look the thing in the eye, see what all the fuss is about."

"Is your church still freaking out?" I ask.

"Oh yeah. They've forbidden any discussion of traveling through them. They believe that Jesus will save us in the Second Coming, not holographic humans from a parallel future. They'd rather us die."

Same as my dad's philosophy, strangely enough. Who knew Dad would ever see eye to eye with a religion?

Dominick laughs out of context from the back seat.

"What's so funny?" I ask. I turn around and see him reading off his phone.

"Sorry, it's just that people are asking the holograms the weirdest questions," he says.

"Like what?" I ask.

"Like 'Can we bring pets?'"

"What's the answer?" Rita asks.

Dominick scrolls down the screen and grins. "They said, and I quote, 'No. Although our photosonic filters are prepared to eliminate malignant human bacteria and viruses from the past, we cannot successfully integrate all of the possible animal species from your planet without knowing how they will interact with our ecosystem. We are sorry for any hardship it may cause.'"

"That's rough," Rita says. "I can't bring Dobby."

Dobby is her feral cat. At least, Dominick and I think he's feral since he attacked us the few times we tried to enter her house. Despite his behavior, she loves him anyway.

Dominick continues. "Next question. 'What kind of food do you have?'"

"Ooh, that's a good one," I say. "What if they eat gross Klingon food?"

"Blah, blah, blah, *Star Trek*," Rita whines.

Dominick ignores her. "Answer: 'We have high standards for optimal nutrition. We provide mostly fruit, grains, and vegetables through rations three times a day. Meat is a rare delicacy.'"

Rita beeps the horn as another driver cuts her off. "My parents will freak that they have something in common with the holograms."

Rations. The word carries the weight of desperation with it and hits me in the gut. Dominick goes quiet as he scrolls through questions.

"You'll have to read through these later," he says. "There are so many already. Some of these are awesome. Like this one. 'What about money? Do you have a monetary system?' Their answer? 'We do not have a monetary system. Everything is free and open.'"

"What the hell does that mean?" Rita asks.

"That means anyone who is rich here will never want to live there," Dominick says.

Dad was right. They do sound like communists.

———

After being stuck in Boston vertex traffic for the next two hours and fighting a massive parking nightmare, we still have to walk for another mile to get even a glimpse of the vertex. When neither of them is watching, I swallow a pill.

Soldiers from the National Guard and U.S. Army form a perimeter around the vertex, surrounded by other local police and media conglomerates. The public stands outside a roped boundary. My chest tightens at the sight of the crowd mobbing the hologram and vertex. I take a deep breath for five counts, hold it for two, let it out slowly, and repeat. The holograms said it is an individual's choice whether to go or stay. The government said we could ask our own questions. How are we ever supposed to get close enough through all the hoopla?

Rita is speechless. Even from a distance she's impressed. By making the vertexes taboo, her church may be inadvertently pushing her toward believing the holograms.

Dominick stays quiet, staring at his phone. I hug his arm. He looks up at me, and I swear I can suddenly picture him as a child. His eyes twinkle with innocence and excitement, like when a kid discovers that baking soda and vinegar react when mixed.

"What is it?" I ask.

"They have a meritocracy."

"What the heck is a—whatever you just said?" Rita asks.

"Question," he reads aloud again from his phone, "'What type of government system do you have?' Answer: 'We have a planetary meritocracy. We believe the most qualified person from each field should rule, not the most popular, for the benefit of the planet. We have a holistic testing system in place to find the most qualified people in every major field, including creative and more physical domains, to represent the people. Our meritocracy consists of one thousand one members at a time, and they must be reexamined every three years. Anyone can take an exam, at any age, every three years. The top person on each test earns a voting seat.'"

"That's better than our system," Rita says. "Remember when Angie beat you for class president? I mean, come on."

Dominick secures his glasses in place. "Thank you for reminding me of my failures."

"I meant it as a compliment. If she had to take a test, she totally would've failed."

He grins. "True."

We move as close to the hologram and vertex as we can manage. It reminds me of the time Rita and I switched seats at a Billie Eilish concert by sneaking closer and closer to the stage. But the main attraction isn't a singer with multicolored hair hitting airy falsetto notes while the stage lights up behind her. No, this is just plain weird.

It's funny how everyone is clamoring to interrogate the holograms. Like we're all searching for flaws with their planet. If we were interviewing ourselves about our world, we'd never pass our own criteria. There are plenty of things we tolerate, know are wrong, and still ignore. Like how leadership is often determined by friendships, money, and gerrymandering and not competence. Weird that we have high expectations for outsiders but low standards for ourselves.

Or maybe, just maybe, deep down we're hoping their planet is better. That hopefully they figured out all our problems by the year 2359, and we can simply travel there and erase our mistakes.

"You know what bothers me?" I ask. "Why do the vertexes only work in one direction? Why can't we go, check out their planet, come back, and tell people about it? Wouldn't that make sense? It seems like an obvious trap."

"True," Dominick says. "But they said it takes a lot of dark energy to keep all the vertexes open for an extended time. That's why they sent holograms instead of coming themselves. Light has no mass. Plus, it sounds like the vertexes are set up to pull us through. It's not a doorway. Works more like a sideways cosmic funnel cloud."

I nod. "I guess. Just seems too convenient." Looking back at the crowd, I realize that there's no way we're getting close enough to ask a question.

"This crowd is impossible," Rita says.

From a distance, I spot the same unruly patient from the hospital, the one they had to sedate, near the front of the crowd. She's wearing oversized jeans with a dingy, yellowed shirt that looks like it came out of a dumpster. She screams at the hologram through a megaphone, but so many people are asking questions at once it doesn't respond. I can't make out all the questions in the commotion, but her voice carries over the crowd like a blow horn through a foggy night.

"Shape without form," she shouts through the megaphone, pointing her free hand at the hologram. It's an indictment, and she's the prosecutor.

"Shut up, lady. Move outta the way." A burly man with a short beard pushes her to the side.

She pushes back and breaks through a police barrier. "Shade without color." She tries to snatch at the hologram. Something in her words makes sense to me, but I can't quite figure out why. Two cops drag her away while she kicks and flails. Bet they'll give her another dose of whatever was in that needle.

She is not alone in her quest to be heard. Another group grabs her megaphone from the ground and starts chanting, "Jesus is the only Lord and Savior. Jesus is the only Lord and Savior."

"Sounds like my parents," Rita says. Her voice has lost its edge. Religion seems to suck the life out of her instead of celebrating how alive and vibrant she actually is.

"If it's any consolation, that woman the police just arrested sounded like my mother when she gets drunk," Dominick says.

Rita smiles, and he pats her shoulder. Moments like this remind me why I'm with him.

I want to ask the hologram my own questions, but the questions I have, it can't answer. *Should I still finish high school? If there is a comet, will I be okay in your world? Should I leave if my family wants to stay?*

———

The government has decided to send a wheeled robotic device through a vertex fitted with a live mini-camera on its frame and other monitoring devices so we can witness what happens when a person steps through to the other side.

The holograms claim our technology is obsolete in their future, and even if our devices were more advanced, the other parallel universe is too far away for our instruments, never mind our minds, to fathom.

Sure enough, scientists navigate the little robot, nicknamed Scout, by remote straight through a vertex in California. As soon as Scout hits the swirling blue energy, it vanishes. So do all traces of it on our monitoring systems. It's a leap of faith.

———

Someone in Florida caught a sparrow on video flying into a vertex. It's all over the internet. In the footage, the sparrow makes a loop in the air, attempts to change direction, and disappears into the blue oval at top speed. The hologram outside the vertex places one hand in front of its stomach and bows low from the waist in a strange show of respect for the deposit.

I find myself thinking about that bird for the rest of the day and writing about it in my journal. I wonder what will happen to it in their world. They said no pets.

CHAPTER 5

QUESTION: What is your view on death?

ANSWER: It is a natural part of life, although the average human's lifespan on our planet is around 250 years due to medical advancements.

Benji arrives at our house in full uniform. He fills it out more than the last time I saw him. It's hugs all around, and I watch both my parents dote over him for the next few hours. My mother cooks his favorite dinner, eggplant Parmesan, and Dad randomly pats him on the shoulder like a football coach with his star player who just helped win the state title.

Benji's been stationed at the vertex in Quincy for security reasons. He won't discuss details, but I know he knows more than he's saying because he keeps avoiding eye contact with me. Dad asks him for specifics, but Benji's a genius at maneuvering around questions and skirting the truth. The military trained him well. Or maybe he was always like that.

The men spend the evening in the backyard drinking beer and talking. Mom cleans up their mess and checks the spare bedroom,

Benji's old room, for the thousandth time to make sure Benji will be comfortable. The gender lines have been drawn, and I don't fit the illustration. It's not until later that night, after leaving the bathroom, that I find Benji still awake in the spare room watching the news and eating popcorn.

"Hey," I say from the doorway. I should know better than to engage him in small talk, but I want more information on the vertexes.

"Hey," he replies.

I enter and sit on a cedar chest at the foot of the bed. Mom's favorite blue and white floral quilt from our great grandmother lays folded over the bottom half of the mattress. It's usually in the chest so it doesn't get ruined. I've always hoped she would give it to me someday, yet here it is spread at Benji's dirty feet.

"Mom spoiling you enough?" I tease, running one hand across the quilt's stitching.

Benji grins. "There's no such thing." He tosses popcorn into his mouth.

"Whatever." I steal a handful of popcorn. "So what's the real scoop? What are you really doing here?"

"I told you. Security." He wipes his buttery hand on the quilt. "Get your own popcorn."

I try to ignore the small grease spots on one of the white squares. "No, really."

"Really." He stares back at the television screen. The news is rehashing the story of the bird that flew into the vertex, except there's an added interview with an ornithologist who predicts the bleak odds for the sparrow in a foreign environment. "Honestly, the government doesn't care if some people leave right now. They're more concerned about what could come out."

I hadn't even thought of that. "But the holograms said the vertexes only work in one direction. You mean like if they're totally lying?" My mind starts to swirl. *I knew it was too convenient. It's the perfect cover. Wait, wait, wait, and then BAM. Alien invasion. Right when we get used to having the bizarre things around.* "You think some futuristic army is going to pop out of the five hundred vertexes and start a war?"

"You never know." He shoves a fistful of popcorn into his mouth. "You gonna freak out now?"

"No. Shut up." A fluttering, dull pain gathers in my chest. "I can't believe they think putting you as a guard is going to help save us."

"Thanks for the vote of confidence." He chews on a few more half-popped kernels. "Tomorrow," he says. His face doesn't move.

His ominous tone makes my insides curl. "Tomorrow, what?"

"Tomorrow it begins."

"Aliens are coming?" I ask, half joking, half concerned after his last comment.

"Well, no. Not aliens. We don't know all that," he admits. "But let's just say tomorrow the world as we know it may change."

"That's all you can give me?" The surface of my skin brims with negative energy.

"Tomorrow," he repeats.

I stay up all night, even after taking a pill. Freaking jerk. Benji and I do not mix well. We're like water and oil. Or more like oil and fire. He knows how to make me burn, and he seems to enjoy it.

The following morning, August 18th, Benji's forecast rings true. The United Nations announces a change—they've lifted the stay on all vertexes within UN countries. We can decide for ourselves whether or not we want to step through to the other side. They warn that there are no guarantees either way, but they admit they must "allow for individual freedom."

The choice is ours. The only catch: all vertexes will be monitored for safety, and they will keep track of those people who leave, "for world census purposes." I wonder if they are telling the whole truth. I wonder if Benji even knows the whole truth. I scramble to write all the details into my journal.

Tomorrow, starting at noon, they will allow the first volunteers to travel through vertexes. I can't imagine anyone daring enough to set foot in one of those things. I mean, for all we know, it's a death trap. Take one step inside and you fizzle up into oblivion.

But across the globe, a small number of volunteers actually come forward to sacrifice themselves to the vertexes. Ex-military, former astronauts, adventurous spirits—all waiting like inmates on death row. Major networks interview them one by one. They must be suicidal.

———

The next morning, Rita comes over to watch the moment with me. Her family has banned all media coverage of the holograms and vertexes. I text Dominick to join us, but he's watching his little brother since his mom has to work. He promises to take me to the movies tonight to make it up to me. How can he think about going to the movies at a time like this?

At noon, the major networks focus on the first U.S. volunteer at the Washington, DC, vertex. The president of the United States stands stoic as the hologram delivers its daily rote warning. Military officials flank each side of the vertex. At the entrance, a soldier holds an electronic tablet, ready to enter those who depart into a database.

I gulp for air from the safety of my bed and grab my journal. Rita comes out of my bathroom wearing a red V-neck T-shirt, jean shorts, a stack of silver bangle bracelets on both wrists, and red, white, and blue earrings that look like falling fireworks. She drags my purple saucer chair in front of the TV on my bureau. The back of her dark head bobs in and out of my view of the screen.

From the living room, Dad's commentary bounces off the walls and makes its way down the hallway. Mom scurries from the parlor to the kitchen to my bedroom and back again, bringing snacks, forgetting things, and yelling from the kitchen, "Is it time yet?"

"I can't believe your brother can't be here," Rita pouts from the chair. "I was hoping to get in some good flirting time."

"He has to guard the vertex in Quincy even though no volunteers are going through there."

She swings her legs up and sits upside down in the saucer, letting her head fall backward. Her feet dangle in my view while her dark hair mops my dusty floor. *The germs that might be collecting on each strand, invisibly crawling up to her scalp.* I bite my tongue to keep from sharing my concern.

"I hope he's safe," Rita says. "Why are guys in uniform so attractive?"

"Grace," Dad's voice echoes. "It's time."

"Ooh, it's starting." Rita flips her body back around in the chair. My stomach and shoulder muscles hurt from anticipating her tipping over and cracking her skull on my wooden floor.

On screen, George Rogers, a former U.S. astronaut, waves to a crowd. He's been a pop culture icon ever since his ex-wife and her lover tried to poison him. The trial lasted months, and the two lovers were found guilty of attempted murder. Rogers became a household name after that. The fact that he's willing to throw his life into a cosmic anomaly while we watch seems like backward poetic justice to me. The media's putting a positive spin on it. They claim he's sacrificing his life to his one true love who never betrayed him: space.

President Lee presents Rogers with a folded American flag, the kind they usually present to families of lost soldiers, an image that I've come to dread. She salutes him, and he reciprocates. Rogers surprises everyone when he unfolds the flag and drapes it around his neck in a final show of patriotism. The crowd in Washington, DC, goes wild.

"Stop treating the flag like a fucking towel," Dad yells from the living room. I sigh. Rita giggles.

"I should shut the door," I say and jump off my bed.

"No, leave it. He's hilarious. My parents never swear. They never say what they really feel. I like this. It's real."

I shake my head and return to my bed. It's not real—it's wrong.

"I wonder how your brother is doing," Rita sighs.

"Stop it. I'm sure he's fine." I hug my pillow. Even though no one volunteered in our area to leave today, that doesn't mean people aren't crowded around waiting in hope and horror for someone desperate enough for fame to step forward.

Rogers steps up to the microphone and gives a quick good-bye speech about life in our world and "the possibilities beyond the stars." The crowd eats it up. I copy it down verbatim. Then he straps on a black backpack with his belongings and spins around to face the vertex. The soldiers on each side of him salute. One soldier types onto the tablet, making George Rogers the first name on the census list of the departed. Cameras zoom in on his face. He closes his eyes, taking a moment. I wonder if it's for himself or for the camera.

I hold my breath. I want to scream *Don't do it!* At the same time, something inside me wants him to go. Wants to push him in and see what happens.

When Rogers opens his eyes, they seem darker. He takes one step forward. Another. Then another. And with one final step his body evaporates into the swirling blue of the vertex like the sparrow. The hologram bows low in respect. The crowd pauses in silent awe, and then a slow clapping and cheering begins and spreads until the noise becomes deafening.

He did it. I can't believe he did it.

"Whoa." Rita's face glows a patriotic blue and red since she's so close to the television screen. "He's totally gone."

"Idiots," Dad comments from the other room. "This isn't the Olympics."

———

Media channels repeat footage from around the globe of the first six volunteers who stepped into vertexes. I jot down the names.

George Rogers age 72 United States
Kun Wen age 86 China
Abani Dhillon age 77 India
Vadim Kozlov age 91 Russia
Nakamura Manami age 82 Japan
Jack Brocklehurst age 75 England

It feels like the beginning of a bizarre space race. Who's willing to sacrifice themselves into the unknown to show they are the bravest, ready to take on a new challenge and represent their country?

Not me.

Plus, according to the government's new Q&A website, the holograms said that people live an average of two hundred and fifty years there, so it makes sense that all the initial volunteers are elderly. It's like a wacked-out fountain of youth. The volunteers aren't brave or suicidal. They're like the 49ers, hoping that the rumors are true, that the grass is greener on the other side. *But who says there's grass or gold on the other side of this rainbow? Why risk it all without a guarantee?*

CHAPTER 6

DAY 19: AUGUST–3,966 HOURS TO DECIDE

QUESTION: DO YOU HAVE SEX TO REPRODUCE?

ANSWER: YES, WE ARE HUMANS LIKE
YOU. WE HAVE SEX FOR REPRODUCTION,
PLEASURE, AND CONNECTION.

That night, the doorbell rings, and I race to answer it. *Fail.* I hear Dad's voice boom, "Nick. Weren't you just here?"

"Can't stay away," Dominick says, stuffing his hands in both pockets.

"Not trying hard enough," Dad responds.

I intervene before Dad gets too cocky. "Hey," I say, stepping between them.

"Hay's for horses," Dad says. He pats me on the back a little too hard. A sweet, all-too-familiar smell radiates from his pores.

"We're going to the movies," I escape out the front door with Dominick before Dad can argue. Dominick still has his hands in his pockets. He's not looking at me. "Sorry. You know how he is."

"It's not that," he says. "My mom had to work overtime. I have Austin with me in the car."

"Oh." I was hoping for some quality time talking and making out.

"I was thinking instead of the movies we could go back to my house? Put Austin to bed and watch a movie there?" His eyes shine with nervousness. Is he afraid of disappointing me or afraid of disappointing himself?

Even though I'm almost eighteen, my parents have a rule against me going to Dominick's house for obvious reasons: A) his mom is never home, and B) they think I'm a virgin, which I am, and they want to keep it that way for as long as possible.

After watching Rogers take a cosmic leap, breaking a parental rule seems super trivial. "Sure, let's do it."

His eyes light up, and a wide grin spreads across his face.

"I didn't mean *that*. Don't expect anything."

"Never," he says. His dimples say something else.

Dominick's little brother, Austin, pulls my hand and offers to show me around their place. He's so excited, I don't remind him that I visited after his father's funeral.

"This is my room," Austin says, giving me a tour. Across one wall, a series of shelves hold a collection of Transformers, plastic figurines, airplanes, other vehicles, and video game equipment, all in strict procession. After my years in therapy and reading about psychology, I recognize signs of obsessive-compulsive disorder when I see them. No kid's room should ever be this organized.

"Nice," I say and point at his Pokémon poster over his bed. "Who's your favorite?"

"I like Pikachu, of course, but I also like Charizard." He picks up a stuffed orange dragon with turquoise inner wings and a flaming tail.

"Why do you like him?"

"'Cause he can fly and breathe fire." He stands on his bed and flies the Pokémon around my head.

"That's cool." I blink as the toy buzzes repeatedly in my face and whacks my nose. I back away to escape the torture.

"All right, time for bed," Dominick announces.

"No. I wanna stay up." Austin jumps off the bed, runs to his desk, and starts coloring an unfinished drawing of a Transformer.

"I'll tell you what," Dominick bargains, "if you hop in bed, I'll let you watch a movie in the dark."

Austin dives into bed, and Dominick sets up the DVD player. Watching their routine together makes me appreciate the full responsibility Dominick feels for his family. There's something both cute and sad about it.

I want to help, so I pull up an airplane-patterned sheet over Austin's legs. "No, it's too hot," he complains and kicks off the sheet.

"Movie's on," Dominick intervenes. "If you get outta bed, it goes off. Got it?"

"Got it." He sits Charizard next to him on his pillow.

"Good. Night, buddy." Dominick clicks off the lamp.

"Night."

We step out of the room, and Dominick leaves the door open a crack. "He's afraid of the dark. The TV helps. He'll be asleep in like ten minutes."

I put my hand on his shoulder. "You're so good with him."

"Someone has to be." He fixes his glasses and changes his tone to a fake kid voice. "Wanna go to my room? I can show you my Pikachu."

"Gross!" I smile and push his chest.

He laughs and says, "Fine. Living room it is."

Once there, he kicks off his sneakers and tosses them under the coffee table, so I slip off my flip flops and do the same.

"We can do shirts next," he offers, lifting his black T-shirt so I see his belt, the top of his shorts, the hair on his navel. So distracting.

I change the subject. "What did you think of Rogers and the other people volunteering to leave first?"

"I think it's absurd," Dominick says, putting his shirt back down. He clicks on the television and channel surfs.

"I know, right?"

"I can't tell if they're doing it for the fame or to escape their lives. I understand wanting to go for scientific reasons, but I still think it's way too early." He stops on a rerun of *The Big Bang Theory* and puts the remote on his lap. So distracting.

"You want something to eat? Drink?" he offers.

"Um, sure. Water."

Once he leaves the room, I put on more lip gloss and glance down the front of my red tank top to check if my cleavage looks even underneath. I shift the underwire of my favorite lacy, black bra to get the right lift.

What were we talking about? Oh, yeah. "I thought maybe it was an age thing," I say loud enough for him to hear me.

He returns with water for me and a can of soda for himself. "What do you mean?"

"Did you notice how they were all older? I looked it up. On the other planet, humans can survive for 250 years."

"No kidding." Dominick takes a sip of cola. "That's a selling point."

"Yep." The cold water slips down my throat. I didn't realize how thirsty I was.

He puts his feet up on the coffee table. "What do you want to do?"

I smile. "Not what you're thinking."

"How do you know what I'm thinking?"

"'Cause I'm psychic. Like Tyler Henry."

"No, you're not.. You're a fact finder. Ballbuster. You're definitely still a Scully."

"Stop it. I am not that cynical."

"Cynical. Skeptical. Sexy. It's all the same." He grins and those dimples reel me in. We kiss and kiss and he climbs on top of me as I lean back. His hand slides up my tank top, and my stomach muscles tense. I stifle a laugh since it tickles. He feels so good and I want to say yes, but I can't make a choice with all these unknown decisions ahead of us. Colleges. Vertexes. It's too much.

"Dominick—"

He must be able to tell by my voice because he stops and lifts off me. "Slowing down," he whispers.

He doesn't realize how much I want him. We started dating in April of junior year. There's nothing we could do about that. You feel what you feel when you feel it. But it always meant that our relationship came with a huge deadline attached. Senior year. College decisions. I don't want our choices to be dependent on each other. With everything else going on, sex will only make everything harder. No pun intended.

I must look upset because he says, "No worries. I don't want to do anything you don't want to do."

That's what worries me. I'm afraid to do so many things, but I'm most afraid of holding him back.

———

Dominick's mom returns dangerously close to my curfew. I get home with seconds to spare and my heart in my throat. Thankfully, the living room is dark, but it's never that easy. I find Dad in the kitchen making a turkey and cheese sandwich.

"How was the movie?" he asks as he spreads mayonnaise on bread.

"Fine," I say.

He cuts the sandwich in half the triangle way. "What did you see?"

"That new horror movie. *The Macbeth Murders.*" I maintain eye contact as long as I can.

"Was it good?"

"Yeah." I shove a slice of turkey into my mouth from the package on the counter.

"Where's the movie stub?"

My heartbeat hammers away, and I can feel it pounding in my skull. I stall, chew.

"It was a digital ticket. Er, on Dominick's phone."

"Huh." He takes a huge bite of his sandwich and chews in loud, wet circles. I can't tell if he's bought it. Now I know why Dominick sticks his hands in his pockets; no one can see if they're shaking. After an awkward minute of the silent treatment, including Dad licking his fingers, wiping his face with a paper towel, and taking a swig of milk, he zeroes in on me, and I can't look away.

"Glad you enjoyed yourself. Hope not too much."

My face feels hot. "Yep."

I escape to my room and lie on my bed. That was close. It's embarrassing that Dad still treats me like I'm twelve. I'm almost eighteen. If I want to have sex with my boyfriend after months of dating and two years of friendship, I will. And my decision will have nothing to do with him and his rules.

But if I want to go to law school someday, I can't let anything get in my way, not my family, not my anxiety, not my boyfriend. Dominick's kisses still linger, soft and tempting. I never expected to doubt myself so much in all three areas, never mind contemplating the future surrounded by holograms and the vertexes.

I wonder if they have lawyers on their planet. No money, maybe no lawyers. Maybe we're in for a rude awakening, and we'll discover that their world works a billion times better than ours. That would be a game changer. I don't know if we're evolved enough to adapt. I know I'm not ready to change everything I've ever known.

What if we get there and bring all our old problems? Wouldn't that ruin their little utopia?

I take a pill so I can sleep.

———

During the next three days, the first major exodus takes place among the homeless, mentally ill, extremely poor, and the sick of the world. I take notes. According to the news, small lines have formed at vertexes in Michigan, New Jersey, Ohio, Kentucky, Florida, New York, and South Dakota. The suicide rate has dropped since many people have jumped through a vertex instead of off a bridge. According to one report, "experts attribute these changes to a newfound hope in another world with better medical treatments and no need for wealth." The mentally unstable who haven't left the planet, however, are checking into hospitals at a skyrocketing rate. Others are disappearing through other means. Experts believe those people have gone off the grid—out to unpopulated, wooded areas, living in tents and bunkers. Their "inability to comprehend the message within the scope of their already intense paranoia" has finally splintered their brains and confirmed their worst fears.

Note to self: keep an eye on Dad. Other than boxes in the basement and more beer cans in the recycling, he's been okay. The light in his eyes is still on. *But at any time, lightning could strike, and he could go on a tirade. Or a power outage, and he could shut down completely.* You'd think the lightning strikes would be the worst, but no, somehow the power outages hurt even more. It's like watching the hope in his soul shrivel up.

A few top astrophysicists, mathematicians, and other adventurous types have also decided to take the plunge. The opportunity was too enticing for them to pass up. I think they're as foolish as the other people, but Dominick disagreed and explained their need to explore a part of space where no earthling has gone before. I can't argue with him when he uses *Star Trek* against me.

Other people have started talking crap about the good the exodus will have on the nation:

"Getting rid of the baggage that's weighing the country's economy down."

"Vertexes are cleaning up the gene pool."

"Dregs of the streets. Good riddance."

Even Dad has gotten onto this train of thought.

I don't understand how people can be so desperate and so mean. Life on Earth must be terrible for those leaving if they are willing to risk everything for the slightest possibility the holograms are actually telling the truth. I mean, we have no evidence there's a comet. It could all be an elaborate trap.

I need evidence. Facts. Ambiguity breeds overreaction. I should know. I'm the queen of biological overreaction. We simply don't have enough information to make a permanent decision. How can people, especially scientific people, make this kind of leap of faith? Can this level of hopelessness and disinterest in our planet really exist?

Maybe Dominick's right. Maybe I really am a Scully. But she always seemed so cool, calm, and collected, not sweaty, shaky, and scattered.

"Come fishing with me tomorrow morning," Dominick asks over the phone. His request catches me so off guard the bowl I'm holding tips, sending a cold dribble of cookie dough ice cream down my bare leg.

"But you said, and I quote, 'I fish alone. Man versus fish.' I remember the lofty speech." I grab a T-shirt from my laundry basket to wipe my leg.

"I changed my mind."

"Are you sure?" I know what he's not saying. His father used to bring him on fishing trips. It was their thing.

"I wouldn't ask if I wasn't sure."

The silent shift in our relationship is palpable. It's a proposal of sorts. He's inviting me deeper into his world, right when it's almost time to let our worlds go.

"Sure," I say. My mind screams *Don't do it!*

"Six a.m. Bring a sweatshirt. It's usually windy."

Early the next morning, I search through my bureau for something appropriate to wear on our fishing date. I choose jean shorts, a Patriots T-shirt, canvas sneakers, and a "Life is Good" hat. My anxiety revs up inside my chest. *I'm forgetting something. I know I'm forgetting something.* Then I remember to grab a navy blue sweatshirt like Dominick suggested. You would think that remembering I forgot something would make me feel better, but instead it justifies my anxiety, which starts a loop in my brain thinking that I must be forgetting something else.

What else am I forgetting? There's something else. I know there's something. Something. Something. If I forget it, something bad will happen. Something really bad. And I won't be able to fix it.

STOP IT.

The loop continues. I dig through my dirty laundry, then open and close every drawer in my room, searching and double-checking for something to remind me what I could be forgetting. My body sweats as I spin in circles.

STOP IT. Everything's fine.

But what if it's not fine? What if I left an iron plugged in? What if I start a fire? What if I go fishing and then come back and the house is burned down? What if my parents and Benji are burnt to a crisp and they have to use their dental records to identify the bodies? What if the police think I did it on purpose? What if—

I take a pill and wait for it to rescue me.

———————

Dominick and I walk along the wide cement pier that extends from New Bedford's Fort Taber into the Atlantic. A metal barrier protects us from falling into the water. Old-fashioned light posts line the left side of the walkway. Even at the early hour, the ocean air is cool but thick with late-August humidity. The wind restores the emptiness inside me from my earlier panic. My old counselor used to tell me that spending more time outside would help my anxiety. Maybe I should've listened, but it always felt counterintuitive since I usually feel safer indoors. As we reach the end of the pier, the wide ocean stretches out for us in full panoramic glory. The Butler Flats lighthouse sits proudly in the water. Sailboats drift past on the horizon. Across the harbor, I can see my town, Fairhaven, marked by two wind turbines in the distance. I can see why the pier was a favorite place for Dominick and his father.

The air at the end of the pier, however, reeks like moldy cat food mixed with fish armpit. If they had armpits. There are always certain summer days when the ocean seems to ripen, and the wind carries the rotten stench of decaying beach life. Growing up here, you would think I would've adjusted. Impossible.

Dominick bought a bucket of live green crabs for bait. Brownish green bodies the size of quarters huddle on top of one another.

"Aw, do you have to?" I complain as he grabs one for the line. "It's cute."

"It's eat or be eaten," he says. "Nature's way." He jabs the underbelly of the crab with the hook. I cringe.

"Can't we be above nature?" I ask.

He gives me that look, the one that says to stop pretending I'm a philosopher to hide that I'm being a wimp. I hate that look.

"Let's get you fishing," he says.

Moving behind me, Dominick wraps his arms around me and places his hands over my hands to show me how to cast the line. My body moves with his body, and I soak in his strength and confidence.

"Do you think the parallel universe has fishing?" I ask.

"Don't know. Probably if they have oceans, they have fish. But I read that scientists believe oceans on other planets might not be made of water."

"What then? Milk?" I tease.

"More like liquid hydrogen. But then the planet wouldn't be habitable for people. Or fish."

I look out at the water. "Imagine if there were alien fish that could survive. They'd be some weird fish."

"The rain would be killer," he jokes. "Literally. Fireballs."

We laugh together and banter under the morning sun. The briny air releases the heaviness in my chest. I reel the line in slowly to tease the fish, but nothing bites. By the third time, I bait and cast the line without Dominick's help.

"You bored?" he asks.

"No, it's nice, actually. Calming."

"I thought you might like it. I hear it's good for anxiety."

It's like he's stuck me with a pin and deflated me. "Stop treating me like Anxiety Girl."

"Sorry, I didn't mean it like that."

"You never do."

He looks away, and I feel bad for wrecking the moment. I laugh nervously. "Anxiety Girl. That's like the worst superhero name ever."

He grins. "I'm sure we can think up worse."

"Like what? Constipation Girl?"

"Puberty Boy?"

"Dandruff Girl."

"Blister Boy."

I move in unnaturally close to him. "Captain Close Talker."

He breathes directly into my face. "Captain HAL-itosis."

I giggle and bite my bottom lip. "Super Lips?"

"Super Lips, huh?" He smiles. "I like it."

He kisses me, and I hold on to the metal railing to keep from falling.

———

After about an hour of kissing and talking nonsense, taking turns with the pole, and staring at the dark surface of the waves, the fishing pole bends.

"Got one," Dominick says and hands me the pole. "Don't reel it in all at once. Pull to the side, then reel. Pull to the side, then reel." He demonstrates from behind me. "Find a rhythm. Don't rush it."

I follow his directions, which sound sexual to me after all the making out we've been doing. Maybe it's just his voice.

Soon, a fish breaches the water at the end of my line. Mottled olive green and mud brown, it's uglier and smaller than I expect after all that pulling.

"It's a tautog," Dominick comments.

"I caught my first fish," I announce. "Take a picture."

I pose while Dominick snaps a quick photo with his phone. As I hold up the fish, I see the bulging lips and gills gape open and close in a desperate attempt to filter the world. I know that feeling. *Gasping for breath. Having your body fail to process the environment properly. Feeling trapped. Helpless. Not knowing how to escape. Maybe like going through a vertex.*

"We have to let it go." I can't get the words out fast enough.

"Alex, I don't usually—"

Before he can stop me, I grab the fishing line with the dangling victim hanging from its end. It flips its tail when I try to touch it, and the spines on its back stick up. I wish I had scissors so I could just cut the line.

"Hold it by the gills underneath," Dominick coaches.

I prop the gills up against my thumb and pointer finger. With my free hand, I try to maneuver the hook from its mouth while avoiding further injury to its system. As it opens its thick lips, a set of human-looking teeth startle me. Our fish are freakish enough on our planet. Its prehistoric face and slimy alien eyes make me wonder if it would try to eat me if it could. I concentrate on the hook, but its slippery body and the smell of rotten seaweed trigger my gag reflex. Right when I'm about to give up, the hook dislodges, and I toss the fish over the edge of the pier to freedom. As it swims away into the dark water, I can breathe again.

Dominick must think I've gone over the edge of the pier myself. I can't look at him.

"Now I know why I fish alone," he says, breaking the silence.

I turn to face him, ready to argue my case, but when I do, I find him grinning.

"Shut up," I say and a smile forces its way on my face.

"I'm sorry. I never knew you had such strong feelings for fish."

"I don't!" I giggle.

"Yet I've seen you eat Filet-O-Fish sandwiches like nobody's business."

I push his shoulder. He grabs me and tickles my stomach.

"Stop!" I say, laughing.

"Hey, you lost me a fish. You owe me."

"Fine, what do you want?" I walked right into that one. Why do I tease him when I know I'm not ready? Am I ready?

He smiles wide. "I'll think about it and get back to you."

"You do that," I taunt and sit on the pier, exhausted.

"I have to say, this is nothing like fishing with my dad." His sentence hangs out in the air like a fish on a line. I'm not sure how to rescue him.

"We can keep fishing," I say to try to help, "as long as I can throw them back."

He thinks for a moment. "I guess you can be the fish liberator."

We fish for another hour. Well, Dominick does most of the fishing. We catch two more, and I free them immediately after snapping a photo. The rush of freeing them becomes a challenge, and even though I wouldn't admit it to Dominick, freeing the fish makes me feel in control for the first time in a long time.

Witnessing each fish struggle to breathe tugs at my memory as I remove the hooks. I don't say anything to Dominick, but it reminds me of when Dad returned home after being honorably discharged. I was eight. For months on end he screamed in the middle of the night, flopping around in his bed like a fish out of water. I watched from the doorway as Mom tried to calm him, but he kept screaming and screaming and fighting with the bedding. When she finally woke him up, he yelled at her for overreacting.

Then one night I found him in the kitchen standing in the light of the open refrigerator. His eyes were vacant, like he couldn't see the world that I was in. I watched him as he wandered out the back door into the darkness. I don't know why I didn't run for Mom, but for some reason I ran for Benji. We watched from the kitchen window as Dad sat in the grass under the automatic security light patting his legs again and again.

"Don't tell Mom," Benji said to me. "It's bad enough. Pinkie swear."

"Pinkie swear."

Over the next few months, when one of us would find Dad sleepwalking, we'd wake up the other one to watch, whispering the code phrase "Zombie Night." We convinced ourselves that it was our secret adventure. We didn't see the real danger until Dad turned on me.

It started as a typical night, Benji waking me up with the code phrase, me jumping out of bed and following him up the attic stairs without question. We spied on Dad as he searched through storage totes with a blank stare.

Then I sneezed, and Dad dove behind the bins. Horrified, I ran to tell him that it was okay and it was only me. Benji told me to stay back, but I didn't listen. I couldn't stand to see my father that vulnerable. As soon as I reached out to him, Dad lunged at me and grabbed me by the neck. I gasped open-mouthed for air the way fish gasp for water. Benji screamed for him to stop, the two of us prying at Dad's thick fingers to pull him off me, but we weren't strong enough. In seconds, the world turned black, my vision closing in like a tube blowing in a television screen.

I heard later that Benji had to bite Dad's arm and draw blood to stop him. It was never clear if Dad actually woke up in that moment or if he broke down in pain. But as my vision returned, I saw him sobbing from where I sat on the floor holding my neck.

Benji ran for Mom. Once she saw Dad's condition and the marks on my neck, she ordered Benji and I back to bed. I listened to Mom and Dad have a huge fight and Dad agreeing to go for counseling and start medication. Mom came into my bedroom to check on me. She gave me an ice pack and said I would need to hide my neck at school to cover the bruises so Dad wouldn't get in trouble. I couldn't sleep the whole night. I wore turtleneck sweaters and scarves for over a week. Haven't worn either since. The Zombie

Nights stopped soon after. That was ten years ago. I've never talked about that night. Ever.

As I set another fish free and watch it swim into the dark waters, I can feel a part of me sink with it, knowing it could be captured at any time and experience the same terror once again. *If a comet actually hits, all the fish will boil alive, flesh and bones falling off and disintegrating while their home evaporates into the atmosphere.* And Dominick thought that fishing would help my anxiety. I wish he'd stop trying to cure me. Trying to guess what will trigger symptoms will only trigger symptoms. Catch-22.

Dominick casts the line with a natural confidence. It's him at his finest. I wish I could find and hold onto that kind of peace inside of me. His father gave him this gift. He'd be proud of his son. I almost say this out loud to Dominick, but on second thought it might be too much to hear.

I chip at my You Are So Outta Lime nail polish. What gift did my father give me? How to swear, argue, fight, and drink? How to worry about the dangers in the world? How to fight against the waves instead of how to ride them?

When a family of five arrives with poles, Dominick and I decide to pack up and head back toward the parking lot. At the end of the pier, I notice a small metal sign off to one side of the barrier, warning to catch and release all fish due to high PCB levels in the water.

"Hey," I say, pointing to the sign. "Did you know this the whole time?" *What if he had taken the fish home, eaten them, and died?*

He shrugs and smiles. "You were determined. I wasn't about to take that away from you."

"I touched all those fish for no reason? You would've done it anyway?"

"You were a pro."

"You're such a punk," I say, bumping him with my hip. "Now you owe me."

"Anything you want," he teases.

His willingness to surrender to me—mind, body, and soul—is both wonderful and terrifying.

Something I don't think I'll ever be capable of doing.

CHAPTER 7

QUESTION: Do you have war? Problems with violence? Weapons?

ANSWER: No, we have evolved into a peaceful society. We have proactive measures in place to deal with possible violence. Your weaponry will not work in our world. We have global technology that can isolate and contain any explosions instantaneously. Your weapons cannot fire here, bombs cannot detonate. (See also question on judicial system and prisons.)

The media is in an uproar. Major credit card companies are asking governments to stop all vertex travel. They want Congress to pass a law requiring people to pay off all credit card debt before leaving the planet through a vertex. It's a verbal war between people and banks. I sit on the edge of the couch and take notes.

People interviewed on TV say it's not fair to technically charge people who want to leave the planet. Companies argue they have the right to collect debt before people leave. One reporter calls the Debt-Departure Debate a "slippery slope." I remember the term from debate team—a type of logic that leads to an avalanche of other outcomes. The reporter mentions other types of debt. Will people have to pay off mortgages? Car loans? Student loans? Even though Dad said he'd never leave, he looks nervous. We have a mortgage and credit card debt. Not sure if both cars are paid off.

Even though I think it's terrifying to leave through a vertex, I don't like the idea of being told I'm trapped and forced to stay, either.

———

It gets worse. Breaking news: fifteen vertexes have been simultaneously bombed in the Middle East, including Iraq, Iran, Israel, Palestine, and Egypt. As reported through every channel and media outlet, extremist groups coordinated the attacks using an underground social media channel and coded messages that passed undetected through all government anti-terrorism checkpoints. I frantically copy the information into my journal.

I can't believe people are so afraid of the unknown they need to attack it. Dad can't believe it didn't happen sooner. Mom believes that it will happen again. I wonder if it has anything to do with the Debt-Departure Debate. The if-I-can't-go-no-one-can mentality.

We are glued to the screen around the clock, watching the bombs blast over and over on replay at each location, watching military officials and people in line to enter the vertex instead get lost in a cloud of debris. But the real reason we are glued to the screen is not the devastation, not the shocking fact that there are people willing to destroy the possible salvation of humanity. What is remarkable and horrific to us all, what we cannot stop watching, is that once the shock and the aftermath of the bombings settled, once the cloud of debris lifted, as others cared for the wounded and retrieved the victims, the blue vertexes and holograms stood untouched. Perfect.

Their invincibility gives us a silent, resilient hope. It also bothers us more than we'd ever admit to each other.

———

I catch Dad staring at the TV in the living room after watching the bombings on repeat. I don't mean vegging out after work; I mean zoned out. Like he's trapped in a dark forest of memory. I know the difference.

"Dad. Dad." No response. Only a blank stare.

My insides freeze. *Is he breathing?* Yes, his chest just moved up and down. At least I think I saw it move.

I wave my hand back and forth in front of his open eyes. "Dad?"

Nothing.

Lights out.

No, no, no. I reach over, grab his shoulder, and shake him back into the here and now. "Dad? Dad!"

He finally acknowledges my presence. "What?" he asks, annoyed, like nothing was wrong.

"You weren't responding."

"I didn't hear you. Jeez."

But we both know that isn't the truth.

I take a pill.

———

According to the internet, the two Massachusetts vertexes were not a target in the bombings; however, not hearing from Benji after his shift has invited what-ifs into our house.

What-ifs are not good for military families. I wish he would answer his phone.

Dad sits in his lounger, drowning himself in beer. Watching him self-medicate is better than watching him get lost in memories. Mom paces the kitchen, frantically dialing her phone. I want to hide in my room, but the masochistic need to watch both parents collapse wins.

I start collecting data in my journal. If I stay in my room, I won't be able to see what's happening, and my mind will imagine the horrible possibilities. But if I record the situation for analysis later, then I'll be able to control it somehow and relax. I sit between the kitchen and the living room, straddling two worlds and reactions.

Dad cracks his knuckles repeatedly in an idiosyncratic dance. He flips through the television stations like pages in a fashion magazine, not even bothering to stop and understand the content. A constant roll of images, all disconnected from the next.

Mom sips a cup of tea, sighs, then checks her phone again. She leaves the kitchen and goes to the bathroom for the umpteenth time. After fourteen minutes, she emerges with swollen eyes and no makeup. She reheats her tea in the microwave, then wraps the cup with a paper towel. She seems older, slower in her movements. There's a carefulness that comes with waiting for news that could shatter you.

No one discusses the elephant in the room. But it's there. I can feel it like running broken glass across my gums. I want to scream for them to speak. But that would break the silence and shatter the illusion that life as we know it isn't on the brink of disaster.

I check the time on my phone. It's getting later and later and still no Benji. I almost text him again, but Mom keeps staring at me, and I don't want her to think that I think something is wrong, too. I pick at my nail polish, and then at a hangnail, making my thumb bleed.

Where the hell is he? Doesn't he understand what not answering does to them? Mom's leaking fluids and Dad's fingers are about to fall off.

Four hours later, Benji crosses the threshold. Dad and I see him first since Mom is in the bathroom once again.

"Hey," he says. "What's everyone doing up?"

"Waiting," I mutter under my breath.

"Your mother's been a wreck," Dad says. He finally stops cracking and wringing his hands.

"Sorry," Benji offers.

"Sorry doesn't cut it," Dad says. He chugs the rest of his drink.

"We had a briefing after the bombings. Then I went out for a beer with a friend."

"You could have called. You'll worry your mother sick."

Mom rushes into the living room and embraces Benji. He returns the hug, and several awkward seconds tick by as two years of pent-up anguish over Benji's decision to serve in the military pour from her eyes.

"Thank heavens." Mom doesn't bother to wipe the tears streaming down her face. "Where have you been? Why didn't you call?"

Benji looks around for help, but Dad has turned his attention back to the television remote.

"Answer me," she begs.

"Mom, I'm sorry. But I'm a grown man. Jeez."

But his face says something different. He avoids eye contact and his lips tighten, like he's fighting an inner battle about not sharing military secrets with us. I store the image in my journal for safekeeping. There's something pressing on his mind, and it's so big he's having trouble hiding it.

I don't know what to say to him. Benji's right, he's a grown man, but he doesn't see how different Mom has been since he left. She used to be a little stronger, a little brighter. An emptiness hangs over the house in his absence, an emptiness I can never fill for my parents.

Benji holds Mom's face in his hands. "I'm fine," he says, kissing her forehead for emphasis. "I'm fine," he repeats slowly.

She hangs her head low, nods, and wipes at her wet face. When she plops herself on the edge of Dad's lounge chair, Dad and Benji share a conspiratorial look as if telepathically agreeing that she overreacted. Like a typical woman.

I don't like it one bit. Dad was just as freaked out. It's not about her. Benji's being selfish as usual, not caring how his behavior affects the family, but since I can't put my finger precisely on what's going on, I don't have a way to argue against it.

———

Governments have decided they cannot play debt police. They conclude that "the right to leave a planet should not be determined by economics." Easy to say when free vertexes appear for travel. I wonder if they'd say the same thing if they had to provide the transportation.

I'd like to say that the decision fills me with tremendous relief. It doesn't. Banks have decided to freeze all credit card accounts until the hologram-vertex prophecy plays out. No new mortgages until February 1st. No new car loans. Guess they're afraid people will go on spending sprees, live it up, and then leave through a vertex. The world has shifted to a cash-only system.

Glad I don't need a student loan until next year, but the whole credit thing leaves me worried about what other problems the vertexes might trigger. Dad immediately empties our bank accounts and buys a safe.

———

The end of August brings my senior year of high school and inevitable decisions. Rita and I spend one last summer girls' night together. We decide to go to a movie, of course, because her religion doesn't allow it. Something about guardian angels not able to protect people inside theaters. Even though many teens in her church openly rebel against the movie rule, she still pretends to follow it in front of her parents.

Before we leave, she changes into a remarkable outfit—a red sundress with a long, beaded, matching necklace and strappy beige sandals. I dress to kill in a peach dress with baby blue accessories but with nowhere near as much cleavage as Rita. I couldn't create that much cleavage with duct tape.

At the theater, a group of guys from our high school whistle and flag us over. Rita grins and strikes up a conversation with Nathan Gomes, the star wide receiver for our football team, whom she's had a major crush on since freshman year. When one of his teammates, a buff guy from my freshman year gym class, tries to make eye contact with me, I move behind Rita and pull out my cell phone.

Dominick texted me a goofy meme of a nerdy cat with a ruler, saying:

Without Geometry, Life is Pointless.

It's not even funny, which makes me giggle more. Tomorrow's our last date of the summer, and I'm ready to have the talk with him about picking colleges.

Rita exchanges phone numbers with Nathan, and then we ditch

the guys and grab tickets, popcorn, drinks, and seats. I snag an aisle seat so I can escape if necessary.

"Sorry about that, but a girl's gotta do what a girl's gotta do," Rita says.

"It's fine," I say and smile. "Just don't do them all."

"Hey," she yells, throwing a popcorn kernel at me. "Not nice. Don't slut shame me. I'm not like that. You know I've only been with two guys. The other one didn't count."

I laugh and throw popcorn back. She returns the favor. "At least I'm willing to do something," she digs.

"Hey, don't virgin shame me. I do stuff." I eat a kernel of popcorn off my lap.

She sips soda. "Define stuff."

I smile but nervousness kicks in. "Stuff," I repeat.

She rolls her eyes. "So have you narrowed down colleges yet with Dominick?"

"No. We talked about Boston again, but I'm still not sure."

"That boy loves you. I bet he'll go wherever you go."

I swallow down the welling tears. That's exactly what I'm worried about. I know his need to accommodate me will hold him back. I can't let him do that to himself.

I push away the negative thoughts and focus on fun. Tonight is about Rita and me.

"You're gonna have so much fun living in college dorms. I wish I was planning to go away instead of living at home and waitressing for my parents at the restaurant."

"Is it still that bad?"

She nods. "Why did I ever agree to go to community college?"

"Remember? Saving money, transferring later?"

"Right. Well, I'm starting to wonder if I can survive two more years taking orders in Jesus land."

The theater lights fade to black, so we have to cut our conversation short. I've spent years complaining to her about how I can't wait to leave my parents, but now that crunch time is here, I don't know what to tell her. She admits to living vicariously through me, but she doesn't really get what it's like to be stuck in my head. The last thing I need is her judgment, too.

The movie ends up being pretty underwhelming. Rita drives us to Panera Bread where she orders broccoli and cheddar soup in a bread bowl, which she admits is not vegetarian since it has chicken broth, but she overlooks it for the cheese. I get a turkey club. It's funny that she complains about her religion all the time, but she'd easily be a vegetarian without the religious guideline.

Back at my house, we change into tank tops and pajama shorts and lay blankets on the floor. We talk and giggle about random subjects while she searches through shows on my television, and I wipe off what's left of my chipped nail polish with remover.

"I miss TV," she announces. "My church told everyone to avoid it since so much of the footage revolves around vertexes. Of course that meant my parents put all the sets in storage and canceled all our subscriptions. Thank God for my phone."

"How's that going?" I ask. "I mean with the church."

"It's impossible. They see the vertexes as the ultimate test for humanity in choosing for or against God."

"But what if you believe God wants to save everyone by sending the vertexes?" I start painting my nails a deep purple color called Midnight in Moscow.

"Exactly." She shakes her head. "The more they talk lately, the more judgmental they sound. You're so lucky your family isn't religious."

Sometimes I'm grateful my parents aren't religious since I don't accept things without evidence, but sometimes I think I'm missing out on its rules and order and community. Makes me feel religiously deficient, like I missed out on spiritual vitamins or something.

When we hear someone close the front door, Rita jumps up from the floor and fixes her hair. "Your brother's home and waiting for me."

"You just got a guy's phone number at the movies."

"Alex, I'd give up every guy in the universe if Benji would give me a chance. Do you realize how hot your brother is?"

"Um, no. Gross!" I throw a pillow at her.

She throws it back, then fluffs up her hair again. "I don't know how he's still single."

"He hasn't had time for a girlfriend. He just got back."

She touches up her makeup in my mirror. "Well, wish me luck. Do you need anything from the kitchen?"

"No. And I'm not going to help you seduce my brother. That's just wrong."

Rita takes a deep breath and tiptoes out of my room like we're in some ridiculous comedy. We would've made awesome college roommates.

By the time she returns, I'm waving around all twenty of my fingers and toes to get my nails to dry faster. She has a weird look on her face that's hard to read. I'd call it disappointment, but that's not quite right.

"What happened?"

"Nothing."

She takes a minute, like she's considering something, then blinks a few times. "He pretty much put a nail in that coffin."

"Ouch. Was he a jerk to you? If he was, I'll give him hell for it."

"No. He's dating someone."

"Oh, I didn't know. Sorry." I feel like I set her up for failure. "He keeps his relationships top secret. You know he doesn't talk to me about stuff like that."

"It's fine," Rita adds. "Like you said, I have a new potential date from the movies. Let's text the number."

And just like that, she moves on. *Why can't it be that easy for me to move on? I get stuck on things. Let them dwell. Feel guilty.* There must be so much freedom in acceptance. I blow on my fingernails. There is so much Rita can teach me about female confidence— something my own mother fails at miserably.

We spend the next hour texting Nathan and laughing. It makes me miss Dominick, but I told him that I wouldn't call or text so I could have girl time with Rita. That was partly true, but mostly it was so I could train myself to start thinking without him. It's not working.

While Rita's busy flirting, I click on the TV. More names of the departed—not dead, simply gone; there's a difference now, and the difference matters—tick across the screen with select footage from sites across the globe. A local reporter takes center screen at the Quincy vertex, reiterating the same hypothesis about people under extreme poverty or with severe mental health problems seeing the vertexes as an escape and hoping for a clean slate in another society.

I've always pictured college as a clean slate where I could rewrite myself and start on a fresh path without the burden of my family to follow me. Until now.

On screen, I spot a familiar silhouette move into the background of the shot. The unruly patient from the hospital is back at the Quincy vertex. I'm surprised she hasn't gone through the vertex, disappeared into the woods, or been sent to a psych ward.

"Turn it up," I ask Rita since she's closer to the remote.

The reporter doesn't realize that the lady is approaching from behind until it's too late. But hey, it's newsworthy material—the reporter adapts quickly and uses every second to her advantage. She shoves the microphone into the lady's face and asks, "What do you think of the holographic message?"

The camera zooms in and catches the lady at a terrible angle, accenting all the wrong features to fill both eye sockets with gothic shadows and outline every wrinkle in her forehead. She might as well be Jack Nicholson in *The Shining*.

"Ma'am?" The reporter prompts again, "What do you think of the holographic message?"

"The hope only of empty men," she mutters.

The camera pans out to normal view. "Interesting," the reporter comments. "So, are you saying we should wait and have hope? Are you planning to stay here?"

The lady dismisses her second question and peers directly into the camera so that her face fills the entire screen. Rita stops texting to watch.

"Paralyzed force, gesture without motion."

The reporter in the background tries to weasel her body back into the frame. "Um, okay. I'm not sure if you answered my question."

"That lady's tripping," Rita says.

"It's the same lady we saw get arrested at the vertex with the megaphone." *Same one from the hospital.* "I feel bad for her. She's not right." For some reason, the lady's words seem familiar to me again. Maybe I'm reaching a new level of paranoia.

For the grand finale, she lets it all hang out, pointing her finger at the camera and crying, "This is the way the world ends." She glances around as if expecting someone to react to her declaration of imminent calamity.

The camera pans back to the reporter, but before she can respond, the lady grabs her and says, "Heroes are born! Heroes are born!"

She pushes the reporter into the camera and runs from the screen. The reporter clears her throat and wraps up the story as if the strange lady is a phenomenon in her own right. I'm sure they'll repeat clips of the interview for ratings.

Suddenly, my brain clicks. I understand why her weird speech patterns seem familiar. "Rita, the way she talks... I think she's reciting a poem I've read before."

"Weird." I look over, and Rita's already texting again.

I search one of the phrases on my phone, and sure enough, everything I've heard the lady spew from her mouth is from T. S. Eliot's "The Hollow Men." Everything except her last line about heroes. That part doesn't make sense. I copy the whole thing into my journal so I can reread it later. I vaguely remember reading the poem during English class sophomore year. It didn't make much sense to me at the time other than having a really depressing tone. I read it over and realize that I understand more of it now since it's appropriate for the current doomsday circumstances. Maybe that's how literature works; you understand more of it as you go through different experiences.

Maybe that lady is not as clueless as she seems.

Dominick and I spend the last day of summer together. We spend most of it at Fort Phoenix beach lounging in the sand and swimming when our bodies get too hot.

Floating on my back while the waves cradle my body is one of the best things in life. Until Dominick pulls me from underneath, filling my nostrils with salt water.

"Hey," I yell and splash him in revenge. "I was relaxing."

He returns the favor, dousing me with water. I automatically giggle like an airhead, but I secretly imagine tying him to an anchor to see how he likes it. *I like breathing, thank you very much.* When he pulls me by my wrist through the water and kisses me with his soft, lingering lips, I forget all about the dunking torture.

Back on shore, we towel off and he puts on his glasses. He really has that superhero alias look down. As the sun catches the light in his eyes and he smiles, I realize that in spite of myself and all I've tried to do to prepare myself for possible college separation, I love him.

I didn't want to become that girl. That girl so attached to a guy that she changes her life plans for him. *So how could I ever let him change his life plans for me?* I can't live with that pressure.

"You hungry?" he asks.

Don't drag it out. Tell him you are not ready. You'll never be ready.

His smile lures me in.

"Sure," I say. We pack up our stuff and go to a local stand for hot dogs and fries. Despite my adamant protesting, he shoves a twenty at the girl behind the counter. I really didn't want him to pay for me when I know what's coming. He decides to feed me a French fry. *No, no, no. I am a terrible person.* I escape for a time-out in the bathroom only to return to see him holding two ice cream cones. Mine, coffee with chocolate sprinkles. My favorite flavor. Each cold lick burns my throat.

At the end of the day, Dominick walks me to my porch. It feels like a walk of death for our relationship. Maybe now isn't the right time. Maybe there's never a right time.

"You've been quiet," he says. "You thinking about tomorrow? Senior year? Shouldn't you be excited?"

Anxiety collects in my chest and throat, like bats leaving a cave. "There's a lot to consider." He doesn't know, can't know, the weight of that statement.

"You mean college? We'll be fine. We're both smart. Probably get our first choices. Get scholarships and take out some loans. Live in Boston together. It'll be great." He puts his arm around my lower back and leads me up the porch steps.

"I think I want to go to UMass Dartmouth. Live at home. Save money."

He stops short and pulls his hand away. "I thought we decided on Boston schools."

I can't look at him. "I changed my mind."

He paces in a quick circle on the porch, his mind and emotions churning before me. "Okay, UMass it is. I can major in math there. My mom will be happy that I'll be around to watch Austin."

"Dominick, no. I knew this would happen. Go to Boston. You've always wanted to go to school there. I don't want to hold you back."

His face drops. "You don't hold me back."

"I will. Maybe you don't see it, but I will. And I can't let that happen."

He rubs his hands through his hair, then sticks them in both pockets. "This is about your anxiety, isn't it?"

"No, it isn't, but of course that's what you'd think." I chip at a piece of deep purple nail polish on my thumb. "I want to save money and commute from home."

"Alex, you can do this. Live in Boston with me. I can help you adjust."

"See, that's what I'm talking about. I don't want to hold you back."

"Damn it, Alex. What does that even mean?"

I shrug. My stomach gnaws at me. I fight the urge to run inside and hide in the bathroom again.

Dominick holds me by the shoulders. "Stop worrying about me."

I knock his hands off me. "You're the one who worries about me too much. That's the problem. You see me as an anxiety case. You're always making sure I'm okay, checking on me, acting like I'm fragile. It's like you assume I'm weak."

He paces the full length of the porch then walks right up to my face. His eyes look wild and sad.

"Alexandra, this is absurd. I don't worry about you because you have anxiety. I worry about you because I love you."

He said it. He had to say it.

He continues. "I love you. Do you get that?" He grabs me by my wrists. "Look at me. I know you don't want to hear it. I know the weight of it makes you feel afraid. I know you. You have to stop trying to push me away. I love you. You don't hold me back. You could never hold me back. You are what drives me forward. I don't want to plan my future without you in it. You are my future. You just have to let me in."

"I don't love you."

The words slip out like a bitter wind across a frozen pond. His eyes lose all brightness. Like Mom's eyes when Benji is away or Dad's during a Zombie Night.

I turn away, hold on to the wooden porch railing, and stare off into the neighbor's yard. I want to rescue him, take it all back, go to a Boston school, stay together, be that girl for him. But I can't. I just can't. To rescue him, I need to set him free. That's the paradox.

"I'm done," he mutters. "You think I don't get it. But I get it."

Without looking back, he runs down the steps, gets in his car, and speeds away. I collapse on the porch and give my tears free rein. Dominick deserves someone who doesn't have my problems. And I need to stay at home to make sure everything's okay.

We have to fall apart so we can both end up whole.

CHAPTER 8

QUESTION: Do you have jobs? Schooling?

ANSWER: Not jobs, employment, or schooling in the way that you understand them. Without the need for money, our people contribute by pursuing their passion and sharing it with others. We have an open education system to anyone who seeks knowledge. Specialized knowledge is acquired by learning from experts in a particular field.

After a sleepless night, I stare at the crack in my ceiling knowing it's time to start my senior year. My mouth feels dry from crying. I check my phone. No messages from Dominick. It's official. By giving him a clean slate, I've cleared myself an empty one.

Ignoring the cute floral skirt, blush T-shirt, and slouchy boots I picked out for the first day, I grab jeans and flip flops and wear the same gray *Star Trek* T-shirt I slept in. My hair revolted during the night into a mane of frizz. Bun it is.

In the kitchen, I pack a quick lunch since, by senior year, I've learned never to eat the cafeteria food unless it's a Friday. I grab a bowl and make oatmeal in the microwave, cutting up a banana and some walnuts while it cooks. Benji comes into the kitchen and searches the cabinets. I was hoping he wouldn't be around in the morning, but I forgot he has first shift today. When my oatmeal's ready, I move to the living room window to eat while waiting for Rita.

The warm cereal settles my acid stomach. I check my phone again. Nothing from Dominick. Not a single word. *Is it really over?* I blink back tears and pop a pill.

Benji walks into the living room and looks out the windows near me. *Please be nice.* I don't have the energy to fight him today.

"I need to talk to you about something." His voice has a sharp tinge to it. Either he's about to deliver bad news about the vertexes or bad news about Dad. Either way I'm hooked.

"Shoot. What's up?" I try to sound aloof while I search his eyes for hidden truths.

He rubs his face before staring out the window and resting his palms on the window sill. I've never seen him so distressed. Whatever it is, it's big.

"You know what," Benji mutters, almost to himself, then says, "I'll catch you later." He pats me on the back. "Have fun. Senior year goes by fast."

What's going on with him? Is someone sick? Is he dying?

"Is everything okay?" I ask.

He nods. "Yeah. Fine." His eyes shift to the left. He's debating with himself. "It's not every day your little sister finishes high school while the world is full of holograms."

"Stay safe at the vertex." I try to smile, but my lips are trembling, my emotions bubbling to the surface. "Are you sure everything's fine? What's going on? Did the government learn something about the vertexes?"

They've discovered an alien army. Scientists are lying, and it's all a conspiracy. I've contracted a vertex disease that has altered my genetic code and will cause me to mutate into a monkey or something.

"No, nothing like that. Everything's fine. Another time." He smirks and then adds, "Don't worry about it."

Don't worry about it. His small comment pierces through my thin skin, and he knows it. Makes me want to push him through the window.

I grab my backpack and escape Benji's emotional teasing. As soon as I step onto the porch, I remember standing there last night. Saying "I don't love you" to Dominick's beautiful face.

Mom steps onto the porch behind me.

"I almost missed it. Benji jumped in the shower before me and threw me off schedule." She gives me a huge hug. "Aw, senior year. Let me get a picture."

Rita's car pulls up in front of the house. "Mom, no," I whine. "Look, Rita's waiting."

"Come on. It's a tradition." She holds up her phone, and I fake a smile before running down the steps.

"Love you. Have a good day."

"Yep." As I walk to Rita's car, I try to set my mind on senior year. My dreams of becoming a lawyer.

Think positive, my brain commands. *Focus on the future,* my mind encourages. *Without Dominick,* my heart reminds.

"So," Rita says, as I climb into her car. "Are you going to explain to me why I'm picking you up and not Dominick?"

"We got into a fight." I buckle my seat belt, and she pulls into traffic.

"About what?"

I shrug.

"Did you break up?"

"I don't know. He was mad, though. Really mad." I flip through the radio stations.

"I don't get it. What aren't you telling me?"

I flip through more stations but eventually slap it off. "I told him that I didn't love him."

She slams on the brakes in the middle of the street. "Well, what'd ya do that for?"

Her words release an avalanche of tears. I bury my face in the bottom half of my T-shirt.

She fumbles to hand me tissues from the glove compartment while a truck behind us blares its horn. She puts on her hazard lights and continues feeding me tissues. Another driver swerves around us and spouts, "Get the stick out your ass and move!"

"Yeah, yeah, a little patience in your life won't kill you," Rita says out the driver's side window.

"Rita, you can't park in the middle of the street." I grab another tissue.

"The hell I can't. My best friend is imploding." She watches me sniffle and wipe then announces, "Okay, woman up. It's our senior year. Save the tears for later years."

I laugh through snot and try to pull myself together. Glad I didn't bother putting on makeup today.

"And as soon as you see Dominick, apologize and tell that boy you love him already."

———

I expected senior year to feel special and a little strange with everything happening in the world, but the hallways buzz with a different kind of energy. Vertexes and holograms. On T-shirts. Not sure how a possible invasion became a pop fashion trend.

"Oh my God, I want one," Rita says, looking around.

"Your parents would have a stroke."

"Oh yeah. Well, what they don't know…"

Is it bad that I kind of want one, too?

"Hey, Rita," Nathan Gomes, the guy Rita's been texting ever since our girls' night, stops and throws his arm around her. Rita's body melts like caramel around an apple.

"Hi," she says. "Long time no talk."

"Sorry, we've been having tons of practices to get ready for the season." He nods to me. "I'm Nathan."

"Alex." I don't remind him that we've met before. What's the point? He won't remember. "Rita, I gotta run. See you later."

"Okay," she says and mouths *thank you* for giving her a few minutes alone with a potential suitor.

I turn into the next corridor and see Dominick at the end talking to one of his friends. I really need to talk to him, but I don't want to start the morning of my senior year crying in the middle of hallway. Before he heads in my direction, I dart into my homeroom.

Mr. Blu, my homeroom and precalculus teacher, passes out our schedules. Students mutter under their breaths and compare.

"I know, I know," Mr. Blu jokes, "you're all excited because you have math first period."

When Mr. Blu speaks, two girls in the front swing their bare legs into the aisle and lean slightly forward on their desks, exposing major cleavage. If Mr. Blu notices, he doesn't show it.

The bell rings, and Mr. Blu shares the class code to access the online textbook. Everyone groans. Dominick told me once that Mr. Blu was his favorite teacher, his reason for wanting to major in math in college. Every time I look at Mr. Blu, I think of Dominick. If we don't get back together, math class will be torture.

Throughout most of the day I manage to keep my head down and my mind focused on listening to teachers' annoying intro-to-class speeches, which somehow all ended up about the holograms and the end of the world. They must've gotten together and decided to incorporate recent events into classes to keep school relevant despite the ticking countdown to destruction. My schedule should really read: Parabolic Precalculus, AP English Apocalyptic & Dystopian Literature, Chemistry of the Cosmos, World Doomsday History, and, well, Phys Ed. I'm exhausted and depressed already.

At lunch I spot Dominick eating at a table with his friends. *Already moving on without me. Probably where he wanted to be all along.* My stomach sours at the thought of tough conversations and the smell of gross cafeteria food. Rita's advice from the morning, however, overrides the need to crawl under a table and die.

"Hey," I say casually, as if I didn't kick him in his balls yesterday.

"Hey," he says. "How's it going?"

"Fine," I lie. "I have Mr. Blu for math."

Another student at the table pipes in. "Oh, he's incredible. Not to mention hot."

I try to smile, but it feels unnatural.

"Can I talk to you?" I ask Dominick.

"Aren't we talking now?" he says and eats a French fry.

"I mean, alone."

"I think you said all you needed to say yesterday."

Everyone at the table looks from me to Dominick and back,

intrigued, trying to read between the lines. I can't be someone else's drama fix for the day.

"Dominick, really. Please?"

He gets up but leaves his tray of food on the table. A sign that I only have a short window of his time. We walk out to the court-yard on the side of the cafeteria. The sun is still blazing hot. Only yesterday we were in paradise at the beach, and today it's textbook formalities.

"I'm sorry if I confused you yesterday. I didn't want to spring it on you like that—not going away to school together."

Dominick doesn't respond, so I continue to reason with him. "We can still see each other. It's only an hour away. I can jump on the train, visit you in Boston. You can come home sometimes, see me and your mom and Austin."

He moves close to me, so close that at first I think he might kiss me. But instead he whispers into my face.

"I would be happy to go to college here or in Boston, wherever, if I knew you were happy. But I know you're only staying outta fear."

"No, I want to stay." I pick at my nail polish.

"Alex, you need to get away from your family. They make you worse."

"No they don't. They need me. My mother is freaking clueless. She doesn't see my dad's symptoms starting back up."

"Are you listening to yourself? You're their daughter. They're the grown-ups. Don't do their job for them. Don't let them control you."

"I'm not. This is what I want."

"Whatever. It's your life."

He takes off before I can respond. I spend the rest of lunch period in the bathroom and the afternoon trying to convince the nurse that I need to go home early. She gives me the last pill in my school prescription, but it can't solve everything.

I count nine cans of beer in the recycling bin that night. Some could be Benji's, some could be from yesterday. Dad sits on the couch nursing one more, and I periodically walk from the kitchen to the living room to make sure he's still conscious and breathing. Benji's not home and Mom's already in bed. Someone needs to be around to call 911.

Loud guitar music from my cell phone forces my body out of its morning coma.

"Ugh," I moan from my bed. I slam my hand across my desk, sending my phone crashing to the floor. Squinting my eyes from the morning light, I fish around on the floor for my phone and hit "Snooze" on the alarm's screen. There are no texts from Dominick. I lie back down, and my body begs to sleep for only a moment or two longer under my plush blanket. My limbs go heavy. I imagine myself sinking comfortably into my mattress.

I wake with a start for the second time. Glancing at my phone, I freak to see that thirty minutes slipped by. I must've hit the wrong button.

"Shit." I jump out of bed and scurry around my room, searching for any clothing that matches. My stomach gurgles. No time for breakfast. No time to pack lunch. Mom opens my door.

"Rita's outside beeping. I told her you'd be right out."

"Thanks," I say, tying my hair back while squishing one foot into a sneaker.

My backpack is still open as I fly out the door. My sneakers sink into the muddy grass as I run to Rita's car. My bare arms shiver in the damp wind. Thank God I pulled my hair back since my curls will rebel in the dampness.

"Let's go, girl," Rita shouts out the car window. "I don't wanna be late on the second day."

"Sorry, I overslept."

She gives me that best friend up-and-down glance. The one that means, "You are a mess, but I still love you."

We make the first bell with seconds to spare. My backpack bounces heavily on my back as I rush up the inner stairs. Down the corridor, zipping past other students and faculty, I skid to a stop in front of room B236. After taking a few deep breaths, I realize that I didn't take a pill this morning. I turn to rush to the nurse's office but remember I forgot to tell my mom to refill my school prescription.

How could I forget it? I take several more deep breaths. *I can do this. I can do this. It's just one day.* Mr. Blu announces that all seniors have an assembly in the auditorium instead of first-period class after homeroom. Some students hoot "Yeet!" The girls in the front row pout.

When the next bell rings, seniors flood the first floor. My body short-circuits as soon as I enter the auditorium. A fire churns my stomach like I've swallowed a bucket of chili peppers.

Rita waves me down. I pretend nothing is wrong and focus on breathing. I creep over several students into the seat she saved for me. It's not an aisle seat. *I need an aisle seat.*

"Awesome. We already get out of class," Rita says.

"Yeah, awesome." *I visualize diarrhea pouring down my jeans in front of everyone.* I search the crowd for Dominick, but there are so many heads I can't find him.

"Have you seen Dominick?" I ask.

"No. Did you talk to him any more after lunch yesterday?"

"No," I peel a layer of nail polish off my pinkie.

We end our conversation as the principal, Mr. Wilson, takes the microphone. After testing and adjusting the volume of the mic and straightening his tie, he addresses the class.

"Welcome to your senior year," Mr. Wilson announces, and the audience hoots and applauds.

My armpits and underneath my breasts pool with sweat, and my heart performs an Irish jig in my chest. *What would happen if the building was suddenly attacked by a lone shooter or a terrorist? Or a rogue hologram? I'd be trapped in the sixth seat in the middle of a crowd. I'd have to climb over people and cross half the room to make it to the closest exit. That's if the shooter isn't blocking the exit. My brains would splatter across the stage.*

The room blurs and softens at the edges. I have no idea what Mr. Wilson is saying or why people are clapping. I fan the bottom of my T-shirt up and down for air, pull the neck area down a few inches. My rapid heartbeat whacks against my skin so hard I swear I've lost the ability to filter oxygen.

My parents would find out I died in a bloody pile. Dad would lose it, get his gun, blow his brains out. Dominick would hate me since my death would trigger memories of his father. Rita would become depressed and suicidal. Or the two of them would get together and have sex on my grave, and I couldn't do anything to stop it 'cause I'd be stuck as a virgin ghost.

"Are you okay?" Rita asks. Her voice is soft and soothing, but the last thing I want is attention.

Ten to twenty minutes. I'm not dying. Ten to twenty minutes.

According to my old counselor, the longest it takes a panic attack to peak is twenty minutes. It's 8:04. I have to convince myself that I'm not having a heart attack or losing my mind for up to twenty minutes.

Easier said than done.

Are they all staring at me? No, they can't be. They can't be. Can they hear what I'm thinking? They must think I'm a freak. Am I saying this out loud? They're watching me like they know. I can't lose it in front of them. I'll never live it down.

I grab my bag and try to squeeze back out of the row. One girl yelps when I step on her foot. I try to apologize, but by the look on the girl's face, I must have muttered something incoherent and asinine.

A guy in the last seat yells, "What's your problem?"

Mr. Wilson stops talking, and everyone turns around. I can feel myself cringing in heat. I run up the main aisle. *It's like I'm in a clear plastic tunnel where everyone is watching and pointing at me, and there's only one narrow exit at the end of the tunnel that may collapse at any second.*

I hide in the nearest bathroom. My skin's burning up and my heart feels like it's going to jump out of my chest like in *Alien*. I collapse at a sink and splash water on my face to cool off. When that doesn't help, I enter a stall, tear off my clothes, and sit on the toilet in my bra. Small red hives cover my chest and stomach. How could I forget about refilling my pills?

I check my phone. 8:12. I really hope I don't pass out and some custodian finds me naked on the gross tile floor. *Probably crawling with foot fungus. E. coli. COVID. Ebola.*

A painful numbing sensation spreads through my fingers. I

shake my hands to stop them from hurting. *Deep breath. Hold it. Let it out slowly. Again.* I haven't had an attack this bad at school since middle school when Rita had to run and get the school nurse as I sat on the cafeteria floor gasping for air.

Why can't I get through two days of senior year?

I grab my phone and almost call Rita. My shaking fingers can't navigate my phone quickly. On my screen I stare at the background picture of the three of us around a fire. Rita winking at the camera. Dominick smiling behind his glasses, those dimples casting shadows on my heart.

My best friends. Rita helped me through middle school, Dominick helped me through high school. I never minded Rita seeing me weak, but with Dominick, ugh, why does it bother me so much?

I play a game on my phone to try to distract myself from the symptoms of death. Any sane person would be screaming for medical help, but I have to sit half naked on a public toilet and play electronic mind games to trick myself into believing that I'm not about to croak.

But what if I'm in real danger? What if this time it's real?

Waiting is the worst.

I hear the girls' bathroom door swing open and shut. I lift my feet off the floor and balance fetal position on the toilet seat rim.

"Alex?" Rita asks, "Are you in here?"

"No." I put my feet down.

Her black floral canvas sneakers appear under my door. "Is it a bad one?"

"As opposed to a good one?"

She doesn't respond. The fluorescent lights buzz at me.

"You don't have to wait," I mutter.

"Not missing anything good anyway. Typical Mr. Wilson speech: 'It's your senior year, blah, blah, blah, respect and responsibility, blah, blah, blah.'"

"You sound just like him," I say, giggling. It feels so good to laugh.

"You would think he would've talked directly about the holograms and the vertexes. Nope. All he mentioned was something like 'in these trying times, character matters.' Please, character isn't going to matter if a comet shows up."

The heat in my body begins to subside, and while my heart still feels sore, the rhythm stabilizes. Reality settles back into my mind. False alarm. Not dying.

"And then the class president talked about the prom and fundraisers to offset the price of tickets. Did you know that hologram gray is the hot trend this year for dresses and tuxes?"

I listen to Rita's voice and get dressed. My insides still feel shaken up and queasy. I exit the stall and rinse my face with more cold water.

"Thanks," I say.

"De nada. Ready to go back? We can sit near the doors."

"I'm never setting foot in that auditorium again. I need to go home and sleep." *And get access to my pills.*

"I'll walk you to the nurse."

My 504 plan legally allows me to skip class and head to the nurse's office or my guidance counselor when my anxiety flares. From the nurse's office, I call my mom. She brings more pills, signs the parental authorization form, and gets me dismissed for the day. She doesn't ask questions. Part of me is grateful. Part of me needs her to shake me until I scream and get it all out of my system.

———

That night, Dominick still hasn't called or texted once. I tell myself not to do it, to leave it alone, but can't stop myself. I text him:

How are you?

As the minutes tick by, my insides burn with embarrassment and regret for pushing him out of my life. I don't know what's going on with me. I check my phone over and over and over throughout the night, making sure the volume is on, the battery didn't die, and I still have a signal. He never responds.

I wish I had my own vertex or TARDIS so I could time travel back to the moment on the porch when my mouth uttered "I don't love you." I need to take it back. If I could rewrite the script, Dominick and I would have sex at his house and promise to stay together throughout college and go to the same graduate school and get married and have kids.

Where's a good space-time-paradox-anomaly when you need one? Even the Enterprise got a few do-overs. Instead, we have these vertexes blinking at us for no clear reason.

Humans are remarkable in the way they adapt to change, even change that makes them uncomfortable. They block out what they can't accept and simply move on with their daily lives, even if that thing stares them in the face. They stop seeing it. Their brains are magical like that. Problems become part of the backdrop, and they just keep going. Maybe that's why I have anxiety. I am bad at adapting. I must not have this gene. I cannot stop seeing the problems. I cannot ignore.

I need to learn to forget.

If I could stay away from media, it would be easy to pretend nothing has changed in the world other than adjusting to senior year without Dominick. Problem is I can't stay away from the news. Dominick was right: I am a Scully. I need to know every bit of information I can get my hands on. Countries that don't have access to media must live in a safe, little, ignorant bubble. Well, maybe not safe.

So I watch the news and take notes instead of sleep. A small but growing number of people have emigrated from the planet each day from various locations across the globe. Sometimes the same people leave several times on recorded, looped news feeds. It's odd to see the same goodbyes over and over again. Kind of like the goodbye between me and Dominick that I can't stop replaying in my head.

———

During the first week of school I develop some nasty habits. I set two alarms so there are no repeat performances at school. Problem is I'm having trouble focusing in classes. Probably from the lack of sleep. I watch teachers' mouths move, but my brain has developed a mute feature that switches on and off without my consent.

Homework is another problem. Not listening in class means I have no idea how to do the work. With due dates approaching, I finally crack open my laptop and settle into bed. An hour later, a text on my phone jolts me awake.

Please be Dominick. It's Rita:

Hey, Nathan just texted me about a party tonight. Wanna come? Might be good to get you out of that funk. Live a little.

No. Absolutely not, the voices of my parents command in my head. I visualize Dad standing with his arms crossed over his puffed-up chest. I wish I could hear Dominick's opinion instead. I think his silent treatment even extends telepathically to my thoughts.

Then Rita's voice takes over. *Live a little.*

I consider my options. I have a ton of homework to finish, but I have the rest of the weekend. And she's right; I am in a funk. The unmatching yoga pant number I'm sporting is something that my mom would wear when she's not expecting company. Including the tea stains on my leg. I can't fade into her.

Sure. Need to change first.

I need to change, in more ways than one. Time to force myself out of my comfort zone. After taking a quick shower, I search through my closet for something party-worthy. The dress I wore the night of the first vertex sighting. *For my date with Dominick.* Might as well.

Looking in the mirror, my wet hair reminds me of poodle road-kill. I grab my blow-dryer and flat iron and set to work. By the time I'm done, my hair looks three inches longer. Not sure if it's better, just different.

Rita knocks on my bedroom door as I pin one side of my hair back with a bobby pin and leave the rest free.

"Your mom let me in."

"Yeah, give me a sec." I spray my hair with anti-humidity hairspray and hope for the best.

Rita borrows the spray. "I told my mom I was sleeping over here."

Even though we have a standing agreement that she can sleep

over whenever, I'm not sure I want her here since I haven't been sleeping well.

"That's fine," I lie. I've been lying to her a lot lately. I still haven't told her that Dominick and I are fighting over me wanting to live at home for college.

"Tonight should be good for us. Get you out and about, flirting with other guys. And I get to finally see Nathan outside of school."

Flirting with other guys. I take out lip gloss and apply it, then take a pill so I don't embarrass myself.

The two of us hop in her car and drive to a Friday night house party. She has to park a block away with all the traffic. As we cross the street toward a huge white Colonial, I double-check my reflection in a parked car's window.

As we approach the front steps, thumping music takes over. The vibrations make my chest hurt.

Inside, Rita yells into my ear, "Let's mingle."

She leads me through the crowd and into a living room area cleared for dancing. She sways her head, arms, and hips to the music. I dance like a pigeon in a park as I try to coordinate my awkward limbs and copy her movements. Nathan asks her to dance and she agrees, leaving me stranded.

A slow song begins, and I dash to sit on an empty love seat in a dark corner. I watch as Rita dances, spooning with Nathan, pushing her butt into his crotch, and slowly rocking in a back-and-forth motion. I wish I could be that daring with Dominick.

Dominick. The thought of him aches somewhere deep inside me that I didn't know existed. A place of escape. A place of solace. *Why did I ever think my future would be better without him?* Nathan's teammate from my gym class plops down next to me. His red face and shiny eyes either means he's flirting with me or he's a little drunk. Maybe both.

"Hey, why's a girl like you sitting here all alone? Let's get that body moving."

I hesitate. He's definitely not my type. I could probably ignite his breath with a match. Rita winks at me from the dance area, and I roll my eyes. Time to live it up, I guess. Take a risk. Besides, my body needs to learn how to navigate and react to situations, even drunk ones. At least he won't care how bad I am at dancing. Good practice. Learning how to relax, fit in, act my age.

I step onto the dance floor, and the guy places his hands loosely around my neck. "My name's Dan," he says.

"Alex. Alexandra," I yell over the music.

"Nice to meet you, Alex Alexandra." His eyes have a needy look, as if he wants to ask something more but can't find the words. He also cannot stop staring at my chest. "Where have I seen you before?"

I can't tell if he means me or my boobs. "We were in the same gym class. Freshman year."

"Oh. Right."

He has no clue. I stare at the floor, over his shoulder, anywhere other than at him until the song ends, then smile as kindly as I can fake it.

"Maybe I'll see you again sometime," he adds as we leave the floor.

"Sure," I say. *Why did I tell him that? Now he'll stalk me.*

Rita and Nathan approach.

"Who's this sweet thing, Nathan?" Dan pats Nathan on the back while looking Rita up and down in approval.

I intercede. "Dan, Rita. Rita, this is Dan the Drunk Dude."

"Nice to meet you, Rita. I see you know my man, Nate G." The two guys fist bump.

Rita tries to hide a guilty smile and fails. She set me up. She told Nathan to have his friend ask me to dance. I'm that pathetic.

A familiar flutter creeps up my chest. I thought my medication would keep my symptoms under wraps.

"I'll be back. I have to go to the bathroom."

"I'll get us drinks," Dan offers.

"Okay. Sprite for me." I have a rule about mixing business with pleasure, prescription with recreational.

I take off to the bathroom. If I can hide away from the crowd, the talking, and the loud music for a minute, I should be okay. Sometimes that's all it takes to keep myself from unraveling. If I catch it in time.

Thankfully, there's only one other girl waiting for the restroom. A painting hangs in the hallway: an image of sharp, overlapping triangles in velvet tones. The soothing warm colors contrast with the harsh angles. It makes me uncomfortable.

Once in the bathroom, I sit and take a few deep breaths. I live too much of my life in bathrooms. I almost pop another pill, but I stop myself since I just took one. I need to pace myself.

Sure enough, it's not even close to a full-blown episode. The feeling subsides within minutes. I lean closer to the mirror to examine my brown eyes, which have dark shadows under them from keeping late hours. My counselor used to tell me how important sleep is for mental health issues. She should've told that to my insomnia.

My curls have already started to revolt against the straightening, flipping at the ends in haphazard directions. The bobby pin has slipped out of place, so I clip it back behind my ear. As soon as I open the door, a gaggle of squawking females flock to the mirror to fix themselves. I have to squeeze near the wall to get out of the room. Like battling for a space to exist.

I scan the sea of unfamiliar faces for Rita. For a moment I can't spot her anywhere. Then I see her sitting on Nathan's lap, making out as if they're sharing oxygen to stay alive.

I'm not sure what to do—never been the third wheel before. I had Dominick. *Oh, wait, does that mean Rita was stuck as the third wheel?* I never thought about how awkward and lonely that must've been for her.

I take a moment to gather my thoughts. Maybe I should say something like "Get a room" and they'll stop. I try not to stare at them, but seeing them kiss like that reminds me of Dominick. I miss that feeling—being so wrapped up in someone else you forget the world exists. Problems melt away. Self-consciousness no longer holds you back from being seen as you really are. That's the measure of any great relationship—comfort.

And then it ends. And you're left with nothing but a flood of insecurity. *I made the biggest mistake of my life. I was too afraid to let him see me.*

Rita heads back to the dance floor. I join in and dance and talk for the next hour. Nathan is still flirting a ton with Rita, whispering and nudging her ear. She's flirting right back by touching his arms and leaning over slightly to show off cleavage. I hide my face behind my soda.

Dan the Drunk Dude barges back over and interrupts. "Hey, you guys down for a drive to the Quincy vertex?"

"I'm down," Nathan says.

"Sure, I'll go if Alex goes." Rita snaps a piece of gum into her mouth and hands one to each of us. When she gets to me, she gives me puppy-dog eyes.

"Fine," I say, sounding more cool and confident than I feel on the inside. *Fake it 'til you make it.* Immediately, another thought undermines me. *What are you thinking? They might be trying to rape you.*

Rita must see the look of indecision on my face because she whispers to me, "It'll be fun."

"Alexandra, you know that's such a sexy name." Dan tosses his arm around my neck, a restriction that irks me to the core. My reflexes almost automatically punch him in the face. He's drunker than before, if that's possible.

I ignore his question. "If we go, who's driving?"

"I will," Nathan offers. "I didn't drink. Football starts tomorrow. Keeping it clean, unlike my friend here."

The two guys lead us away from the party. They approach an old Ford Explorer, and Nathan opens the front door. "Ladies first."

Rita sits up front with Nathan, leaving me in the back with Dan. *Great.*

"Are you applying to college?" Rita asks.

Nathan starts the truck. "Yeah. Hoping to get a football scholarship. Got a lot riding on this season."

"What do you think you'll major in?"

"Haven't decided yet. Chemistry, maybe." He drives away from the party and into the dark night.

"Is that a pickup line?" Rita flirts.

He chuckles. "No, I'm really interested in working in a lab someday. What about you?"

"I don't know yet. Maybe business."

Listening to them reminds me of Dominick. I thought I let him go for his own good. For my own good. But now that we're apart, I can't see who it's helping anymore.

I was mean to him. Like unforgivably mean. I am a terrible person. He doesn't deserve to have someone horrible like me in his life.

Dan the Drunk Dude puts his hand on my knee, and I take it off. "Don't be a tease." He tries again.

"I'm not being a tease. I have a boyfriend."

"Then you are a tease. Come over here." He tries to pull my legs to his side of the back seat.

"Not a chance in hell," I say, kicking at him.

He shoves my legs away as if I had been the one putting them near him. "Bitch. Great night this is, Nathan. We picked some real winners."

"Speak for yourself," Nathan replies.

"Hey, Alex is amazing," Rita adds. "She's gonna be a lawyer. Maybe she'll rescue your ass from jail someday."

"A lawyer, huh?" Dan the Drunk Dude peers at me and winks. "Like with sexy heels?"

He is everything that is wrong with the male species.

The rest of the ride on the highway is just as awkward. I thought parties were supposed to be fun. *How come all I want to do is escape to my room and rot there?*

And then finally, looming through the darkness, a beacon of uncertainty and infinity—the vertex. Even from here I can tell that the hologram is exactly the same as every televised version across the globe. Same gray outfit. Same androgynous face. Weird. It's like a clone war, except they're not clones exactly and there is no war. *Not yet, anyway.*

Witnessing one vertex affected my sense of the world, at least for a few weeks until nothing else happened. Seeing the vertex again after so much media coverage cements the impact of the event in our lives. Something has shifted in the universe. The media is not making it up. There really are five hundred of them spread across the globe, waiting for us. We don't know what to do about it yet, and since we can't process the significance, we pretend it's nothing. "Business as usual."

Like with ending my relationship with Dominick. I need to go numb and hope in time it won't burn so much and have drastic, lasting consequences.

It's late enough that the major crowds near the vertex have diminished. Within a half hour, we are in the front and have access to the vertex to ask the hologram anything we wish. Several guards stand by, including one with a tablet in case we decide to take the leap and he needs to record our departure. Thank God Benji has the morning shift.

Dan the Drunk Dude approaches the hologram and pokes it. His finger goes right through even though it appears to be a fully realized human being.

"Cool. Hey, sweetie," he calls to me. "Come here. I promise I'll be a gentleman. I want to show you something."

Great, he wants to show me that he can poke a hologram. I'll play. I kind of want to touch it myself.

"What?" I ask as I get closer.

That's when he lifts me off my feet and onto his shoulder. Staggering forward, he carries me closer and closer toward the vertex.

"Time to go into another world. Bet you won't be a tease there."

My whole body reacts at once. I flail my arms and kick my legs and scream and pound on his back with every ounce of energy and anger and fear inside me. My heart hammers like it does during a panic attack, only this time the threat is real.

"Put her down!" Rita screams.

The guards surround us at gunpoint and command Dan to release me. As soon as my feet make contact with the ground, I run and shield myself behind Nathan and Rita. The adrenaline inside me surges at every nerve ending like lightning trapped in a jar. I cannot believe he did that. I cannot believe I fell for it.

The officers handcuff him while lecturing about underage drinking. They are being way too easy on him. Charge him with attempted…something. Something more than underage intoxication. Attempted vertex kidnapping. If Dad and Benji were here, they would've beaten the snot out of him.

Dan the Drunk Dude announces to everyone, "People, it was a joke. Relax. Don't get your panties in a bunch."

"Sir, do not address them. Step this way. Please be careful." The officer holds him by the elbow to guide him.

Dan snorts. "Be careful? Ooh, the vertex will get you. It's nothing but a glorified lava lamp. Harmless."

He sticks his foot into the vertex to demonstrate. The swirling mass envelops it, and Dan's face contorts in confusion. He loses his balance. With his hands in cuffs, he can't stop himself from falling forward. The closest five officers grab hold of his body. A massive tug-of-war begins between Dan, the officers, and the vertex—muscle versus technology. The hologram doesn't flinch.

Then in a blink, the vertex wins. Dan's T-shirt rips, and a few of the officers stumble back.

Dan's body is sucked into the vertex, pulling two officers with him. *Gone. Swallowed. Poof.*

Just like that.

"OH MY GOD!" Rita covers her face.

Nathan takes a moment to comprehend what happened and then yells, "He's my teammate!"

The hologram lowers its head graciously for the transaction.

Part of my brain wants to laugh. It's ridiculous. *Who loses their football buddy to a black...er...blue hole? Karma's a bitch. Jerk.* But there's a bigger part of me that recognizes the shock and horror of the moment, no matter who he is.

Was. Is.

And a deeper part of me realizes something else, and I can't escape it: *That could have been me.*

He could've easily slipped while still holding me. And this truth I cannot accept.

I'm never going near those damn things again.

CHAPTER 9

QUESTION: What do you do for entertainment?

ANSWER: Entertaining is one of our many forms of contribution. We have alternatives for celebrating and bonding that have evolved from similar sporting events and other pastimes on earth. The skylucent, a theater in the heavens, is one of our most popular attractions.

Dan the Drunk Dude's departure ends up on the news. It's the first accidental vertex incident that we know of, and people must talk about the ramifications from every angle and perspective. His family's devastation plays on a looped media feed. *How many times will we turn other people's private grief into a morbid spectacle?*

The most common question the media asks the family is whether or not they will have a funeral for him. It's such a rude question, but at the same time, will they? It is a loss. He's lost to them, at least for now anyway. *Will they mourn his loss like a death? Will a priest say that Dan the Drunk Dude has gone to a better place? I mean, did he?* Nobody knows. I guess nobody ever knows, so what's the difference? We don't have the religious traditions in place for this type of loss. Traditions need to evolve when we discover new scientific ways to live and ways to die.

One prying reporter asks Dan's mother if the family will join him. Oh, the look of horror and guilt on her face. I can't believe he asked that question to a grieving parent. Although, they could choose to join him.

Even worse, Dan the Drunk Dude's accidental exodus inspires some racist groups. They've begun an online "Purge the World" and "Throw 'em In" campaign. I've decided I'm staying in my room where it's safe. I tried to live a little and almost died, well, almost got sucked into a vertex.

Under a warm cocoon of cotton blanket and extra pills, I visualize my safe place. *Bright blue island sky. White rope hammock tied to palm trees. A book waiting for me. Pages flipping in the breeze.*

Rita keeps texting me. Her parents never found out she was at the vertex because she wasn't named. The police notified my parents since I was the "underage victim" in the case. But there is no case without a defendant.

Mom gives me space like I knew she would. Dad avoids me, which means he's slipping into his own oblivion. For the first time in a long time, I don't have the energy to focus on him. It's liberating and scary. It means I am slipping, too. And I don't care. Slipping means finding comfort in a dark place where nothing can touch you.

I ignore everyone, toss back more pills, and sleep the time away. My phone beeps, waking me up from my medicated bliss. The harsh light from the screen blinds me. Squinting, I see Dominick's name and text flash before me.

Are you okay? Why were you with him?

His words knock me off my sedated rocker. I want to cry. I want to text him that I need him, that I miss him, that I love him, that I'm an insecure idiot who doesn't deserve him.

Through a cloud of hazy tears, I manage to text back:

I'm fine. Don't worry about me.

I don't answer his other question. I don't have an answer.

———

I miss school for the next few days. Okay, maybe a week. The edges of time become fuzzy when you're highly medicated, forming a weightless dream world that protects you from the sharpness. A place of absolute freedom.

Then Benji crashes my pill party.

He kicks open my locked door, yanks the blanket off me, pulls me by my ankles. My tailbone whacks the floor and sends shock waves through my sleeping body.

"Get up. Pity party's over."

I wail and chuck pillows at him. "Get out of my room!"

"No. Mom called a counselor. You have an appointment in an hour."

"What? No, not that quack again." My bed beckons me. I climb back under the lavender comforter. Bed is soft. Life is hard.

Benji grabs me and hoists my body over his shoulder. Hot panic sears through my veins. "No, no! Put me down! Dan, stop!"

Benji doesn't flinch or let me go even when I start clawing at him. My thumbnail bends backward. The sharp pain serves as a momentary distraction while Benji carries me into the bathroom.

Before I realize what's happening, he tosses me into the bathtub fully clothed and turns on the showerhead.

"Argh!" Cold water runs over my head, soaking my long T-shirt and pajama shorts.

"Get dressed. One hour. No excuses. I'm driving."

He leaves the bathroom. Through the stream of water, I see Mom in the doorway, watching the whole ordeal. She closes the door without speaking. Dad's nowhere in sight.

"Where's Dad?" I ask Benji in his truck.

"Dad doesn't need your crap," he says. "The last thing he needs is for you to stress him out with bullshit."

Bullshit? I already want out. If I don't go to the counselor, what can they do to me? Ground me? Send me to my room? Good. I should make a run for it. How hard could it be to jump out of a moving vehicle?

Skin smearing on the cement like melted butter across burnt toast.

Benji continues. "Dad's like he is because of war. He has a real reason. He was in actual battles where people died. Blown up. Body parts burned and scattered. Friends lost. You have no reason to be like this. None. You overanalyze everything. You think seeing Dad screwed up made you screwed up? Give me a break. I grew up here, too, and you don't see me copping out or breaking down. I mean, my life's way more stressful than yours, and I'm still standing. Yes, that kid fell into the vertex. You didn't. You're fine. Get some perspective and grow up already."

I try to hold back tears, but they don't listen. Benji thinks this is all news to me, but I've lived with these same thoughts about myself. What he doesn't understand, though, is that more than anything, I'd love to function like him, to be able to roll with life's punches. I know my thoughts get irrational. But when they are happening, they are as real as my body reacting to a flame. Making me feel guilty for having these feelings only makes me feel invisible and angry and lost.

Benji parks near a small church that was converted into office space. It isn't my old counselor's office.

"Did my counselor move?"

He shoves a note at me that has A. Riley and an address on it. "Your other counselor isn't in practice anymore."

"Good," I mumble. Probably screwed up some case and got his license revoked. *What if he screwed up on me? Hypnotized me and implanted some chip inside me that misfires at certain sounds?*

Even though my brain wants to flee, my body refuses to exert that much energy. I crawl out of the truck and drag my sore, atrophying muscles inside.

Benji sits in the waiting room while I search for an office door with RILEY on the plaque. Her heavy wooden door looks like it belongs in an English Victorian novel. It's cracked open, but I knock anyway.

"Ms. Riley?"

"Hi," she mumbles through food in her mouth. She holds up one finger while she swallows, pointing her other hand to the peanut butter crackers on her desk and gesturing for me to have one. I can't remember the last time I ate.

"Sorry about that. Pregnant. When you need to eat, you need to eat. You must be Alexandra Lucas." She holds out her hand to shake mine. "Call me Arianna."

"Yep." I hate it already. First-name basis. Establish familiarity and trust. I know the drill.

"Have a seat, Alexandra."

I sit while "Arianna" retrieves the appropriate paperwork. Her pregnant belly hits the file cabinet drawer when she opens it. She has to pull the file sideways in order to free it. The tab at the top rips off. She doesn't notice, or at least she fakes it well. Her competence is underwhelming.

"Your mother called and thought we should meet to see if I can help get you through your senior year." She reads through the small file. "It says here you want to go to college for pre-law?"

I really don't like small talk with counselors. This is a paid conversation through health insurance. Get down to business. "I thought we were here to discuss the tragedy."

"Tragedy. Is that how you see it?"

I exhale. "Don't do that. I've been in counseling before. I know the whole turning-what-I say-into-questions-so-I'll-analyze-myself bit."

Ms. Riley doesn't flinch. They must teach that in counseling school. Never look shocked, even if a patient discusses wanting to hack off people's limbs and put them into milkshakes.

"What were you in counseling for before?"

"Generalized anxiety disorder. Depression. Panic attacks. I still take Ativan sometimes." *Sometimes. Ha.* I popped one before getting into Benji's truck.

"Does it help?"

"Yeah." Is she really going to waste my time debating whether or not a prescription for anxiety helps my anxiety?

"What other techniques do you use?"

I sigh loudly to let her know I'm over the conversation already. "Visualization. Breathing. Exercise." Well, two out of three isn't bad.

"Good. And is your anxiety getting better?"

"Yes." I twist one loose curl around my middle finger. My lie sinks into the area rug and permeates the room.

"Good." She pauses for a good thirty seconds. "Then why do you still need the Ativan?"

The lining of my stomach sinks to my sneakers. *Don't you dare, lady.* "For emergencies. Panic attacks."

She nods. "Do you consider what happened to Dan Tatterwort an emergency?"

Was that his last name? "Yeah." I cross my arms over my chest and keep twisting my hair tighter and tighter.

"Why?"

How do I answer that question? What am I supposed to say? *That he vanished into a cosmic abyss and almost brought me with him?*

I shrug.

"Let me rephrase. Have you been feeling anxiety since Dan left?"

I can't help it—a loud, rude, obnoxious, uncontrollable snort escapes me, and my mouth lets loose.

"In case you haven't noticed, lady, there are alien holograms with vertexes across the planet, telling us the world is coming to an end, and some drunk guy tried to throw me in." My voice starts to waver, and my laughter loses its edge. "And then he tripped and actually fell into God knows where? And he almost took me with him." My voice booms louder than I expect. A ball of fear rises in my throat, traveling from my heart to my brain.

"Has there ever been another time where you felt your physical being was in danger like that?"

I shake my head no, but my throat constricts, my heart takes over all brain functions, and tears escape my face. Traitors.

She repeats. "Has there ever been another time where you felt your physical being was in danger?"

Usually counselors wait a few sessions, try to establish a

relationship of trust. I don't even know her, and she's hitting the nail on the proverbial head on the first wild pitch. I want to fight her on her methods, but the emotions rush out of me before I can stop them. My hands and body shake and shake like I've been pulled from icy waters. My throat closes as my father's hands lock around my neck in the attic that night.

She hands me a box of tissues. "We have all day if you need it."

After the session, Benji and I drive home in silence. I'm angry at him and kind of grateful. Those two feelings don't mix well. The grateful side serves as fuel for the anger in a strange loop. It means he has helped me, and I am indebted to him. It sits like a burning rock in my stomach, a rock that I wish I could vomit and then throw at his smug face.

Benji drops me off. Dad's car isn't in the driveway, but I spot Rita's car parked out front. All I want to do is crawl back into bed.

Mom stops me on the way to my room.

"Rita's here," she says, wiping her hands on a towel. "She's waiting in your room. I'm making dinner. You must be starving."

"Why is Rita here?"

"I invited her."

Good old Mom, sweeping things under that silent, mental health rug of ours.

As I head down the hallway, I try to remember the condition I left my bedroom in. It's a blur.

Rita's sitting in my purple saucer chair surrounded by piles of laundry, empty food containers, and moldy cups.

"You're alive," Rita says.

"Alive and kicking." I collapse on my bed and wish I could sleep the rest of the day away.

"Missed you at school. Your mom said you went to see a counselor. That's good."

"Yeah, the counselor's nice. She gave me a medical excuse for missing classes, too."

"Good. You know it isn't your fault."

"What isn't?"

"If I hadn't invited you out…"

I sit up and poke her shoulder with my sneaker. "Stop it. It wasn't your fault. You were being a good friend and trying to get me out of the house. Even if you also wanted to spend time with Nathan. You couldn't have known Dan was that much of an idiot."

She smiles unconvincingly. "Nathan is old news. Turned into a jerk per the usual." She glances around. "No offense, but your room is rank. You want help cleaning? It would help me with my guilt."

After a quick peek at the garbage piled around my bed, I face facts. I need to be more honest with myself. I need to learn to accept help from people. I hold so many feelings down deep they seem to go haywire at the wrong time. Maybe if I learn to let them out at the right time, my system will reset itself.

"Sure," I say, "if it'll help your guilt."

Together we get my room in order. I take garbage and dish duty while she gathers and sorts laundry. At the bottom of one pile, she finds a printout of Dominick holding up one of the fish we caught.

"You buried Dominick?" she asks, raising one eyebrow.

On seeing his smile in the photograph, a wave of emotion hits me that I have been keeping at bay.

"Don't know why you let him go," she states. "He's a catch, pun intended."

I shake my head and chuckle at her bad fishing joke, and I wipe a stray tear. *Why did I sabotage the strongest relationship in my life? Because he cared? Because he'd sacrifice anything for me? Was I afraid that I would have to change to be enough for him?*

"I told Dominick I want to stay here for college, and I want him to go to Boston."

"Since when?" She stuffs an armful of T-shirts into my hamper.

"That's why he's not talking to me. He offered to stay here, too, and I said no."

"Wait, why do you want to stay?"

I shrug. She whistles low and long while tossing a white sock into the pile.

"Alex, listen. I've known you forever. If you suddenly want to stay here for college, you really are screwed up." She sits on the corner of my bed. "What happened to becoming a kick-ass lawyer and taking Boston by storm? Leaving your family that stresses you out? You said your father randomly goes wild or numb, and your mother is pathetic and naive about it. Never mind how much Benji tortures you, which I cannot believe with a face that gorgeous. Why would you want to stay here when Dominick"—she picks up the picture and shoves it into my hands—"brings out the light in you?"

"I don't know," I admit. "But I can't see physically separating myself from them. I can't do it. And I don't want to stop Dominick from going to school in Boston."

"Just promise me," she says and hands me a tissue from my bureau, "that you will at least apply to some Boston schools. Keep both options open in case you change your mind."

I nod. She means well, but she doesn't understand the hold Dad has on me. Like a tractor beam in *Star Trek*, pulling a ship out of its journey to safety. There's a pull inside of me, and I cannot break the connection.

———

Over the next month and a half, Arianna and I meet on a weekly basis. She explains that what happened when I was younger with Dad has gotten stuck inside me, and I react to other situations as if that event is happening again. The vertex incident with Dan only made it worse.

She does a form of therapy called EMDR. By following a back-and-forth pattern either with your eyes or by tapping your legs or arms and thinking of a traumatic memory, you can rewire your brain to deal with it with less and less fear and pain. It sounded like bullshit to me at first, but somehow it works.

Arianna taught me how to do EMDR to myself in moments when I feel major fear about something. It's not a cure for anxiety since anxiety can be environmental and genetic, but it will help me to manage it. If my panic attacks continue, she also recommends taking an antidepressant. Certain ones can be effective at eliminating panic attacks. I'd rather not go that route if I don't have to because the last time I took them, they made me feel terrible. My Ativan prescription gets to stay, but I'm noticing that I don't need it as much anymore. I can't believe I didn't get this kind of therapy sooner. It's like superglue for the cracks inside me.

———

"How's school going?" Arianna asks. "Did you bring your grades up?"

"School's been fine. Boring, actually."

"Boring's good. How's your anxiety? Have you been exercising? Breathing?"

Of course I've been breathing. Otherwise, I'd be dead. "Yes, I've been walking around the block after school."

"Good. And how's the situation at home?"

I take a deep breath. "My dad's avoiding me by working longer hours. He's drinking more, too. I triggered him again. I'm keeping my distance until I can pull myself back together."

"Wait, it's not your fault. You are allowed to need help. You are both different people."

I nod and stare at my hands.

"Alex, you are not your father. You are not responsible for your father. You are only responsible for yourself."

I nod again, but deep inside I know that's not true. I'm his daughter. I'm supposed to care about him. Look out for him. I think about Benji and how he doesn't seem to care like I do. How he can simply move on with his life.

"I've been wondering how come other people can cope better than I can. Am I a weak person?"

She smiles. "No, you're not weak at all. You're sensitive. Sensitive people are some of the most caring, creative, greatest thinkers of our time. Sensitivity is only a weakness if you let it be. You have to learn to see your sensitivity as strength. Sensitive people can see through fakeness. They spot problems others overlook. And while they want to help others, when they feel threatened or hopeless, they have trouble processing the stress. But that doesn't mean you are weak. It means you are human. The world needs sensitive people like you to stay in balance."

I consider her words.

"I feel so out of control when my negative thoughts take over and start looping and my body reacts. How can I turn that into a strength?"

"How about this: Have you ever heard of a mantra? Like a catch-phrase? Memorize the line, 'Don't get tricked by a thought.' Got it? 'Don't get tricked by a thought.' Try saying that to yourself when you have an irrational thought."

Seems too easy. "I'll try it."

"Also, some people find it useful to write in a journal when their brain feels overwhelmed. You could try writing all your thoughts and feelings down. Don't worry about grammar or spelling. Free write, scribble, doodle, whatever. You can even take it a step further and slam the book shut to swish those big feelings into mere flat words on a page. Takes the power away. Or rip or burn the pages. Thoughts are meaningless, fleeting, random ideas with no power unless you give them power."

"I have a journal that I use sometimes." *Understatement of the century.*

"Good. Keep it up if it's working for you. Also, exercise. Exercise is a powerful stress management tool. Following a healthy plan for managing your symptoms is the first step to becoming your strongest self." She pauses, then asks, "Have you started applying to colleges? That's always a stressful time for seniors."

"Not yet." I think about what Dominick and Rita said to me. I'm still not ready to face that decision.

On Halloween weekend, I take a bus to my new job at the Techno café. I enter the restaurant and try to sneak by Xavier, the manager, but the bell over the door gives me away.

"You're a half hour early. Keep it up and you'll be a manager in no time."

"Great," I mumble. "More responsibility." Arianna thought a job would be good for me, seeing as I feel out of control in crowded spaces. Face my anxiety.

So far so good. It's been a week.

I take orders from college students, professors, and elderly folk. Most of them only want coffee or lattes to sit and chat over. I hate coffee. I don't understand how so many people could be addicted to the diarrhea-colored liquid. It tastes like dirt. Plus, I'd be up all night between the caffeine and insomnia. But I'm happy to serve it, as long as the tips help me save for college and distract my brain from overreacting.

Minutes turn to hours, and soon most of the customers leave. I work until 6:00, and around 5:30 the manager tells me to refill the napkin dispensers. I hear the bell over the glass door ring, which means I have to serve another customer before I leave if I want the tip. Great. I slowly push a handful of napkins forward onto the metal platform inside the dispenser. Without looking up, I ask, "Coffee?"

A familiar male voice answers, "Nope. Just you. And maybe a jelly doughnut."

Dominick sits at the counter. Oh God, I forgot how good he looks when he smiles at me. I bet he feels better than I remember, too.

"What are you doing here?" I ask, trying not to smile. "How'd you know where I work?" I hand him a doughnut wrapped in wax paper.

"Rita demanded that we follow through on our Halloween pact for senior year. Said you forgot about it with everything going on. She's waiting in my car."

He takes a bite of doughnut, leaving a trace of powdered sugar on his bottom lip. "She's been worried about you."

"Were you worried about me?" I hand him a napkin.

He grins. "Not falling for that one. I'm here because it's Halloween, and we have a tradition."

I laugh. "Seriously?"

"Completely. And I still want to know why you were with that guy." He licks his thumb and pointer finger clean.

My manager clears his throat. I start filling salt shakers. "Jealous much? We aren't even together anymore."

His smile fades. I meant to say it in a flirty tone.

"I'm sorry. I didn't mean it like that. The guy thing wasn't my fault. Okay, so it was partly my fault. I tried to avoid him, but he wanted me to poke the hologram."

We stare at each other, and then we burst out laughing. The manager clears his throat again.

I move to the next table and pick up a pile of napkins. Dominick stands awkwardly, fidgeting with his hands in his pockets. The bell over the glass door pierces the silence as a mustached stranger strolls into the café and sits at the counter. I take his order for a cup of coffee and a bagel. While my back is turned to toast the bagel, I hear the bell ring again. I turn around to see if I have more last-minute customers only to discover that Dominick is gone, his cash left on the counter.

Every particle in my body screams to go after him. He drove here, found me at work. I need him back in my life. But I also need to be protective of myself and learn to be in control of my emotions. I just started getting myself on the right track, trusting my own instincts. Yet there's something about Dominick that fills me with peace instead of worry. I just don't want to fill him with a sense of burden.

My heart bangs against my ribs to escape, and I can't stop thinking about running out the door, chasing after him, and screaming his name down a lamplit alley. *Dominick! Dominick, wait!* And he'd turn around in slow motion like in a corny romantic film, and we would speed toward each other and embrace in one swoop and kiss. Oh, and kiss the juiciest kiss known in the history of romantic moments captured forever in books and movies. And then it would downpour, of course. But no, I'm not that kind of girl. I can't take risks in love or life. They backfire. Besides, this is real life, and I still have customers.

By the time I leave the restaurant, a giant knot grows in my stomach. I made the wrong decision. I should've gone after Dominick when I had the chance. Why do I keep sabotaging my chances with him? I whip out my phone, but before I can even type a message, Dominick's familiar black Honda Civic, his father's old car, pulls up beside me with Rita in the passenger seat.

He stayed.

"I thought you left," I say as I hop in the back seat. The TARDIS air freshener that I gave him still dangles from the rearview mirror.

"Your manager kept giving me dirty looks, so I thought I should wait outside."

Rita throws a plastic bag at me. "You didn't think we'd forget you? It's Halloween. It's our tradition."

Inside the bag is a short-haired ginger wig, a robe, and a wand. I stick the wig on my head and throw the robe over my clothes. Freshman year, the three of us unanimously wanted to dress up for Halloween like Harry Potter, Hermione Granger, and Ron Weasley. Only none of us wanted to be Ron. Dominick had argued that he should get to be Harry since he's a guy, and that Rita and I should just both be Hermione since we're girls. That gender logic was never going to fly with us. So we compromised and made a pact. Every Halloween we would rotate characters. I thought we were done since Dominick and I aren't together, but apparently I was wrong. Thank you, Rita.

Rita places a pair of dark plastic glasses on her nose. My red wig itches. Dominick tosses on a long brown wig.

"Dude, you are the ugliest Hermione ever," Rita says, laughing. I giggle along with her, and Dominick turns to grin at me. His shadow of facial hair combined with the bad Hermione wig and his glasses turns my laughter into snorting.

"With that wig and your glasses, you kinda look like a strung-out Harry." Rita and I both get louder and more hysterical.

"Shut up or I'll curse you with my long wand," he says in a deep voice and waves his plastic wand.

"Long? Really?" Rita asks. I smile and bop her on the head with my wand from the back seat.

We drive to Buttonwood Park, ditch the car, and for the next two hours we act foolish, cursing random people, saying inappropriate things, hiding in leaves to scare kids, and sometimes trick-or-treating when houses seem willing to hand out candy to older teens.

In a fake Harry Potter voice, Rita asks a random group of girls, "Would you like to whomp my willow?"

Dominick chuckles and walks by my side, sometimes brushing up against my arm. I want to reach out and hold his hand. It always made me feel safe. Its absence hangs between us like an abandoned friend.

As the cold settles into the night, we head over to the Dartmouth Mall since they let kids trick-or-treat there. It's so dead for a weekend, I wonder if it's actually closed and we somehow broke in. I chalk it up to Halloween parties elsewhere, but the more we walk around, the more I sense something isn't right.

"Something's rotten in the state of Massachusetts," Dominick announces. He swings his wand in the air. "Where is everyone?"

"Right? It's too quiet," I mumble, chewing on a Starburst.

"Maybe the vertexes sucked them all up," Rita says. She tosses back a mouthful of Nerds from a box.

"Not funny," I reply, and I don't laugh this time. None of us laugh. The mall is never this still. I'm waiting for a giant tumbleweed to roll past Old Navy.

We decide to go to Walmart instead, and again, it's eerily quiet. We finally spot a crowd of parents and costumed children gathered in the back electronics area. They stare at the wall of glowing television sets, all with the same vacant look in their eyes.

"What's going on?" I ask a row of people in front of us.

No one answers. It's never a good sign when you ask a silent crowd a question and no one flinches. Especially when you're standing there in a ridiculous Ron costume. *I wonder if the vertexes have suddenly turned them into zombies or taken over their brainwaves, and somehow the three of us are immune.*

I watch too much sci-fi.

We face the television screens. It's all over the news. NASA's Planetary Defense Coordination Office, or PDCO, has confirmed that a comet, ten miles wide, is on a trajectory for a direct hit on Earth, most likely on the Atlantic Coast, within the next three months. Governments are warning everyone not to panic. The United Nations has been working on a three-part plan with NASA and other space engineers around the globe to adjust the comet's course.

But the media stresses there are no guarantees the plan will work and debates whether the vertexes are a more viable option.

This just got real.

PART 2
MESSAGE TWO

Doubt thou the stars are fire,
Doubt that the sun doth move,
Doubt truth to be a liar
But never doubt I love.

–WILLIAM SHAKESPEARE

CHAPTER 10

DAY 92: OCTOBER–2,211 HOURS TO DECIDE

QUESTION: How do you handle natural disasters on your planet?

ANSWER: Since we are able to regulate atmospheric conditions with our technology, we do not experience the harsh temperature changes, storms, floods, or droughts of earth. Our structures have been built to withstand any seismic activity with little to no impact.

The entire store erupts from silent trauma mode into ants-on-fire mode. Everyone is in an uproar about the comet. How did the government not know a ten-mile-wide comet was only three months away from hitting us? *How do you miss something like that?* In the vast cosmic universe, is it really a proverbial needle in a haystack? Is it really something as easy and diminutive as forgetting to dot an *i*, cross a *t*?

All I know is there's a comet. Fact. According to the hologram countdown app on my phone, we have two thousand two hundred eleven hours left to decide. Now what are we going to do about it?

Phase two begins instantaneously: people begin to scatter. Without even discussing it, Dominick, Rita, and I push past other shoppers, run out of the store, gowns and wands flying behind us, and flee to the parking lot.

The lot is flooded with foot and tire traffic, honking horns, adrenaline. The government warned us not to panic.

Panic: from Pan in Greek mythology, a satyr who has known to create irrational, sudden fear in people for fun. Something that happens to everyone when the world announces that an Earth-crushing hot mass barreling toward the planet may likely kill us in three months.

"Where did I park?" Dominick spins slowly in a circle like a broken compass.

"Over there, maybe?" Rita points to the left. I have no idea where we are, where we are going, where we've been. I follow her lead.

In times of complete panic, people move. *As if we can move out of the way of global disaster. It's not hide-and-seek. Annihilation is absolute.* The strange thing is that everyone has the same reaction. Move. Go home. Is it to be with our families? People who have known us since the beginning? Born together, die together?

Giving us time to move around and pretend we're not helpless— it's irresponsible. Rude almost.

We cannot run from this one.

We could go through a vertex.

My phone vibrates, snapping me back into my body and out of my head. It's my dad. I hold up a finger to quiet Dominick and Rita, then answer.

"Alexandra!" It's wartime, and I'm standing in the line of fire.

"Dad?" My voice shakes to match his.

"I'm coming to get you. Where are you? I want you home. Now."

Home. Everyone has the same gut response. Will it really help? *Will we hug as we burn?*

"Alexandra!" His voice booms through the receiver.

"You don't have to come get me. I'm with Rita and Dominick. They can bring me home."

"Where are you?" he barks at me again.

"We went out for Halloween." *Is he really going to argue with me when the world might be ending?* I pull the Ron wig off my head and fan my face with it.

He must hear the edge in my voice. "Alexandra, don't worry about the comet. They have nukes for shit like this. I'm more afraid of how people will overreact. You need to come home so we can hunker down. Make a plan."

Hunker down. Make a plan. The comet's no big deal. Dad's lost it.

"I'll be home soon," I reassure him. "We're leaving."

"I'll be waiting at the door."

After hanging up the phone, Dominick, Rita, and I find his car. Dominick fumbles to put his keys into the ignition. Rita starts crying softly.

"My parents are never gonna let me leave through a vertex," she says. "They'll make us die here."

You and me both.

"It'll be fine," I say, trying to believe it myself. "The comet's three months away. You'll have time to convince them."

It's weird to say she has plenty of time before the world might end. *But how else do I have conversations? What matters and doesn't matter now? Doesn't everything other than death become petty and small and equal in unimportance?*

Three short months.

Dominick touches my shoulder and snaps me out of it. How did I ever think that I could survive without him?

The typical twenty-minute ride home takes forever. Traffic clogs the highway. We take turns driving, pulling over to the side of the highway every half hour or so, running around the car like there's an emergency, and then sitting in slow-to-unmoving traffic once more. The TARDIS air freshener spins in midair, teasing us.

We turn on the radio. The same breaking news spouts on every station. NPR claims that media sources are investigating a possible cover-up to see if governments had prior knowledge of the comet and were keeping it from the public. They report that several online bloggers claim they had warned about the comet for years and no one listened. NPR discredits their evidence, explaining that the bloggers produced doctored photographs, and some of their older blog entries originally professed the images were alien spaceships, not comets. Instead, the reporter provides a scientific explanation. Something about the sun's alignment with Earth blocking our direct line of sight of the comet until now.

I want to scream. Does it matter who's right and wrong here? This is bigger than conspiracies and rhetoric. It just *is*.

"Did either of you see the movie *Armageddon*?" Rita asks.

"I think I did," Dominick says. "Was that the one with Bruce Willis?"

"Yeah, and they have to blow up a comet, or maybe it was an asteroid? Anyway, they blow it up but the pieces still do major damage." Rita's eyes begin to grow wider and wider with concern.

"That's Hollywood, though, not real life," Dominick says. "In real life, scientists would rather move it off course."

"Hollywood, right. They can do anything. Governments, not so much." Rita snaps a piece of gum like she's trying to beat it into submission.

"It's not the scientists' fault. NASA hasn't been funded properly for years," Dominick argues.

"I wasn't blaming the scientists." Rita looks back at me in the back seat for help.

I can't debate. Not this time. My mind seems to be overprocessing all information. I can't cry. I can't truly comprehend it. Even my anxiety is too confused to kick in. I'm like a computer stuck on the little spinning hourglass instead of an arrow cursor, trapped in time instead of moving with direction and action. Maybe I'm not capable of understanding certain levels of devastation. Maybe we're not supposed to fathom it ahead of time. Maybe it's just too damn big.

We drop Rita off first since her house is closer. Mom calls me to see what's taking so long. When I finally get home around 11:15, Dad opens the front door as soon as my foot hits the bottom porch step. When he says something, he means it. He's been in sentinel mode, waiting up for me. Not good. Mom appears behind him, groggy and sober. She hugs me, then returns inside.

The stars fill the night sky with foreboding. Nothing is safe. Dominick turns to leave with a wordless wave.

"Dominick." I try to figure out what to say and how to say it. I need to apologize, need to kiss him after everything that's happened, but it's awkward enough without Dad watching on top of it. I try to give Dad a can-you-give-us-a minute-alone look, but he stands vigilant.

"It's late," Dad announces. "Nick, it's time to head home."

"Thanks," I manage to say to Dominick, my voice wavering with so many more important things to say but without a way to say it in front of my dad.

"No problem. I'm glad I was with you." He turns to leave.

"Wait," I squeak. It's now or never. "I'm so sorry for what I said. I didn't mean it. I miss you." He nods, and the hint of a smile lifts the corners of his mouth. *Screw it.* I take a quick step forward and kiss him. At first the kiss feels hard, desperate. But once he responds, it changes to a soft, wet, deep yearning.

Dad clears his throat. The kiss goes on and on anyway. It's all that matters. "Enough already," Dad says.

Dominick and I break away, grinning like amused children who share an amazing secret.

"Sorry, Dad," I say. "No disrespect, but the world's ending." And I walk into the house after one more quick peck and wave at Dominick.

"The world is not ending," Dad yells.

That same night, after a few short hours of restless sleep, I wake up to find Dad sitting on his throne, drinking. Black splotches of paint cover his arms, hands, and shirt. Despite the news repeating the contrary, he still thinks the world's not ending and people will lose it once the doomsday prophecy approaches. He's decided the basement will be our safe spot, so he's blackened the windows. I pop a pill.

I keep asking myself the same question: *Why did I come back here?*

And the same answer: *Where else was I supposed to go?*

Across the globe more people have gathered at vertexes to take the plunge. News of the comet struck a nerve in everyone, but some people have reacted immediately and want out. Others, like me, are frozen with indecision. Or, like Dad, they are stubborn until the end.

The following afternoon, my cell phone rings. At the sight of Dominick on my screen, the heat of our kiss returns to my mouth. I wonder if he felt it, too, and if it was enough for him to forgive me. I mean, what's the point of arguing about college choices when the world could explode?

"Are you watching the news?" Dominick asks.

"No, I shut it off for a break." I stare at the ceiling in my bedroom. The crack above my bed grins at me, mocking me for assuming the call was about our lost relationship.

"Turn it on," he says. "The hologram's message changed today at noon."

"What?" I sit up, my open journal falling off my chest, and fish through my blanket and sheets for the remote.

"Watch it. It's on replay."

As soon as I click on the television, the image of a hologram fills the screen. It takes me a few seconds to find a source that has the message from the beginning.

A hologram stares out blankly at a crowd gathered in front of it.

"By now we hope you understand the urgency of our message. The comet should be visible with your technology. In three of your calendar months, that comet will strike your planet and destroy your people. This is your known destruction; there is no way to prevent it.

"We hope we have answered all questions to your satisfaction.

We are waiting and able to help. Simply walk through the vertex. We will be on the other side.

"This automatic message will repeat once a day at each vertex location. You have approximately two thousand one hundred ninety-six hours to decide. The vertexes will remain open until then.

"Consider. Save your people. Save yourself before it is too late."

I click off the television. My heart can't handle more.

"You there?" Dominick asks.

"Yeah. For now." I take a deep breath and let it out slowly.

"You okay?"

"Yes," I lie, chipping off a piece of OPI & Apple Pie from my ring finger. I should be upset that he's worrying about me again, but with a coming cataclysm, I guess it's time to get over it. Everybody's worried. Two thousand one hundred ninety-six more hours of worry to go. *And that message was taped an hour ago.*

"Want me to come get you?" he asks.

My heart leaps to the crack in the ceiling. Maybe that kiss meant something to him after all.

———

Dominick and I sit in his car staring out at a moody, November Atlantic Ocean. Being with him has never felt so hard before. We aren't talking. The world has definitely changed.

As I watch the waves, my mind tries to examine my relationship with Dominick, my relationship to the world, my relationship to existence. I try to examine every variable. Decisions are coming. I need to do the right thing.

"Should we all just leave?" I blurt out.

Dominick looks at me from the driver's seat. "You mean through a vertex?"

The last time I saw a vertex, I was almost its victim. Now I'm wondering if it's time to let it swallow my life. I nod.

"We just found out the comet's real," Dominick says. "I'm surprised you're already throwing in the towel."

"But the comet changes everything."

"We still have three months to decide. Ninety-one more days after today. Why not wait it out a little at least, see what scientists can do first? I thought there was more of a fighter in you."

I nudge his shoulder with my elbow. He fake flinches. "There's my girl."

As soon as he says those words, he turns away and stares out the window. The silence returns to the car. The kiss from yesterday lingers between us, an answer to an unasked question.

"I love you," I say. "I always have."

"I know." His eyes stay on the beach. A seagull circles the area and swoops out of sight. "I just want everything to be back to normal."

I don't know what to say. "I'm sorry for pushing you away. I went to a therapist, and she helped me deal with my anxiety better. I needed to get myself together. To be worthy of you."

He gives me a dirty look. "You are worthy of me."

"No, I'm a mess. And the comet thing has made me even worse."

"Alex, you're not a mess. You're stronger than you realize. Everyone's freaking out. You're not alone."

I'm stronger than I realize. Everyone's freaking out. You're not alone. I like the sound of those words coming from him. *Is that what he really thinks?*

He continues. "And sometimes I worry about you, but it's not because I think you're weak. That's what people do when they care."

I let his words wash over me like the cold waves crashing in front of us. I know his words are true in my mind. I have to get my heart to believe him.

"I realized something when we were apart," he adds.

"What?" I swallow hard. His tone carries weight with it.

"You're not really a Scully."

I'm so used to fighting him on the annoying nickname, I open my mouth to protest. "Wait, did you say I'm not a Scully?"

He grins. "I've decided since the world may be ending, that I'm more of a David Tennant. And you're more of a Rose."

It's the most romantic thing he's ever said to me without sarcasm.

"He was always my favorite Doctor," I comment. "But what about us as Rory and Amy? Would you wait two thousand years for me?"

He rolls his eyes.

And just like that we fall back into each other.

CHAPTER 11

QUESTION: What types of transportation do you have?

ANSWER: For limited travel, we prefer walking. For longer distances, we have an elaborate network of self-navigating magnetic pods, or magpods, that work using a similar technology to the electrodynamic suspension used in the few maglev trains on your planet. For even longer distances, we use a technology similar to the vertexes on a smaller scale.

The United Nations releases more information about their three-part plan. I record every detail into my journal. Classified under the CORE project, part 1 involves immediately launching a series of modified nuclear missiles to detonate at specific coordinates in hope that the blast pushes the comet off course.

If that doesn't work, a smaller group of scientists have proposed part 2: send an unmanned ship, *Hera II*, to try to alter the comet's trajectory using the gravity of the ship. *Hera II* will attempt to pull a chunk off the comet to increase its gravitational pull. Most scientists don't believe this will work, because *Hera II* was originally built to deal with smaller asteroids and plenty of time, not a colossal comet in three months, but others believe they've solved the issue. NASA is willing to improvise and compromise. The might-as-well-try-it-Hail-Mary-pass approach.

In the meantime, NASA's PDCO will be preparing part 3, which they are not releasing the details about yet. *Makes me wonder if there even is a third option.*

It sounds like they are scrambling to piece together the technology in time. Apparently, we weren't as prepared for cosmic flotsam as we like to believe. The scientists said if CORE isn't successful, the comet will most likely hit us on January 31st, give or take room for error and time zones. Around midnight here. Same date the holograms predicted.

———

People begin migrating. It's weird that when we have time to live, people separate, but during times of crisis, we gather. Wouldn't it be nicer to always live with the people you would choose to gather with at the end? Or is the gathering more out of duty and guilt than actual desire?

My maternal grandmother, Penelope, has decided to fly up from Florida once she finds an available flight, and she doesn't exactly get along with Mom and Dad. She thinks Mom wasted her life by marrying Dad before he went into active duty overseas. Over the phone, Mom happily informs Penelope that she will have to stay at a hotel since Benji took the guest room. Benji offers to leave and stay with a friend, but Mom shoos away his proposition.

Dad's brother, Uncle Henry, calls from Texas. He's staying put with his wife and three kids, but he checks in to make sure everything's "hunky-dory," as he likes to say. I overhear Dad talking to him about "stockpiling" and "hunkering down." Sometimes I think they both have the paranoid gene, and Dad passed a version of it to me.

As days pass and the truth of the comet begins to sinks in, a strange hope begins to spread across the globe that we can do something about it. We have three whole months. Three months for the best scientists in the world to make a plan and divert the thing. It's better than thinking of us as sitting ducks who aren't ready to fly south even though winter's coming.

I want to talk to Arianna, my counselor, about everything that's happened, but she hasn't answered my phone calls. *I Maybe I said something that offended her. Or maybe she quit her practice like my last counselor, me being the common denominator. The ultimate lost cause, destroyer of the psychiatric community.* I replay our last few sessions in my head and search for possibilities that could've been misconstrued.

Mom tells me later that Arianna is on immediate maternity leave because she went into early labor and had an emergency C-section. The baby isn't doing very well. I feel bad that I kept calling her when she was dealing with her own trauma, and I almost want to call her again to apologize. But I don't. I wonder if she will head through a vertex with her baby, get futuristic medical treatment, and start a new life in another world.

I stop going to school, and my parents don't fight me on it. In fact, a slow exodus begins from schools and workplaces across the country, probably across the world. From what I hear, only some administrators, teachers close to retirement, and students with bad family lives have been attending my high school. Rumor has it that they gather in the cafeteria to talk about life and play games. Too bad school wasn't like that before. They've transitioned all courses online so students can complete work from home. It won't last.

How do they expect us to focus? I don't bother to log in. The government keeps saying "business as usual," but come on, we all know that's impossible at this point. This is the closest to the end that we've ever come. Why would we work away our time?

Dad says that kind of talk is like drinking the Kool-Aid. I don't know what the hell he's talking about. He thinks we need to prepare to defend our lives until the end.

I say nothing matters anymore because every moment matters.

A week later, my mother ropes me into going with her to pick up Penelope. She says something about the Lucas family sticking together. I almost remind her that technically Grandma is not in the Lucas family since her last name is O'Donnell, but I let it go when I see her searching the house for her lost keys. She finds them in the refrigerator. The stress of Penelope's visit is already affecting her brain.

Boston Logan International Airport has so many people inside, you'd think they were giving away free tickets. I heard it's the opposite, though. Prices have skyrocketed, and people are using up their cash to get where they want to go. Mom and I stand in the middle of the airport looking over the crowd searching for Penelope's peppery hair and leathery skin. Her plane landed an hour ago. Of course, she refuses to carry a cell phone. Minutes tick by, minutes of my life I may never get back. Funny how much time means to me now there's a countdown. *Come on, Penelope. You're killing me.*

On top of everything else, Mom's in a bad mood since all the hotels in our area are full to capacity already. So despite earlier plans, Penelope must stay with us for the remainder of the possible apocalypse. Benji's bunking with a friend after arguing with Dad about not wanting to crash indefinitely on our couch. *Just how I always wanted to die. Watching my family argue.*

"Over here!" Penelope, as my grandma insists I call her, waves us over to a tower of red luggage with gaudy gold hardware. I swear she brought her entire house from Florida.

"I went a little overboard," she admits, probably after seeing the look of horror on our faces. "But how do you pack for something like this?"

"Light," I mutter under my breath.

"Alexandra, you look so big. I believe someone has an important birthday soon." Relative-speak. She pats me on the head like a good puppy. "Wow, turning eighteen. You must be excited. There's a present for you in one of my suitcases."

I half smile. I'm sure she bought me assorted socks and floral perfume like she sends every year. She turns her babbling comments toward Mom. I tune her out and start wheeling and weaving two of her six suitcases through the crowded airport.

The ride home could compete for the longest, most tedious hours of my eighteen years around the sun. The vertex in Quincy clogs traffic from both directions, so it takes double the time to get home, plus Penelope doesn't take a hint when Mom turns up the music.

My mind drifts from thought to thought, whirling and twisting apocalyptic fiery endings with blissful times spent with Dominick and Rita. If these are the last days, I cannot spend them with my biological family. I can't waste time being the nice daughter who does whatever they expect. The minutes are ticking down.

I make a decision there and then about Dominick. I can't wipe the smile off my face.

As soon as Penelope sets foot in the house, things heat up. Normally, I would like having someone on my side watching Dad's every move, but Penelope's rude to him. While I usually observe the lion, and Mom soothes or ignores the lion, Penelope provokes him for sport.

"Ben," she pats him on the head like a sick child in a hospital. "How are you feeling?"

"Fine." He turns up the volume on the television with the remote.

"Are you sure? You don't look well."

"I'm fine, Penelope. How's Florida?"

She runs a hand through her wispy skunk hair. "Florida's fabulous. Warmer than this hell."

"It's November. It's New England. Whatcha expect?"

"It's horrible. Too bad you never moved the family down to Florida. Never could save enough, I guess. How's the store?"

Dad's nostrils flare, and he vise-grips the remote. Penelope belittles him effortlessly, like a queen toying with a serf, and she's only been here a whopping five minutes. I can't believe Mom left me alone with them to go shopping.

"The store's fine. Everything's fine." His face grows red. With everyone else, Dad's blunt with his words and quick tempered. I've never figured out why he doesn't blow up on Penelope like he does with everyone else. Guess it's a respect thing since she's his mother-in-law. Dad plays by social rules and order. Unless his PTSD kicks in, which I'm afraid Penelope might trigger if she doesn't lay off.

"Well, everything's not fine, or I wouldn't be here," Penelope continues. "I'm surprised you're still working—no one else seems to be."

"People need groceries," Dad says. "Food's not a luxury."

"Well, I should hope not." She sits on the arm of the sofa, giving him no elbow room. "Let's not sweep this thing under the rug. There's a comet heading straight for us, and if scientists can't do anything about it, we have temporary escape routes available. If you ask me, I think we should leave now."

Dad laughs aloud at her comment. My shoulders tighten with each chuckle. *Oh God. This is bad.*

"Leave now? Why? We have time. We have weapons. We can deal with the comet ourselves without the help of alien outsiders."

"Spoken like a true military man."

Somehow Penelope is able to flatter and insult him in the same sentence.

I need to get out of the line of fire. I text Dominick for an escape. I'm done being the neutral buffer in the family.

Dominick's mother is working the night shift as a home care worker, so we put Austin to sleep again. It makes me feel like we're a married couple putting our son to bed. I think about my ride home from the airport and the decision I made. It still feels right, and it's nice to make a major decision and stick to it in a world of uncertainty.

Dominick sits next to me on the couch and grabs for the remote. I take a deep breath and announce, "We should have sex."

He fixes his glasses as if his eyesight has something to do with his hearing. "Repeat that?"

"We should have sex. Tonight. Now." I don't look away and

will myself not to grin out of nervousness. I want him to take me seriously.

He responds, "Okay."

I thought he might joke around a little, ask questions, make sure it's something I really want to do since I swore I didn't want to do it before college. I mean, there's pregnancy, and STDs, and everything else the school scared me with in health class. But the threat of death is a different kind of departure, one that requires checking off certain boxes, experiencing all that life has to offer. Just in case. Time to be brave. We have no idea what the future will bring—no one does at this point. Maybe no one ever does. All I know for sure is that we have tonight. Nothing else is guaranteed.

I slide closer to him and kiss him slowly, softly. He kisses me back, touches my face. His eyes ask if I'm sure. I respond by undoing his belt.

We kiss, and without stopping somehow he blindly leads me into his bedroom, bumping into the doorframe and the side of his bureau on the way.

I want to do it. Surrender to him. The world might be ending.

We still use a condom.

———

I lose track of time, and Dad yells at me for missing curfew. His words bounce over me like I'm wearing an invisible shield. I never realized the power in letting go.

I'm not sure what I expected, but something is definitely different between Dominick and me. I thought when people said that, they were exaggerating. But I know him now. Like really know him.

And he knows me. Like really knows me. No matter what happens, we will always have this between us. Always.

We will just know.

I'm thinking that maybe everyone should have sex before time runs out. Then again, they probably already are.

———

Rita laughs when I tell her.

"About time! Damn, you made that boy wait."

"It's only been a few months," I protest.

"You've been friends for years. He's loved you for years."

"But we broke up."

"Please. It took world annihilation for you to give it up."

"True," I say, and we burst into laughter.

———

Carpe diem is a dangerous concept.

Dominick and I can't keep our hands off each other.

———

The first snowfall of the winter season floats down from the sky. I wonder how many more snowstorms we will see before, well, before whatever ends up happening. Even though it's only a dusting of snow, the blanket of white magic inspires Dominick, Rita, and me to head to the local indoor skating rink for some winter fun. I know it's ludicrous to ice-skate when the world could be ending, but it's also equally ludicrous not to ice-skate when the world could be ending. Doesn't everything other than death become significant and enormous and equal?

We decide skating is a perfectly acceptable world-might-be-ending activity, healthier than taking drugs like most teens are bragging about online. Not as fun as sex with Dominick, but we have to come up for air sometime.

The rink is packed. See, good idea. The three of us lace up pairs of rented ice skates. Rita taught me to skate when I was in middle school. She used to take lessons when she was younger, and she can skate backward and do spins and jumps like in the Olympics. Okay, I'm exaggerating, but she's that good compared to me.

The skates dig into my ankles. Before we hit the ice, Rita taps me on the shoulder. She pulls a pink box out of her backpack and flips open the lid. Inside are three gorgeous pink lemonade cupcakes with fluffy white frosting and candy lemon slices on top.

"Happy birthday. We know you'll be celebrating with your family tomorrow, so we figured it would be a good surprise."

"You didn't have to do this," I say and take a cupcake.

"Oh, shut up and eat," she says.

I take a huge bite, rolling the soft, sweet tartness across my tongue. "Ohmygoditisogood."

"What was that?" Dominick teases.

I grin and swallow. "So good. Thank you."

"Time for presents." Dominick and Rita hand me two small gift bags.

I open Rita's first. It's a silver charm bracelet with one heart charm that says FRIEND. She holds up her arm. The word BEST dangles from her wrist.

"Awesome." I hug her in gratitude. "We always talked about getting them."

"I know. I figured with the world ending…" She chuckles.

I look at Dominick, and he hands me his bag. My stomach aches. We usually give each other gag gifts, but our relationship has shifted. *What if he gives me something ridiculous? What if I hate it? Should I pretend to like it so I don't hurt his feelings? What if it shows that he doesn't really feel what I'm feeling?*

I reach into the bag and pull out a small box. Inside sits a silver ring with a ruby heart stone. "I love it. It's my favorite color." I slip it onto my ring finger.

"I know you don't like to wear necklaces, so—"

"It's perfect." I kiss him until Rita starts fake coughing.

"Enough with the pecking, lovebirds, and finish your cupcakes. I want to skate."

We laugh together, scarf down the remaining desserts, and step onto the rink. As I glide across the ice, I'm not as afraid as I used to be even though I'm just as rocky. Usually I cling to one of them for support. Today, I put my arms out in mock *Titanic*-style and glide across the ice. It lasts a few glorious minutes until I stumble over and fall on my butt, taking them both down with me. In the past, the embarrassment would have triggered my anxiety. Instead, I find myself laughing and laughing until I can't breathe.

So what if I fall? SO WHAT? The world's ending. I never thought that annihilation would free me to live. That's kind of pathetic. Kind of sad. Kind of awesome.

The next day, my family gathers for my eighteenth birthday. Even Benji shows up. Since Penelope's arrival at our house, Dad has disappeared more and more, spending time in the backyard, in the basement, at work. Wherever she isn't. It's funny how Penelope traveled to be closer to family, and instead we are spending more and more time apart. Except for my birthday.

Mom bakes me a gorgeous pineapple cake with almond-coconut frosting, my favorite. And yes, Penelope gives me socks and terrible perfume, and I act surprised and grateful. Mom and Dad give me a new phone. Exactly what a girl needs during an apocalypse. Benji hands me a folded fifty without a card. Nice, I guess.

I thought I wanted to spend less time with my family, but with the pending disaster, I need to know they're there. I'm worried that the comet will come when I'm stuck in public somewhere, and I will die surrounded by strangers. Dad's right in one respect. If I'm going to die, I want to die surrounded by people I've always known, even if I don't necessarily like them.

———

That afternoon, I find Dad hiding from Penelope in the basement sorting through supplies. With his supermarket and military knowledge, the basement has been stocked, shelved, and categorized. There's canned items, including soups, vegetables, beans, and processed meat that I would rather die than eat. Another shelf has cereals, pasta, rice, and nuts and liquids, like dry milk, juices, sodas. A whole section is devoted to bottled water, and of course, there are other supplies, such as matches, batteries, oil, and—I notice today—gasoline in containers. That can't be safe. Add a cash register and we might as well be a mini-store ourselves.

"Wow," I say, impressed.

Dad immediately covers up a pile with a sheet and clears his throat. He knows he's gone overboard.

"Shelves keep emptying faster than we can refill them at the store," he explains. "Shipments haven't been arriving on time, people not showing up for shifts. Shoplifting's been rampant since there's not enough manpower to control it. The gas station at the store has cars lined up around the perimeter of the lot. Bet they'll be out of gas soon enough." He points to the gas containers in the corner. "I don't like storing it down here, but we don't have a garage or a shed. I should've built a fallout shelter years ago."

As he pulls another sheet over a section of canned goods, my heart acknowledges how hard he's trying to protect us and how much time he's wasting.

He clears his throat again. "I want to be prepared for anything. I keep thinking that I forgot something."

I hate to admit it, but he sounds like me.

"Dad, you can't prepare for everything. It's impossible. Nothing like this has ever happened before."

"True. But serious trouble's brewing. Have you heard the saying 'Desperate times call for desperate measures'?"

"Yeah."

He pulls the corner of another sheet to cover his treasure. "We can be our own worst enemies. Our own sources of destruction. We don't need a comet."

His comment carries with me for the rest of the day. Despite how much I want to refute or ignore him, sometimes Dad strikes a note that resonates and cannot be unheard.

One of my earliest memories is hearing that Dad had been discharged and was coming home. Benji and I spent the morning coloring a huge Welcome Home banner in a rainbow pattern to hang across the porch. I remember waiting in the front window, holding a bouquet of handpicked wildflowers from our backyard. By the time he walked through the door, most of them had wilted.

"Daddy!" I cried.

He crushed me in an embrace. "I missed you so much."

"I missed you, too. But the flowers…"

He took them from me and tossed them on the coffee table. "It's okay, Alex. Flowers die."

He moved over to hug Benji, and I was left staring at the table, wondering what happened to the daddy I remembered, the one who loved when I gave him flowers, who would squish and dry them in books and save them in a cigar box.

Sometimes I feel like that little girl in the window, still waiting for my old daddy to come back.

CHAPTER 12

QUESTION: What do you do with people who break the law? Do you have a judicial system? Do you have prisons?

ANSWER: Most people do not break the law because they are happy. If someone is exhibiting violent or other disturbing behavior that infringes upon the rights of others, we have medical knowledge of the brain's thought pathways to reroute the misfiring neurons. It is called brain regulation mapping and thought reconditioning. It is rarely used. It is rarely necessary.

Each state has been asked to vote on a timely debate.

Should prisoners have the right to decide whether or not to leave through a vertex? If not, should they be forced to stay? Or should they be forced through a vertex?

The last one has been popular in North Korea and parts of Africa.

The question also has variations depending on the crime and sentence. Since I just turned eighteen, I'm allowed to vote. I never thought my first ballot would be about choosing whether or not to let convicts travel to a future parallel universe or fry in an apocalypse.

I make a serious list of crimes in my journal to help me decide how to vote. Who deserves a chance to leave, and who faces a comet?

Terrorism/Hate Crimes
First Degree Murder
Second Degree Murder
Involuntary/ Voluntary Manslaughter
Kidnapping and False Imprisonment
Rape and Sex Offenses
Larceny
Burglary
Fraud (Identity Theft, Credit Card Fraud, other)
Aggravated Assault and Battery
Arson
Drug Distribution/Possession
Criminal Possession of a Weapon
Human Trafficking
Other?

The voting will take place in one week. I thought the list would help, but it's making me realize that it's simply another decision I don't feel qualified to make.

And I want to be a lawyer.

Thankfully, I find out on social networks that the voting won't list specific crimes, but instead will be based on the amount of time they were sentenced.

Dad says they should all stay, but he thinks everyone should stay put. Mom thinks that only heinous criminals with sentences over ten years should stay. That seems like an arbitrary number to me. Dominick thinks we need to let the prisoners decide, especially since the holograms say they deal with crime through brain regulation mapping and thought reconditioning, whatever that is. Maybe the prisoners can be reformed. *What if it's alien rhetoric for forced lobotomies?*

I guess it's good that the government is allowing us to vote on the issue, letting people decide what's ethical in a world apocalypse versus exodus situation, but at the same time there are some things that no one is qualified to answer. I think the government wants us to decide to take the guilt off their conscience. The good old Pontius Pilate approach. And we know how the masses voted in that decision.

Maybe there's something to the meritocracy in the other world. They make the hard choices.

They keep all the blame.

———

After dinner that night, the debate begins. "Vote no. No choice. Period. Easy decision."

Dad has spoken. Benji nods his head in male agreement. Mom stays silent as usual. I take the bait. I can't let his obstinate opinion go unchecked, especially when Benji's present.

"Are you saying that someone addicted to drugs deserves to die in an apocalypse?" I question.

"Yes," Dad says. "Absolutely." He sips his beer.

"Fine," the debater in me thinks up an argument. "Let's say it wasn't vertexes and holograms and a comet. Let's say an area is flooded. Would you evacuate the prison in that situation, or would you let all the prisoners drown?"

Dad stares at me. His authority is being ruffled. "There's a big difference."

"Yeah, big difference," Benji echoes.

I look from Benji to Dad and back again. Apparently, we're playing on teams. Two on one. Boys against girl. Mom begins to clear the table. She's not even bothering to play referee. Where's Penelope when I need her? Napping. Figures.

"What's the difference?" I ask. "In both cases, their lives are in jeopardy."

Benji traces his finger on the kitchen table like he's writing an invisible battle plan.

"First of all, yes, we evacuate during flooding. There's time. And prisoners would be evacuated in a timely way, all at once, under guard." He slides his finger down the table and back around again. "They would then be relocated and put back in prison to finish serving their sentences. But in terms of the vertexes, you are allowing choice, allowing them to escape one at a time before the threat of danger even becomes real. And then you are allowing them possible asylum on another world."

Dad takes a long, proud swig of his beer. I want to knock it over and spill it onto both of their laps.

"But if the comet is real," I continue, "then the threat is coming. We don't know if the government's plan will work. If it fails, then what? They blow up? Shouldn't prisoners have the right to live? To at least get to choose?"

My face is hot. I'm starting to wonder if I'm fighting for prisoners' rights or mine.

"What about murderers?" Benji goes off. "Rapists? Terrorists? You would let them have a choice? Most of them should have life in prison or death sentences anyway."

"Bingo." Dad eggs him on.

I burn with frustration. They're not listening. They're playing their military loyalty card. I can play that game. "In some countries, people would consider you a terrorist." I point in Benji's face. "Did you ever kill anyone?"

Dad turns red. "Alexandra, you never ask a soldier that question. Ever."

I've never seen Dad so flustered. He takes a sip from his beer, slams the bottle on the table, and doesn't release his grip. Then he takes another long gulp.

Benji stares at the table. Then he whispers, "No."

Dad slams the bottle down. After a pause, he replies, "Count yourself lucky." Then he walks out of the room. The empty bottle sits on the table.

"You had to go there," Benji whispers and follows Dad's exit.

I've cleared the room. I think this is called winning the battle but losing the war.

———

Late that night I wake up to noise coming from the kitchen. Groggy, I stumble down the hallway and find Mom pouring boiling water into a mug from a teakettle. A tremendous weight lifts from my chest, accumulated worry that Zombie Night had returned.

"What are you doing up?" I ask while I rub my eyes. The time on the microwave reads 2:54 a.m.

"Your father had a nightmare again. He hasn't had one in years. I think it's because of seeing Benji again, knowing that he's still manning the vertexes after those bombings. Don't tell your brother that, though," Mom adds quickly. "I think seeing him return from duty is bringing up old wounds."

I nod as if that's true, but I know it's because I pushed the limit. Maybe Zombie Night is coming next.

"Want tea?" she offers.

"No thanks. I heard noise and wanted to see who was up."

"Alexandra." She pulls out a chair and sits. "I've been wanting to discuss something with you."

"What?" I join her at the table.

"How do you really feel about the vertexes?"

It's a loaded question. It's choosing between living and dying. Between lover and family. Between fact and faith.

"I don't know yet. I just know that I want to decide for myself. I don't think it's a decision that should be made for me."

She smiles. "We are more alike than you know." She means it as a compliment, but it's not what I want to hear. I want to be independent. I want my thoughts and decisions to be completely separate from her. Her focus has always been on Benji. And now, after all these years, she thinks we're alike? No, we're not alike. I never would've become so self-sacrificing. So damn invisible.

CHAPTER 13

QUESTION: Do you live in families?

ANSWER: Yes, we live in communal housing situations with like-minded people if we choose. Some also live alone and prefer a more solitary lifestyle. We do not have the same static definition of family as you do.

As the weather in New England shifts from fall to an early winter, the neighborhood landscape also begins to change. While hotels and motels remain full, more houses are empty. It's hard to notice during the day, but at night the streets are darker than usual because fewer and fewer houses have lights on in their windows. The news calls it the "Great Vertex Migration," more people traveling to be with family, staying closer to a vertex just in case, or leaving through a vertex and abandoning property. Normally, the homeless would squat inside the homes, but most of the homeless have left via the vertexes as well.

The darkness gives my neighborhood a more sinister atmosphere, like a town of haunted houses, abandoned after torturing families. *Where there's emptiness, there's space where things can hide and come out to attack you when you least expect it.* I've never been afraid before to walk home at night, so at first I think my anxiety is acting up. When Dominick insists on staying inside after dark, I realize my fear is rational.

———

The day of the prisoner voting question I almost skip it and let other people deal with it. But the more I recall Dad and Benji discussing the need to leave all the prisoners behind regardless of crime because they gave up their rights long ago, the more I wonder if that's what I want to happen. My vote matters, damn it. I decide to wield my invisible sword and cast my first and maybe last public vote.

Dominick has to watch his brother, so Rita and I decide to meet up and go vote together. She shows up at my house an hour later than we planned. I could've walked to the high school by now.

"Sorry," she apologizes. "My parents were being difficult. They think I'm at the library." She grins deviously. "Check this out."

She unbuttons her black wool coat to show me her latest acquisition of HoloVertex fashion. Companies have been cashing in and profiting off the phenomenon, creating merchandise like cups, T-shirts, hologram dolls, and key chains, both in favor of the vertexes and against them, to appeal to all consumers. Rita proudly displays her new T-shirt. Across her bulging chest is the slogan HOLOGRAMS ARE SEXY in white bold letters against black. The SEXY is in red, of course.

"Like it?" she asks, grinning and driving. It's her mini-rebellion.

I know, like me, she's putting up with her parents and their beliefs. Doesn't mean she can't have a little fun of her own in the meantime. Like I am with Dominick. Like most people are.

"I bought a different one for you," she says, smiling. "I figured since you and Dominick have been so amorous lately..." She points to her bag on the floor of the passenger side.

I reach inside and pull out a hot pink shirt with the slogan THE END IS COMING—ARE YOU? followed by a smiley face.

"I can't wear this!" I laugh.

"Why not?" Rita asks with a grin plastered on her face. "It's innocent."

"Yeah, sure it is." I fold the shirt to hide the front. "Thanks."

"Welcome."

"I'll wear it. As pajamas. When my dad's not around."

"Chicken." She starts making clucking sounds.

"Fine." I pull the shirt over my tank top. It kind of feels empowering, to be honest. "Stop teasing me. I don't see you wearing your shirt in front of your parents."

She stops clucking. "So true."

By the time we reach our voting area at the high school, the line snakes out the door and around the corner. I'm not surprised to see people holding signs, some for the rights of prisoners, some against. After Rita parks the car, we wait in line for what seems like a millennium.

All these people. Perfect location for another bombing attack like at the vertexes. I search the line for potential terrorists—everyone looks suspicious.

"It's hard to believe we're waiting to get into the high school," Rita jokes, "when we couldn't wait to escape."

"I was thinking the same thing," I lie. "Weird how the building looks exactly the same as it did freshman year but how much has changed with us."

"So true. Hey," she says, pointing, "Isn't that your brother?"

"I doubt it. He's supposed to be guarding the vertex site." I search the line for a Benji look- alike.

"It's definitely him. Up front with the sign." That's when I spot him. Benji's with the protesters.

"I forgot how good he looks out of uniform," Rita comments.

I roll my eyes. Benji's taking his anti-prisoner stance seriously, taking work off and everything. But then, from a distance I read the sign that he's holding: PRISONERS ARE STILL PEOPLE.

What? Since when is he on their side? My side? *After he freaking made me argue in front of Dad, giving him nightmares again, and possibly sending him back on the PTSD zombie train? What was the point?* A wave of anger overpowers my reason. I don't know whose side I'm on, what side I stand for, but the next thing I know I'm at the front of the line screaming in Benji's face.

"Hypocrite," I yell and whack his sign with an open palm. He fumbles to keep it upright. "Chickenshit!"

"Alex, relax," Rita says, grabbing my arm.

"No, let go of me." I can't control myself. I am a banshee fighting for the life I deserve. Benji tries to block me with his sign, but I push it away. In front of Dad he always makes me the bad guy when I'm the only one who looks out for him.

A cop monitoring the voting area steps over to intervene.

"Ma'am, calm down." He places his body between me and Benji, one hand on his belt, one outstretched to block me.

"I am calm!" I cannot believe Benji was for prisoners' rights all along and harped on me in front of Dad to look good. How could he do that, side with him and cast me as the villain?

The officer doesn't back down. "Ma'am, if you don't calm down, I will have to arrest you."

The word "arrest" knocks me back into reality, if reality exists anymore. *Handcuffed and charged with domestic assault. Stuck in a concrete prison. The shortest sentence given by a judge would still serve as a death sentence unless voters release me to a glowing vertex ready to devour me alive.* I take several deep breaths to regain my composure. Benji stands there, eyebrows furrowed and silent, still holding the sign.

The cop asks, "Are you able to act civilized and stay in line, or do I have to escort you off the premises?"

"I'm fine. I want to vote." I say it as evenly as possible, but I really want to spit the words into Benji's face.

"I'll be watching you," the cop adds. "One more step out of line, and you'll be gone."

I head to the back of the line. Rita follows me and stays quiet. I know she has a million questions to ask me, but she knows it's not the time.

It's ironic that after screaming at Benji, I'm about to vote in favor of the rights of the prisoners to choose their own destiny. *I don't want to vote the same as him.* It's a childish thought, and I know it, but it's the truth. It's weird to fight with someone when you're on the same side.

As the anger subsides, my anxiety fills in the space. I look at all the signs around me, for prisoners' rights, against prisoners' rights, for holograms, for Jesus. Even my T-shirt carries its own agenda. There are too many signs nowadays, blatant and hidden, distorted and clear. How people look versus what they say. What people say versus what they mean. What they mean versus how they feel. How they feel versus how they act.

How do you know what's real and what's a cover? Do you listen to the voices around you, the one in your head, or the one in your heart? Do hearts even speak anymore when the world becomes so damn loud?

Twenty long minutes later, I enter a voting booth and cast my vote.

———

Rita and I walk back to the high school parking lot after we vote. Benji leans against his car, waiting for us.

"Can I talk to you?" Benji asks me.

"Why?" I ask. "What can you possibly say to me?" The anger rises inside of my throat.

"Rita, could we have a minute alone?" Benji requests.

"Sure," Rita says. "I'll be in my car."

I read her face. She wants me to spill everything later.

"Thanks," Benji says to Rita.

Who said I wanted to talk to him? Even though I'm fuming, something seems off. He was actually polite to Rita for once.

Benji begins. "Alex, I understand why you are upset. I get it."

"Do you really?" The words come out sharper than I expect.

"Yes, you think I'm a hypocrite, like you said."

My full anger bubbles over. "You're so fake. You sided with Dad and then totally voted the other way."

"Alex, you don't understand."

"What don't I understand? That you can totally ream me out to look good in front of him? That you like to torment me? That you blame me for my anxiety and for making his worse? Yeah, I get that. I so get that."

"No, you don't understand. Not really."

He takes a deep breath, and his eyes focus in on me. "Alex, I'm gay."

What? My brain feels like it traveled in time and hit a loop. *WHAT?*

"Since when?" I almost wonder if he's lying to distract me from being pissed at him. Except his face has softened with vulnerability. "Since always. Mom knows. Dad doesn't."

A burning sensation bubbles up from my stomach and settles in my heart. My tongue tastes like iron. Instead of being the sister I am totally capable of being—instead of flooding him with support—anger and worry, hot and wild, floods my veins.

His hopeful eyes wait for a response. I can't tell him what I'm really feeling because the only overwhelming emotion I feel is betrayal and I don't know why and I don't know how to explain that to him. I really want to shake him. Hard. Behind that feeling, however, is a bewildering sense of disappointment in myself for feeling betrayed.

Everything I've ever thought about Benji feels wrong. All my memories, interactions, everything, feels like a lie. *How could he hide it from me?* I have so many questions. My heart aches that he could hold on to the truth all these years and not tell me, his only sister. *Why didn't he trust me?* Then fear settles into my stomach.

Dad's gonna have a tirade.

And that's when I begin to understand. As much as I hate Dad when he gets going, he's so proud of his militant, all-American son. The knowledge will shatter the perfect image of his son and trigger Dad's PTSD. That's the one thing Benji and I avoid at all costs—crushing Dad's universe.

Benji's been fulfilling his role for years. For Dad. For Mom. For me. He's been the glue holding our broken family together.

I hug him for all those years. I can't remember the last time we've hugged, but I've missed it.

What happened to us? When did we stop being allies? When did our lives become about protecting Dad?

———

I rehash the conversation for Rita on the ride home. There's a long pause, and then she says, "I knew. He told me."

"What do you mean you knew?"

"Remember our last sleepover? He told me that night."

"And you didn't tell me?" My anger resurfaces.

"He told me he was gonna tell you before school started. And then he didn't."

"You should have told me. You're my best friend. He's my brother." My hands start to hurt, and I realize that I'm twisting the bottom of the T-shirt she gave me with all my might.

Rita sighs into the steering wheel. "I know. I'm sorry, but it wasn't for me to tell. I wasn't going to out him to his family."

"Whatever. I would've told you."

"No, you wouldn't have."

"Yes, I would've."

"You're being childish and emotional."

"You're being a bitch."

That does it. She drives me back home in silence. Best friends should tell each other everything, sometimes through mental telepathy. I feel duped by both Benji and Rita, and I'm uncomfortable with the knowledge that my small world could contain such important secrets—and I missed them. *What else am I missing?*

———

That night Dominick and I have sex in his car since his apartment is no longer parent-free. His mother has been let go from her job as a home health aide since many of the elderly and sick have left through vertexes or have moved back in with their families.

Afterward, we sit and look out into the growing darkness of the city.

"My mother's freaking out about losing her job," Dominick says. "She doesn't really have much cash saved. I have a couple hundred dollars in my bureau, but that's not much to live off."

"It's mid-November. The doomsday deadline is set for the end of January. How long can you last?"

He shrugs and looks off into the distance.

"Well, I doubt the landlord will evict you since there's no one else to move in." When he doesn't respond, I change the subject. "I can't believe Rita didn't tell me about Benji."

"Alex, stop." A blue vein in his temple looks like it's about to burst. "It's not about you. For one second, can you think about someone else for a change?"

His words slap me across the face, and the imprint stings. Tears well up from being silenced by him. I don't like it, and I don't know what to say back.

Then I see him wipe a tear from his face. He's always been my rock. My heart sags seeing him break down.

"I don't know what to do," he admits. He's starting to sound like me.

I rub his shoulder. "Is this about your father?" I ask.

More tears fall silently from his eyes. He removes his glasses. "He told me to step up and protect them for him." He can't wipe the tears away fast enough.

"Dominick." I hug him and rub the back of his head. "Your dad didn't know you'd be facing an apocalypse."

He laughs through snot and smiles. I hug him more, clinging to him for comfort and support—mine or his, I can't tell. Maybe it doesn't make a difference anymore.

Back at home that night, I sneak into the basement and fill a garbage bag with food and supplies for Dominick's family. I take a little of everything so Dad won't notice.

The results of the voting are in. I copy them into my journal. It boils down to crime and prison sentence:

Should those with five years or fewer to serve have the right to decide to leave immediately? Yes. 75%.

Should those with more than five years but fewer than fifteen to serve have the right to decide but should have to wait until January 10th to allow free citizens to exit first? Yes. 61%.

Should those with more than fifteen years but not life sentences have the right to decide but should have to wait until January 20th to allow free citizens to exit first? Yes. 53%.

Should those with life sentences have the right to decide but should have to wait until January 30th to allow free citizens to exit first? No. 90%.

The debate continues on television and online. The numbers follow how I voted, so I guess I'm okay with it. The newscaster predicts that the Supreme Court will review the "validity of the voting" and whether it's legally binding for the public to basically determine death sentences and technically overthrow rulings that put people behind bars in the first place.

Victims' rights advocates are up in arms, warning about "the detriment and emotional scars the voting has unmasked in those affected by serious crimes." The majority of prisoners who had five years or fewer to serve have opted to leave through a vertex immediately.

I watch on television as armed vehicles drive the first waves of prisoners to the closest vertexes. Each prisoner enters the vertex still handcuffed and shackled. I wonder what the people on the other side will think when they see them arrive. Family members of the prisoners wait near the vertexes to journey with them to the other side and live out a happy, free reunion. Well, everyone assumes that's what will happen.

The camera scans the crowd to display the police barricade where protesters hold signs. One sign in particular catches the eye of the camera, and it zooms in. A HOLOGRAM FREED MY RAPIST. I swallow down the hard fact, knowing it's how I voted. I never considered how it would affect individual people. There's a difference, and the difference matters. I shut the television off. I can't watch anymore. No matter which way I turn, which battle I fight, nothing is making a difference.

I miss Rita. She won't text me back.

CHAPTER 14

DAY 120: NOVEMBER–1,546 HOURS TO DECIDE

QUESTION: Do you celebrate holidays and traditions?

ANSWER: Every day is a holiday or a tradition for someone on our planet. We no longer have similar holidays and traditions, other than birthdays and deathdays, but we are happy to incorporate and appreciate those holidays and traditions that you choose to celebrate.

Thanksgiving this year feels more like the Last Supper. The kitchen brims with an odd tension. It's the first time I understand the expression "Too many cooks spoil the broth." Dad has a grim smile plastered on his face as Mom and Penelope start prepping all the food. He keeps muttering things like, "We could've lived off this stuff for a month." At the same time, however, he doesn't stop them. Even though the supermarket has received fewer shipments and products each week, Dad helped commandeer specific ingredients for Thanksgiving from the supermarket's stockroom before customers had a chance to buy out the front shelves. He stalks the kitchen like a hunter making sure his prey hasn't escaped.

"You should baste the turkey more often," Penelope says from the counter, brandishing a potato masher. "I don't understand why you won't follow my old recipes. They work."

She doesn't seem to notice that Mom starts chopping vegetables faster and louder and in less uniform chunks. I think Mom's imagining my grandma's fingers on the cutting board instead of carrots.

"Alex, you and Benji set the table. Use Nana's china."

In the dining room, Benji and I find the table already dressed with Nana's heirloom red tablecloth, matching cloth napkins, and a silver candelabra centerpiece. We retrieve the "good" plates—the ones that live in the dining room cabinet except on holidays. Each piece belonged to my great grandmother, who died weeks before I was born so Mom named me after her. Looking at Nana's old decor, I think our names are the only thing the two of us had in common. The white china rimmed with a blue flower scroll design reminds me of an uptight English tea party. The delicate porcelain feels like bird bones, and my fingers tremble as I try not to let them clank together. The sound gives me chills, like tiny teeth clicking against each other.

As Benji and I carefully lay each place setting, I can't help feeling like we are dressing the table for our funeral. If our Thanksgiving was an actual tea party, our dinner would not be a snobby affair. More like a rendition of *Alice in Wonderland*, including Dad as the Mad Hatter, Benji as the March Hare, Penelope as the Cheshire Cat, and Mom as the Dormouse. I'd be stuck as Alice, witness to the fact that everything, even time, has become unpredictable.

Benji clears his throat and whispers, "I need to tell you something."

"What?" I ask. My insides turn like they want to become my outsides. After his last confession, I don't know what else to expect from him. *Is he about to reveal some secret government insight about the vertexes and holograms? Are we about to be invaded? Am I really adopted?*

"I've invited my friend Marcus over." He lays down a plate and moves to the next place setting.

Phew, that was underwhelming supersecret info.

"Okay. So we need another place setting? Does Mom know?"

"Yes. And yes. And Marcus is gay."

I follow Benji's lead and provide the last setting with silverware. "Okay."

Benji clears his throat again. "Alex, we're together. I'm going to tell Dad. We're getting married."

My heart starts pounding in my ears. I have just gotten used to the idea that Benji had a whole life I didn't know about.

"You're gonna tell him today?" My mind starts reeling with possible Dad reactions. Nuclear war comes to mind.

"Why do you think Mom's going overboard with all the food?"

How can she be dealing so easily knowing what's about to happen? "You're gonna put Dad over the edge."

"It's not about Dad." He puts down the last plate and turns around in a circle, like a dog sniffing for more. "It's about me. It's finally about me. Besides, Dad's already over the edge, and it's not my fault. I've always stayed the line to protect Dad, but you always make him worse by freaking out over everything."

"Me? I'm the one who actually cares about him. You take off and constantly remind him of his past."

And there it is. Benji and I, fire and oil. Dad is gasoline. Penelope's gunpowder. What does that make Mom?

I know I should congratulate him, but he's about to turn our possible last Thanksgiving into chaos. I already feel chaotic enough inside. *If the world's ending, why cause more havoc? Why not ride it out peacefully? Why not let things be?*

Maybe because to him, Marcus is his sense of peace. Maybe I make everything worse by worrying in circles about it. Maybe I need to let things be.

Benji and I both jump when the doorbell rings. While he races to the door, I race to my room and swallow a pill before returning to the unavoidable drama that's about to unfold. I pour myself a glass of water and drink half of it in one long gulp.

I'm not prepared for what happens next. When I reach the living room, Mr. Blu, my homeroom and math teacher, greets me with a fabulous white smile. Next to Benji, he's slightly shorter with light brown hair and striking eyes.

"Mr. Blu?" I say.

"Alexandra, nice to see you again," he says and sticks out his hand. "Call me Marcus." When I reach out to shake his hand, the glass in my other hand slips and drops to the floor. It shatters into a thousand pieces like a diamond exploding.

"Crap," I mutter.

"Let me help." Marcus crouches and picks up larger chunks. Benji sighs deeply for my benefit. Mom and Penelope rush into the room and see the broken shards.

"Oh, no." Mom kneels down next to the glass like someone has collapsed on the floor. "It's one of Nana's."

I roll my eyes. Penelope catches me and shakes her finger in my face.

"I'll get a broom," I offer, a chance to help and a chance to escape. In the kitchen I retrieve the dustpan and broom stored in the small space on one side of the refrigerator. By the time I return to the living room, Dad has cornered Marcus.

"So, what do you do?" he asks, arms crossed over his chest.

"I'm a math teacher at the high school," Marcus answers. "Was a math teacher, anyway, before the holograms basically shut the schools down."

Dad nods in respect. "You'll be back to work in no time."

"Alexandra was my student this year. Always quiet and very conscientious."

"That's my girl," Dad says.

My face burns as if there's a spotlight blazing on me. I sweep up the remaining glass into the dustpan and escape to the kitchen to toss it into the trash. The back door looks like a great escape route. I take several long breaths and hold them, slowing my heartbeat. *Ativan, don't fail me now.* I can't believe Mr. Blu is Benji's boyfriend. *Did he know I was Benji's sister when I was at school?*

I hide in my room, waiting for the food to be ready. There's no way I'm listening to their small talk. That's an anxiety explosion waiting to happen. Thirty minutes later, I hear Mom's voice call for me.

Everyone has gathered in the dining room and chosen seats. The only open seat is between Dad and Penelope. Fun.

Penelope offers to say grace. I didn't realize she knew how to pray.

We pass the food around the table as cordially as any functional family, but my hands begin to shake with the weight of the mashed potato bowl. I'm afraid I might drop something else.

Benji drops the bomb instead. He stands up, holding a glass of wine. "I have an announcement."

Dad automatically plasters a grin across his face for his son. He probably thinks Benji has won some type of military honor. I drink more and more water to hide my face behind my cup.

"Despite all the changes happening in the world, there is one thing that I know to be true. I am in love. With Marcus."

Everyone stops breathing at the table. Chewing sounds. Mastication. Horrible word for the horrible wet squishing sound that fills the room and bounces off the nice china. Under the table I try tapping my knees with my fingertips in a back-and-forth method like Arianna, my new counselor, taught me.

"We are getting married." He gulps from his wine like it's a liquid life force and sits.

The clink and scrape of a fork on a plate, the swallowing of liquid from a glass. Everyone waits. I worry about the fate of the dishes once Dad explodes.

I swear a whole minute ticks by before anything happens. Maybe that makes it worse. Then Dad stands, turns, and in one quick motion punches his fist through the wall behind him.

"Goddamn it!" he yells, cradling his fist as he retreats from the room. We can hear his footsteps down the hall and my parents' bedroom door slam close. I stare at his empty chair, his plate of food sitting there getting cold when I know how much he doesn't want to waste food right now. I tap my knees in rhythm, trying to calm the electric feelings coursing through my body that are commanding me to run out the back door and hide.

Benji and Marcus cast furtive glances at one another, reading each other's feelings and thoughts like an old couple, filling in the silence with the unspoken language of time spent together. I don't know which of them will cry first, but I can feel the spillage coming like the crisp smell of snow on a cold day. Maybe the one who's about to cry is me.

What is he doing in the bedroom? Is his gun in there? What if he tries to shoot himself? What if he comes out here and shoots Mr. Blu, his brains splattering across our Thanksgiving dinner?

I remember Arianna's advice, and start repeating in my head,

Don't get tricked by a thought. Don't get tricked by a thought. But my thoughts seem plausible. He could do it. No, no, his gun is always locked up in the attic, and Mom has the key.

Penelope breaks the silence. "Is one of you pregnant or something?"

Marcus burst out laughing. His laughter is bubbly and infectious, and soon everyone is laughing. Everyone except Mom.

Penelope continues, "I mean, in my day, that was the only reason to rush a marriage. That or"—she clears her throat—"someone leaving for the military. But I guess the world ending is reason enough."

Mom points accusingly at Penelope. "Now is not the time." She removes her fancy napkin from her lap and tosses it on the table. "Are you two okay?" She asks Benji and Marcus.

They nod unconvincingly.

"Then excuse me for a minute," she mutters and follows the wake Dad left to the bedroom.

"I thought it was funny," Penelope offers and sips a glass of wine.

"It was," Marcus adds.

But I know that military comment was a dig. Mom married Dad when she turned eighteen before he left for duty and against Penelope's wishes. Mom leaving the table has thrown me for a loop. I assumed Dad would lose it, but not Mom. I wish I could hear what was going on in the other room, but I can't hear Dad's voice for a change. *How am I supposed to know if everything will be okay if I can't see what's happening? What if he shoots her?* My medication is having trouble doing its magic.

"I thought if anyone around here would be getting married," Penelope says, "it would be this beautiful girl sitting next to me."

"Me?" The look on my face must be priceless because the three of them laugh again.

"You're eighteen now, and I've seen you with that boyfriend of yours. With all that's going on in the world… Like mother, like daughter."

"Um, no," I say, cutting her off. "I don't even know if I believe in marriage."

"What the hell does that mean?" Benji asks. Marcus turns and stares at him. I don't think he's ever seen the side of my brother that likes to fight me on everything.

I take a sip of water to stall. "I think it puts too much pressure on people. The forever concept. Freaks me out."

"Smart girl," Penelope says. "Smarter than her mother."

Smarter than my mother. Her comment should make me feel proud, but instead I feel smaller. Benji glares at me from across the table, my brother and my adversary.

Penelope drags her knife back and forth over the meat and makes a face. "Turkey's overcooked." She shoves a piece into her mouth. "Dry. So when's the wedding?"

"December 12th," Marcus says. "City hall, nothing fancy. We wanted to do it as soon as possible, but there's a waiting list."

Benji pipes in. "Apparently everyone's lining up to take the plunge since forever might end sooner than we thought." He shoots me attitude.

What can I say—forever scares me. Love scares me. I mean, forever? People change. And then what?

When we hear the bedroom door open, the four of us flinch and sit up straight. Footsteps shuffle down the hall toward us. Mom returns, followed by Dad. I sit farther back in my chair as if the wooden back can provide the support I need. Instead of a gun in his hand, it's wrapped with an ice pack and a hand towel.

Benji stands up. *What're you doing?* my brain screams. *Sit down.*

Dad and Benji face each other, father and son, military men. Dad's hands are balled into fists at his sides, and so are Benji's. It's like a western movie where someone must pull the trigger first or die. I don't know who will win. I grip my fork like a weapon in case the action somehow turns on me.

Mom sits in her seat and places the napkin back in her lap. "Ben," she addresses Dad. "I think you have something to say to your son."

Dad clears his throat. "Family sticks together. We're a family." He puts out his right hand to shake Benji's. I still expect him to deck Benji with his left, ice pack and all. Benji's body starts to tremble uncontrollably, so Dad abandons the handshake and delivers a quick, one-armed hug with several strong pats to Benji's shoulders. I wait for Dad's sneak attack.

"Now let's eat," Dad announces.

Sometimes people hide their true feelings while guests are present. Sometimes people give up their predilections since the world's ending as they know it anyway. And sometimes, people shock you. In Dad's case, I don't know where to put his reaction in my list of possibilities. Like the vertexes and holograms, it's something I could've never predicted in my wildest dreams.

As everyone eats, I stare at the hole in the wall, the hole that everyone else has managed to forget. Everyone except me. I look over at Mom. She's smiling and talking to Marcus as if nothing happened. *How does she manage to ignore things so easily? How did she manage to get Dad to come back out here and be civilized?*

That's when I figure out something—I know what Mom is. If Benji's fire, I'm oil, Dad's gasoline, and Penelope's gunpowder, then Mom is sand. Boring, adaptable, gentle, loyal, warm sand. Able to shift landscapes, put out fires, and battle the ocean.

Benji and Marcus's wedding announcement subdues Dad for the next week. He goes to his job at the supermarket, but when he returns he doesn't say much anymore. Maybe he's following that saying, "If you can't say something nice, don't say anything at all." I'm trying to be optimistic. It's not easy. I notice that when he comes home from work, he collapses into his chair and doesn't move for hours. He used to take a shower, grab a beer, put on the television. Now he just stares into space. Like Zombie Night in the daytime. I keep trying to snap him out of it, talking to him about sports, the vertexes, his stockpile of food. Nothing works. He craps out in the middle of conversation. And Benji doesn't live here anymore to talk Zombie strategies, and Mom doesn't seem to notice that Dad's disappearing down the rabbit hole again.

The first inkling of the city's breakdown comes as a knock on our door in early December. I answer the door assuming it's Dominick. We've been spending more and more time together since his mother's home to watch Austin. Instead, standing on the threshold is a young couple with a toddler. The mother holds the child on her hip, a little girl gnawing at her thumb like it's a lollipop. The father, maybe in his late thirties, stands behind them. They look harmless enough except for a wide-eyed, empty stare. It takes me a second to realize their deprivation.

"Please," the woman begs. "Do you have any food?"

Her request catches me off guard. Of course, we have extra food, thanks to Dad's hoarding.

The poor little kid is about to eat her own hand. "Hold on," I say. "Wait here."

I shut and lock the door—something inside me senses the beginning of a danger that needs locking out, but I'm not sure exactly what it is yet. I walk down the basement steps and remove the sheet from one section of stored food. I take a deep breath and focus on my mission. I think about that little girl and search under sheets until I find a box of Cheerios, a can of beef vegetable soup, some peanut butter, bread, and a large container of apple juice.

Satisfied, I cover up the piles with the sheets so Dad won't notice the difference. By the time I return upstairs, they have already left the porch and are standing on the sidewalk looking defeated. I can tell by their faces they assumed I wasn't coming back. I jog down the stairs and hand over the items. They react like it's Christmas. The mother embraces me and starts to cry. The kid rips a hole in the top of the cereal box like a burrowing rabbit. The father avoids eye contact. The tops of his ears turn bright red.

"Thank you," the mother mutters. "Thank you."

"No problem."

They scurry away like overgrown squirrels hiding a secret treasure. I should feel happier inside about helping them, but I have a sinking feeling in my stomach that I'm putting a Band-Aid on a carcass.

CHAPTER 15

DAY 131: DECEMBER–1, 284 HOURS TO DECIDE

QUESTION: Do women receive equal rights?
ANSWER: Yes.

On December 9th, the United Nations releases a statement that part 1 of the CORE plan, the series of nuclear missiles, did not affect the trajectory of the comet according to NASA data. *Hera II* has been launched, and they'll know by Christmas if it achieved its mission. If it fails, they'll activate part 3, which is still confidential and super annoying, and by January 15th they should get word whether or not CORE was successful in diverting the comet. I can't believe it will take that long for them to get it together, but they said they want to ensure its success by taking all necessary precautions. They are especially concerned with the possibility that the "gas pressure blowing off the comet" will damage *Hera II* or push it off course. They are trying to compensate. *Compensate: going around a problem and trying to deal.* I know what's really going on—they've never had to do something like this before. It's "unprecedented", which means it's never happened or been done before. I'm worried it means they have no clue what they're doing.

———

Benji and Marcus's wedding has become Mom's only focus. Doesn't matter if there are holograms and vertexes and a comet crisis. Her only son is getting married in three days. She sends me and Rita on a mission to find flowers in the dead of winter.

"Who cares about flowers during an apocalypse?" I argue. "No flower shops are still open."

She replies, "Flowers are celebrations of life. Necessary. Not luxuries."

She would never win in any courtroom, but I hate when she wins arguments with me simply because I don't understand her cryptic responses and I'm usually left speechless. Maybe that's her plan. Confuse and deflect.

Even though I hate driving, I borrow her car. Rita and I have been texting polite nothings since our last face-to-face blow up. I need to find the right time and apologize in person. When I pick her up, she bounds forward and unbuttons her coat, showing off another T-shirt underneath. There's a cartoon of a pimped-out hologram in a purple fur coat and feathered hat charging admission at a vertex site, with the caption COME INTO MY VERTEX.

"Rita, that one's terrible."

"What're you talking about? This one's my favorite. Look at the colors in the graphics. It even has an old school hologram effect."

She moves from side to side, and the pimp's coat changes from purple to royal blue and back again. It also bows and tips its hat. I shake my head and laugh.

We drive to several florist shops, but each door has a closed sign and the windows are dark.

I guess Mom's wrong. Flowers are one of the first to go.

We park in downtown New Bedford and walk the old cobblestone area to see if any local businesses are still open. Rita leaves her coat open even though it's freezing out so she can show off her slogan while she's out of the house. Again, the small shops have CLOSED on their front doors. We change course and head up Union Street, where we find one coffee shop with lights on. We are the only customers.

"Hello?" I ask.

The owner's head appears from the kitchen area. "The bathroom's around the corner."

"Could we order?" Rita asks from the counter.

"Do you have cash?" he asks.

His rude question catches me off guard. "Yeah. Would we order food if we didn't have money?"

"Okay, then. Let me see the money first."

"Why?" I ask, looking around at the empty business and wondering if he's planning to jump us for cash. "What's the problem?"

"People keep coming in here to use the bathroom. Then they beg for food. Don't have no money. This is a business. Well, was a business." His eyes stare at the vacant wooden tables.

Rita pulls out a five-dollar bill. "I have money."

"Sit yourself down then, ladies, and give me a sec. What would you like? I'm all out of pastries and bread, but I still have coffee."

"I'll take a coffee," Rita says.

"And you? Coffee?"

His lack of hospitality and supplies concerns me. I wonder if I should really eat or drink anything he's serving. *Probably curdled milk, ants crawling through the sugar, maggots waiting to hatch.*

"Tea for me." I'm hoping he can't taint boiled water and a tea bag.

"Sure, coming right up." The owner disappears behind the counter. Rita and I find a seat near the windows. Cars pass by every now and then, but not as often as they did before the comet warning.

"Did you ever think your life would turn out like this?" I ask Rita in all seriousness.

She smiles. "Did you ever think you'd ask me that question at eighteen years old? You make it sound like our lives are over."

"Rita, everything's screwed up. The world's starting to crumble. Schools are closed, businesses are folding. People are getting freaked out and desperate, including me."

She strums her fingers on the wooden table. "If it's so bad, maybe we should leave."

My heart skips several beats. "Are you serious?"

"Alex, it's December. By the end of January, either the comet comes or doesn't. Say we actually stop it—what kind of world's gonna be left?"

My heart stops. She has a point. I've only been thinking about survival, not about the aftermath and consequences of surviving. "So you're ready to leave?"

She sighs. "I wouldn't say 'ready.' I'm willing. I just don't know when to pull the trigger."

The owner brings over two steaming cups—one with coffee, one with tea—and a ceramic creamer. "Enjoy, ladies. You'll probably be my last customers before I close for good."

I search the sugar for signs of movement before stirring some into my cup. Not touching the creamer. "Why?"

"Can't get food supplies on time. Can't get regular paying customers. Lose-lose situation. Time to call it quits."

"Here," Rita hands him the five, and I add two dollars. "Keep the change."

"Thanks," he says, pocketing the money in the apron wrapped around his waist. "No rush. Stay as long as you want." He returns to the kitchen, and I see him pick up a book and read.

"That was nice of you," I say. I stare at the brown liquid in my mug, wary to take the first sip.

"My parents' restaurant has been hurting, too. The only reason it's still open is because members of the church have helped to keep the business afloat."

I nod. "How's that going? The church stuff."

"Getting weirder every day. I don't wanna talk about it." She sips from her black coffee. "How's your dad been with the wedding coming?"

"Okay, I guess. Quiet." I take a sip, following her lead, and let it linger. The warmth settles my insides, giving me courage. "I'm sorry about getting mad at you about the Benji thing."

"I know," she says. "It's fine."

"No, it's not. I wasn't being fair to you or Benji."

"No, you weren't. But you were feeling left out and ambushed. It's a major change to wrap your brain around." She takes a long swig of coffee and sighs deeply. "I mourned the loss of my future husband for over a week."

"I shouldn't have taken it out on you."

"That's what friends are for," she says, grinning. "For better or worse." She gazes out the window. "What's with all the cars?"

A slew of vehicles have parked along the road up the street. More and more arrive and search for a space.

"Something's going on."

"Wanna check it out?" Rita asks.

"Sure," I say, glad to abandon my half-drunken tea. I wait as she downs the remainder of her coffee.

We leave the café and follow the gathering crowd to the public library two blocks away. The wintry air nips at my nose and makes it run. I don't have tissues with me, so I have to resort to wiping the drips on my sleeve.

Inside the warm library, people line the walls and sit on the floor. A man with a cropped white beard rigs a microphone near the circulation desk.

"It looks like a rally or something," I say.

Rita leads me to a corner near the side exit. From here I can watch from a safe distance with a clear escape route if necessary. I lean back and let the wall hold my weight.

The man with the white beard steps up to the microphone. The audience goes silent.

"Thank you all for being here. As a community we need to address the growing violence in our city and discuss ways to combat the problem. In the past week alone there have been twelve home invasions, and last night the mall was looted clean."

Rita and I glance at one another, horrified. I didn't see that on the news. Then again, I've been avoiding it lately to help with my anxiety.

Rita pokes me and whispers, "We could've grabbed so many clothes."

I stifle a giggle. A woman nearby clears her throat and gives us the evil eye. Rita's face changes from happy and defiant to mortified.

At first I assume it's because of the woman's attitude toward us, but when I follow her gaze, she's not looking at that woman; she's looking at the side exit near us.

Both of her parents are staring at her. Through her. Fuming. If they were cartoon characters, they'd have steam coming out of their ears and speech bubbles with symbols instead of words.

Her mother points at her and then points out the door. Rita flees the room, and I follow. As soon as she reaches outside, her mother grabs her arm and pulls her aside.

"Margarita Ann Bernardino!" her mother declares. "¡Mira!" Her mother points at her chest. "¿Qué es esto? ¿Qué llevas puesto?"

Rita's face burns scarlet. She fumbles to button up her coat, but it's too late. She crosses her arms in front of her shirt to block the slogan.

Her father doesn't speak, but if looks could talk, he'd be swearing like my father on a bad night. Or any night.

"Mami," Rita whimpers, her face pleading as it runs with tears and mascara. "¡Lo siento!"

Her mother continues to berate her. Some people stare. Some feign obliviousness. I'm not sure what's worse: staring at someone's demise or ignoring it. I'm watching the humiliation of my best friend, and even though there's nothing I can do, I don't want to be a witness to her destruction.

"Please," I try to intervene, "Mrs. Bernardino, it's not a big deal."

"Not a big deal?" Her eyes bulge. "We don't run our house like yours, Alexandra. We have God in our household, not guns and sex and violencia. Margarita, get in the car. No quiero mirarte."

Rita jumps into the back seat of their car. As they drive away, I see Rita bawling with her hood up. She doesn't look at me. I'm left on the sidewalk with my hands shaking and the familiar dread building in my stomach and chest. I know my body must be reacting to Rita's mother, but an irrational worm has burrowed itself into my mind and won't stop repeating: *The tea. The tea in the shop was poisoned.*

I pop a pill and sit on the curb, rocking and repeating to myself, *Don't get tricked by a thought. Don't get tricked by a thought.* It takes all the energy in my body not to flee to the hospital and demand a complete blood and urine analysis.

———

Rita's cell phone is non-responsive to my string of texts and phone calls. Dominick says she's probably grounded. Maybe that's true. I replay the last conversation we had at the restaurant. For better or worse. Was she being sarcastic? Did I ever say sorry? My fingernails become a minefield of missing polish. I'm a terrible friend. What else is new?

———

The next day, all I can think about is Rita and how she must still hate me, so when the doorbell rings and Dad answers it, I think nothing of it until I hear him yelling. I run to the living room and peek out the window. A crowd of people has gathered in front of our house.

"Go away," he shouts through the half-opened door, the chain still in place. "We don't have any food to spare. I have my own family to feed."

Someone responds, "But earlier this week a girl here gave us food. She had long brown curly hair? Please, sir, we're starving."

"If you're that desperate, go through a goddamn vertex and leave us alone." The door slams. "Alexandra!"

His voice has never sounded that sharp before, and that's saying something. For a split second, I think of fleeing into the backyard like a two-year-old. But by the time I reach the kitchen, he's behind me. I think of grabbing something to defend myself, but the only thing I see is a dishrag.

"Alexandra, did you give our food to people?"

It's too late to lie. "Just one family." I remember the hope and sadness in that little girl's eyes. I had to do it. She would've had no fingers left.

"Alexandra, what were you thinking? I've stockpiled for a reason. To help our family. No one else's."

I attempt to nod, but my neck feels stiff. The oxygen seems to have left the room. I need to escape. I need air. My heart convulses over and over like it's being squished in a vise. I grab onto the counter.

"Are you even listening to me?" he yells louder. "Sometimes I think you've got a good head on your shoulders. Other times you make the worst decisions."

The room begins to spin, and I can't hold on anymore. I feel like I'm having a heart attack.

Dad catches hold of me and guides me over to the table to sit. "It's okay," he says. "Breathe."

I listen. I try to focus on the chair, the wood grain in the table, anything other than what's going on in my body.

"Alex, breathe. Where's your medicine?" he asks.

"In my purse. On my desk." My body is on fire. If Dad weren't here, I would take off my clothes. *I'm not dying. Ten to twenty minutes. Ten to twenty minutes.*

He runs out of the room. I start tapping on each leg in a back-and-forth pattern. It's not working. Dad returns moments later, and I swallow a small pill of hope. The wave of swelling panic starts to plateau after several minutes. Dad sits with me and rubs my back. I feel like a child again when he does it, but I still like it.

"Are you feeling better?" he asks.

"Yeah, it's fading."

"Good." He pours me a glass of water, and I take small sips.

"We still need to talk," he says and sits next to me. "Anxiety or not, you cannot give away our food."

I drink a big gulp and manage to say, "They were starving. They had a little kid."

He rakes his fingers across his face. "I get that. I do. How do I explain?" He stares off into space. "Do you remember that story of the grasshopper and the ant we used to read to you when you were little?"

"Yeah, the ant does all the work in the summer while the grass-hopper plays music and goofs off. Then winter comes and the grasshopper is screwed."

"Well, that's what's happening around us," Dad explains. "I planned for the food crisis. Other families didn't."

"It's not the same," I say. "They didn't know winter was coming for sure."

"Fine. Okay, remember at the end of *Titanic* when the people on the lifeboats don't help those in the water?"

"Yes, I hated that part." *An image of drowned carcasses invades my mind.* I put my water down.

"Yes, but that's survival. The people in the water would have flipped over the boats if they tried to help, and then more people would die. Is that what you want?"

"No. But I don't want to sit in the boat feeling guilty, either."

"Alex, we can either feed everyone who comes to our door for a week or survive as a family for a year. Once the UN defeats the comet—"

I roll my eyes at his government optimism.

"Once we defeat the comet," he repeats, "I'm not sure how long it will take to reestablish order. Food's crucial."

My mind understands what he is saying, but my heart still debates if it can watch people starve while I eat. *Can I live at the expense of others?*

CHAPTER 16

QUESTION: Do you have different races? Prejudices?
ANSWER: We are the human race.

On December 12th, my family and I gather at city hall for Benji and Marcus's wedding. Other brides and grooms fill the corridor waiting for their turn to take the plunge and bind themselves together. They must be triple-booking appointments. There's an old man around seventy wearing a black tux with a girl no older than twenty-five wearing a white slip dress. I'd say she must be marrying him for the money, but since money is slowly becoming irrelevant with fewer things available to buy, I really don't understand. Two older ladies in pastel pantsuits hold hands on a far bench, happiness radiating from their faces. Someday I hope to feel that happy.

Benji stands with his chest puffed out, attempting to look composed in his white dress shirt and red tie. Underneath his militant stance, I know he's nervous. When most people are nervous, they pace or tremble. When Benji's nervous, he's as still as a statue. Marcus, wearing a blue dress shirt and red tie like Benji's, sits on a bench. There's no question that Marcus is nervous since his legs are shaking, and I respect that he lets it show. They look cute together, and the thought surprises me since I never would have considered matching Benji up with a guy, never mind my teacher. Go figure.

Benji said I could invite Dominick and Rita, but only Dominick shows. Since Mr. Blu was his all-time favorite teacher, he's thrilled that he gets to witness his wedding to my brother. Rita is still missing in action. If I don't hear from her soon, I'll have to plan a rescue and apologize mission.

Mom and Dad meet Marcus's parents and his older brother, Curt. Dad shakes their hands and acts polite as Mom presses her hand on the middle of his back. I'm not sure if it's for moral support or as a push forward. Whatever, I guess. He's behaving.

Both Benji and Marcus have invited their closest friends. Miranda, Benji's date for prom and one of his best friends since elementary school, hugs me, and I introduce her to Dominick. Miranda is the opposite of Rita but just as likable. She's soft-spoken and tends to dress sleek in all black and gray. She's so laid back that I used to think she was on drugs all the time, but Benji swore that wasn't true. I don't buy it, but I still like her anyway. Benji also invited Tommy, his creepy friend who tried to kiss me once when he slept over. He winks at me from a distance. I pretend not to notice and grab Dominick's arm.

No one introduces me to Marcus's two friends, so I never catch their names. Both male, they are taller than Marcus and more athletic looking, but Marcus is definitely more attractive. He has the kindest face and eyes that light up over the smallest detail. I can see why Dominick admired him as a teacher. Since school shut down so quickly, I never really got the chance to like him.

The ceremony is as promised—low-key, short, but special enough. Dominick squeezes my thigh and leaves his hand there. I didn't think I believed in marriage, but with the right person, maybe forever could be nice. I wonder if marriage could be in our future, if there is a future. It's sad that it took world annihilation to let myself fall for him. Even sadder that it took world annihilation for Benji to get to be himself.

Throughout the short ceremony, I keep my eyes on Dad longer than on Benji and Marcus. Dad doesn't seem to know where to put his arms—across his chest, down by his sides, hands clasped on his lap. *He reaches into his jacket, pulls out his gun, opens fire.* Oh, wait, that was only his phone.

Mom cries, but what mother doesn't cry at the wedding of her child? If the wedding had taken place a year ago, she would've made them get married in our backyard and then thrown a reception there afterward. But with the worsening food situation, instead everyone is going back to the house for a homemade white cake, Mom's gift to the couple. If the world doesn't end next month, maybe they'll get real presents.

By the time we return home, I'm so hungry I could probably eat the entire wedding cake myself. Dad heads up the front steps first to unlock the door. As he's about to put the key in the lock, his back straightens. He backs away slowly, waving at everyone to shut up and back up in silence. For a split second I think it's some sort of surprise party and we're supposed to scream on his cue.

"What is it?" Mom asks, concerned.

"The door's open." Dad's face changes. I can see the paranoid thoughts cloud his eyes.

"I probably left it open," I lie. I can't let him unravel in front of Dominick and the wedding guests.

"No, Alex, there's damage to the frame." Dad's eyes still seem distant, searching for answers inside his turning brain.

"I'll call the police." Mom searches through her purse for her cell phone and frantically dials. Benji and Marcus arrive along with the other guests.

"Why's everyone out here?" Benji asks.

"Break-in," Dad murmurs.

"Seriously?" Benji asks.

After Dad exchanges a few whispered words to Benji, Benji walks back to the car and returns with a handgun. Dominick pulls me back at the sight of the firearm. The sight of the gun doesn't trigger my anxiety, but its location does. *It's supposed to be locked safely in the attic. Mom's supposed to have the key.* I turn to complain to her, but she's on the line with 911.

Dad and Benji nod to each other and start to creep toward the house.

"I'll go," Marcus offers while hugging himself.

"No, wait here," Benji says over his shoulder. "You don't have training."

Marcus doesn't offer twice. Benji and Dad step onto the porch, automatically falling in line with each other. Once a soldier, always a soldier. As much as Dad might think they are different now, they are still the same.

Dominick wraps his arm around my waist. I rub the back of his hand but avoid eye contact.

"I hope everything's okay," Penelope says, applying more lipstick to her already pink, wrinkled lips. Mom sighs deeply in the phone.

When Dad and Benji don't return after ten minutes, Mom starts pacing up and down the sidewalk.

"Maybe we should go inside," Marcus says to his wedding buddies.

"I'll come," Dominick offers. I pull his arm and try to convey my not-on-your-life stance telepathically. Before Dominick and I have a chance to argue, Benji appears in the doorway with a hardened expression in his cheeks.

"It's clear," Benji announces flatly. "No sign of anyone. But all the food's gone."

I release Dominick's arm and race inside. *No, please no.* On the dining room table where Mom left the wedding cake lies an empty platter of crumbs and smears of excess white frosting.

Dominick catches up with me and touches my shoulder. "The whole cake's gone?"

Before I can respond, my disappointment in the missing cake dissolves as my mind goes into high alert about my bedroom and the basement.

"My stuff—" I fly down the hallway, and Dominick follows me into my room.

My television still sits on my bureau, the purple saucer chair poised companionless. Everything seems to be the way I left it. I wonder about the pile of clothes in the corner. I kick it to make sure no one is hiding underneath.

"Is anything missing?" Dominick asks, searching the space.

"I don't think so." I take a few deep breaths knowing my stuff hasn't been stolen. I prepare myself for the scene in the basement. "Wait here."

"Why?" He shifts his glasses back onto his nose.

"Please, just wait here." I guarantee that Dad is in the basement, and I don't want to subject Dominick to his unpredictable reactions.

"Fine," Dominick says with a slight attitude. "But I thought your dad didn't want me in your bedroom."

I shoot daggers at him. This is not the time. He slumps onto my purple saucer chair, faces his palms in the air, and adds, "Okay, okay. I'll wait here."

The basement door is wide open. I scramble down the stairs and find Dad with his eyes glazed over. The basement's condition is the opposite of my bedroom. Strewn across the cement floor, the sheets lie flat like deflated ghosts.

Everything is gone. The canned soups, vegetables, juices, cereals, pasta, water, matches, batteries, gasoline. Picked clean. Like a giant eraser rubbed away our supplies, leaving behind the sheets as useless eraser shavings that we must brush aside and discard.

This is all my fault. Those people. I led them here. They knew we had food. Dad tried to warn me.

I want to reach out to him, but I can't move. I can't even feel my legs. I can't console him. I can't rescue him. I inadvertently touch my neck.

Mom runs down the stairs and gasps. She grabs the sheets and tosses them into a pile, trying to remove the evidence of the crime as swiftly as possible. By the time she's done, they look like an innocent pile of laundry, not the reminder of Dad's failed attempt to keep us safe.

She reaches out to him, and I flinch. When Dad's not okay, I'm not okay. I'm the freaked out barnacle along for the ride.

I can't watch. I must watch.

He won't look at her. She puts her hand on his chest, over his heart. Kisses his cheek. *I feel her lips. I hope he doesn't strangle her, too.*

"It'll be okay," she says softly, stroking his face with a feather of words.

It doesn't work this time. He charges over to the pile of sheets, screaming and grunting like a beast trapped in the wrong cage, and throws them over and over at the cement walls with all his might. She gives him space.

Together we watch him explode.

———

It takes the police forty-five minutes to arrive. When we hear the sirens, Dad refuses to leave the basement and talk to them. Mom and I return to the front porch to see the cops with weapons drawn, screaming at Benji.

"I'm military," Benji yells back with his hands raised. "This is my family's home."

"Keep your hands up! All of you!"

The entire wedding party has their hands raised in the air, even Penelope and Dominick. Apparently, Dominick was uncomfortable waiting in my room.

"He's telling the truth," Marcus pipes in, his hands up.

Mom and I stand aside in the front doorway. One officer moves forward slowly, gun drawn. His partner covers him from the car. I'm not sure what's going on. I want to yell, "He's my brother," but I'm afraid I might startle the cop into shooting him.

The officer moves closer and closer until he reaches Benji, then he reaches forward and removes the revolver sticking out from the front of Benji's dress pants.

Idiot.

They handcuff him as Marcus's face turns red. "No, no, you have it all wrong. He's innocent."

Congratulations, Mr. Blu. Welcome to the family of unpredictable chaos.

———

Penelope sits in the living room staring at a black television screen while the police officers search the house and take notes. Mom answers most of their questions. Dad's safe full of cash is still stored in the back of their closet, untouched. She downplays how much stuff was hidden in the basement. At first I wonder if it's because she doesn't know about the gasoline and other stuff Dad was storing, but I doubt it. She's not out of touch with the family; she's more in control than I ever wanted to admit.

Before the cops leave, they confess that most likely nothing will be recovered. I'm glad Dad is still stewing in the basement and couldn't hear them say that.

———

I wake up to banging. Disoriented, my body wanders the house in search of the sound. It's coming from the living room. I peek around the corner and see Dad.

He places a piece of wood across the window and nails it in place. It's four o'clock in the morning. I almost think it's another Zombie Night until he looks over his shoulder clear-eyed and says, "Want to help? I'm boarding up all the windows."

I rub my eyes. "Sure." It's my fault he's freaked out about our safety. I might as well help.

Wordlessly, I hold wood in place as he hammers each corner of the board into the window frame. I notice he taps the nail in place with the first hit, then hits it once more and he's done. Two hits. Once we finish the living room, we move past the dining room area, where the hole in the wall still haunts me, and on to the bathroom. The bedrooms will have to wait until Mom and Penelope wake up. He must've already boarded up the windows in the kitchen since it's pitch black. I wonder what Mom's going to think about the covered windows. I wonder if he's walling people out or walling us inside.

In the bathroom he hands me the hammer. I try to mimic his method: one hit to steady the nail, one hit to flatten it all the way. My first tap keeps it standing. Then I whack it as hard as I can, and it bends sideways.

"Take it out. Try again," he says.

I pry out the nail with the back of the hammer and attempt it again. *Fail.* I expect him to get angry at me, but he grins.

"Tap it in lightly. You don't have to do it like me."

I know that, but I want to try. I attempt the two-hit method again, and it works.

"You're hired." Dad pats me on the shoulder, and I can't help but feel relieved.

By the time we finish, it's impossible to tell whether it's day or night. The clock on the microwave reads 6:31. Dad and I collapse on the sofa from our work.

"Look at the two of you." Penelope glares at us from the living room doorway. "I've been up in my room waiting for you to stop all the racket. Do you really think that this," she points to the boarded-up windows, "is going to help?"

Dad gives her a death stare. Even though I'm tired, I have to intervene. "I feel safer already," I say.

"You would," Penelope mutters.

What does that mean?

"So what on earth will we eat for breakfast? Tap water?" Penelope complains.

Dad grins. I think he's going to kill her and make us eat her rationed body parts. *Grandma casserole, anyone?*

"Ben, oh my goodness!" Mom's squeal from the kitchen has us all on our feet. She's standing in front of the kitchen counter. Spread across the faux granite top is a small assortment of food items.

Penelope clams up. Dad walks like a peacock strutting his feathers. "I had a few things put aside at the supermarket. Just in case."

My mother bear hugs him and doesn't let go.

"There's more, too," he adds, "I couldn't get it all in one trip. It's not nearly as much as before, though." A shadow of disappointment returns to his face. "It's gonna be rough."

Mom cries tears of relief. "It's wonderful. Thank God."

Penelope saunters over to the items and picks up a wrapped Pop-Tart by the edge of the foil packaging as if it's contagious. She never gives him any credit.

———

Early that afternoon, Mom returns from the mailbox with an envelope addressed to me. Lately, the mail only arrives once or twice a week due to lack of workers and physical mail. I never get mail. There's no return address on the envelope, but I recognize Rita's handwriting. I rip it open. We haven't spoken since the day at the library when her parents reamed her out in front of everyone.

Inside is a letter from her. I read it silently even though Mom stands nearby waiting to know who sent it.

Alex,

By the time you get this letter, I'll already be gone. I can't live like this anymore. Me and a group from my church have decided to break free and escape while we still can. Our church is too rigid in their view of the Second Coming and their hatred of the vertexes. I can't sit back and let them make this decision for me. It's my life. I love my parents and I know this might hurt them, but staying will hurt me. Religion should fit a person like a second skin. When it doesn't fit, it's stifling (and you know me and outfits) .

I really hope there's something on the other side and we're not jumping off a hidden cliff. In any case, it's my cliff to jump. I'm sneaking Dobby in my backpack and bringing him into the vertex with me. Even though the holograms said no animals, I can't bear to leave him behind. I'm sorry I didn't say goodbye in person, but we needed to leave before anyone got suspicious. I couldn't text or call you 'cause my parents took away my phone. Our church leaders are telling members to keep subversive people, as they like to call us, constantly monitored, saying the devil is attempting to control us. I don't even believe in demons (at least not supernatural ones).

You've been my best friend since the day you shared your lunch with me after I forgot mine in first grade and was too embarrassed to tell Ms. Hall. You stood up for me when Billy kept making fun of the long skirts my parents used to make me wear every day (until I discovered a sense of style and the power of the bathroom ☺). Remember those ugly things? I hope things work out and we see each other again on the other side. I will miss you so much. Te quiero como a una hermana.

Para siempre,
Rita

P. S. Tell Benji I said congratulations. Tell Dominick I said good-
bye and to give you a hug for me.

I read the letter several times before it sinks in that she's gone.
It's not until Mom grabs me by the shoulders and asks me what's
the matter that my chest starts convulsing and I sob like someone
has died.

CHAPTER 17

DAY 135: DECEMBER–1,185 HOURS TO DECIDE

QUESTION: Do you have religions?

ANSWER: Yes, we have religious freedom. If you would like to believe in something, you may. We have many religions, new ones every day. We believe religion is a personal choice. However, no religion is allowed to promote inequality or judgment toward others. We do not consider intolerance to be a religious, moral, or spiritual philosophy.

My tears over Rita's departure turn to anger at her church, so I search online for as much information as I can about different religious views on the vertexes so I can be pissed off at all of them. Knowledge is power, after all.

According to the internet, the Pope says that sometimes "prophets come in many forms, as do false prophets," and it is up to our "hearts" to decide what is right for us. He mentions the story of Noah and the flood, how people in Noah's time were skeptical and lost their lives for it. He explains that "faith is a feeling and an act." He asked everyone to "pray for clarity." When asked if he will leave through a vertex, he said he will "leave that decision to God." The Catholics aren't sure what that means.

The Church of Jesus Christ of Latter-day Saints claims it's not the end, that "All prophecies must be fulfilled" before "that great and dreadful day." Like a comet isn't prophecy enough? They also believe that "no man shall know the date," and the holograms gave us the date. Mormons not already living in Utah are heading to Salt Lake City in great numbers, while some splinter groups head to Adam-ondi-Ahman, wherever the hell that is. Rumors have it that they're combining their stored food into one massive armed food bank at Welfare Square to protect it from raiders.

The Jehovah's Witnesses believe that the comet and vertexes "mark the beginning of Armageddon." They predict the United Nations will fail in their attempt to divert the comet because "God has sent it to cleanse the earth." Like Rita's church, they believe in waiting for the "inevitable destruction and redemption that await them for fulfilling the scriptural requirements for selection into God's kingdom." They don't seem worried, expecting the Rapture to save them before any comet hits.

Jews have begun a slow, mass exodus through vertexes. They've been here before, and they aren't taking any chances.

Muslims, like the Mormons, believe that the end "date will be hidden," not posted on a countdown clock at every vertex. The comet, however, represents an environmental disaster marking the "Last Hour." They cannot agree on whether or not the holograms represent the figure Dajjal or Mahdi.

Unitarian Universalists assert that it is "up to individuals to discover the truth for themselves." No judgment either way.

Bottom line as I see it—no one knows what the hell to think or do.

Dominick reads over Rita's letter in his car while I watch the ocean. I still expect her name to pop up on my phone screen and request some quality girl time. It can't be real. If it was that bad at home, she could've hid in my basement. God knows there's plenty of space.

But she didn't even ask. I should've said sorry.

He folds the note and hands it to me. "She's got guts to leave her parents without telling them."

"I couldn't do it." The ocean ebbs and flows, a vast space full of goodbyes and returns. *Where is she now?*

"She was always like that, though," Dominick says. "Remember April Fool's Day freshman year?"

"Yes, the sticky notes covering the faculty room! That was all her idea."

"And sophomore year when she accidentally started a fire in chemistry?"

"We had to evacuate and got to miss the next two periods. For the next week everyone called her Firestarter. I swear she liked it."

"I warned her not to crank up the Bunsen burner to save time. Didn't listen. She liked figuring out things on her own terms. She was cool like that."

Talking about Rita in the past tense bothers me. I want the memories to make things better, but the more I talk with Dominick about her, the worse I feel.

"She might be right to leave now," Dominick says.

Not him, too. "Are you serious? I thought you said we should wait it out. Give it a little time."

"Food supplies are getting lower."

"Yeah, we're lucky that Dad works at a grocery store. He gets first pick on any new shipments." I see his face, and it finally occurs to me how badly his family might be struggling. "Wait, you'd leave?"

"We might have to."

———

By the time Dominick drops me off at home, the stars glitter in the winter sky. I wonder if one of them holds Rita in some vast future, or if instead she's been swallowed by the cosmos.

On my front porch, my frozen fingers fumble with my keys. The first key I choose doesn't fit, so I automatically flip through the other two. No, that was the right one. It takes me a few seconds before I notice that the whole lock's been changed. After ringing the doorbell several times, I hear my mother's muffled voice yell from inside, "Go around back."

I skirt the house through the metal side gate and walk up the back patio. The last time I hung out here was with Dominick the day after we were decontaminated at the hospital. I remember him trying to explain how the vertexes worked. Bouncing the basketball. He was excited then. Now he seems as uncertain as I feel. How much has changed in only a few months.

Mom waits for me at the back door.

"Your father blocked the front door. He's trying to make the house more secure. One entrance and exit only."

I swallow hard.

"Alex, he's trying."

In the bitter darkness I kick the tarp that covers the patio furniture. With Rita gone, I can't take any more change.

When I don't respond, she adds, "He loves you. He's not the same man he was that night. Before he got help with his flashbacks."

"Yep." The light in the yard casts weird shadows across the dead grass.

"Alex, seriously, he's changed. You're the one who hasn't. With everything that's happened, don't you think it's time to let it go?"

"Why?" Unexpected anger boils up inside of me. She's taking his side over mine, accusing me of having the problem. "He's never even talked to me about it."

"That's because he's ashamed. He can't believe he hurt you that night. He would do anything to protect you. That's why he worked so hard to get himself together."

"I really don't want to talk about it with you." I push past her, flee down the hallway, slam my bedroom door. My heart dances in my chest, pain ripping through my ribcage.

I take a pill to escape from today. When it doesn't help, I take a second before I hit the pillow.

———

I dream of the other world through the vertexes. Well, my subconscious version of it.

Up in a purple sky two suns blink in and out like giant, winking eyeballs. I'm in the middle of a strange rainbow city. People from different parts of the world float past me with plastic smiles plastered on their faces. They wear the same ghastly uniforms as the holograms. I look down and see that I'm wearing my pajamas. I walk from person to person, waving my hands in front of them and trying to communicate. No one flinches.

Then I spot Rita in the crowd. Tears flood my cheeks as I run and run and run toward her and she moves farther and farther away with every step. My feet begin sinking into the white pavement.

It's like standing in liquid marshmallow. I scream her name to get her attention and apologize once and for all for being a jerk. She doesn't turn around.

From behind, someone grabs me around the neck and drags me into an alley.

"Still a tease?" Dan the Drunk Dude breathes into my face. I squirm and kick to get away from him, but the ground slips under my feet. When I glance down, I see a sheet of ice beneath me.

I scream for help with all the energy in my chest, my desperate attempt to escape failing as each second passes.

Then like a superhero, Dad appears with a machine gun and blows Dan to smithereens in a fantastic spray of violence and machismo.

"Family stays together," he says. We hug in the double sunlight.

As he leads me out of their world and back home, I look at my feet. The ice is gone. The white pavement is firm. Everything will be okay.

He heads toward a massive gate with a black, swirling mass inside it. A return home. "What about Rita?" I ask.

Dad doesn't respond, doesn't look at me. "Dad?" I ask, pulling him back.

He won't budge. I look at his feet, checking the white pavement for signs of struggle. That's when I notice Dad doesn't have a shadow.

He turns his face to look at me, and instead of eyes his sockets twist like blue, liquid metallic vertexes.

I jolt from my bed, my curly hair clinging to the sides of my face with sweat.

It wasn't real. It wasn't real. Don't get tricked by a dream. The clock reads 3:44. I take another pill, click on the television, and watch

Stranger Things while scribbling in my journal to escape the growing fear and gripping indecision drowning me.

By morning, I feel like a zombie has been snacking on my brains for breakfast. The only consolation is that I probably won't need any more pills today no matter what since I'm too tired to feel anything.

———

For breakfast I have a piece of toast smeared with peanut butter and a glass of water. My pajama pants sag at the waist, so I roll the top to keep them from slipping down. I used to love the view of the yard from the kitchen sink. Now all I can see are wooden planks blocking out all traces of daylight. The sun would've hurt my overtired eyes anyway.

Apparently after we went to bed, Dad barricaded us in the house. The inside of the back door is blocked with a makeshift contraption of wood wedged into the bottom, another piece of wood and metal crowbar jammed crisscrossed across the door, and a piece of rope tied to the knob, the other end attached to the refrigerator. Calling it overboard would be a massive understatement. And Mom thinks he's fine. I call bullshit.

Mom enters the kitchen and makes a cup of Lipton tea.

Dad follows and pours a bowl of cereal with reconstituted powdered milk. I watch each of them circle each other, Mom handing him an extra spoon as she gets the sugar out of the jar, Dad scooping some dry milk into her teacup. I never noticed how much happens between them without words. Comfort and acceptance in the little things.

Penelope comes in and announces she's leaving.

"Leaving?" Mom takes a sip of tea. "Back to Florida?"

Penelope stands firm, one suitcase in hand. I wonder where all the rest of them are. "No, through a vertex."

She's serious.

Dad laughs. "Good luck to them."

"Ben!" Mom throws a dishrag at Dad, then focuses back on Penelope. "You can't just leave."

"The hell I can't. Look at this place. It's a prison. Look at the food." She points at the counter. "What happens when all this is gone?"

"I have more at the store. In the back room. Not as much as before, but it's enough."

He's lying. I know him. He may have food at the store, but when he said "enough," he cracked his knuckles.

"It doesn't matter. I've had enough drama to last a lifetime. You all ought to come with me, but I know he won't go" —she talks about Dad like he's not in the room—"and if he won't go, you won't go."

"No one's going anywhere." Dad slams his fist into the table. "We have to stick together. Hunker down. Let the government handle it. We just have to wait."

"Wait? Wait and worry and then what?" Penelope points in his face. "Die together? I don't understand how you cannot put your family first over your love and trust in this damn country."

"Mother, back off." Mom steps between them. Dad storms out of the kitchen. Their bedroom door slams.

Penelope smiles a sad smile, kisses Mom on the cheek, leaving behind hot pink lip prints, and whispers, "I knew he'd be your downfall."

Mom's fists ball up, but she doesn't respond.

"I love you," Penelope says to her. "Take care."

She moves from Mom to me.

"Bye, sweetheart." She kisses me on the forehead. "You can come with me, you know. You're eighteen."

I shake my head and refuse. I don't know if it's the right decision, but I know it's not the wrong one. At the moment. As much as Dad irks me, and as much as I'd love to see Rita, I can't see myself stepping into the unknown with Penelope, and especially without Dominick. There's still another month before the comet arrives. The government could come through, like Dad said.

"Oh, Alexandra, I know you love your father, but leaving is your decision. If you want to stay, that's your prerogative. But don't stay because of him."

A car horn beeps. Penelope picks up her bag with one hand.

"Marcus offered to drive me. I didn't think a send-off at the vertex would be a good idea. Didn't think Ben would react well. I was right." She lifts up her suitcase higher. "Traveling light. No choice. You can do whatever you want with my other things."

As she hugs me goodbye, behind her my mother struggles to stay calm. Her eyeballs look ready to burst. She could use one of my pills.

Mom begins to cry, and Penelope hugs her one more time.

We have to un-booby-trap the back door to let her free. And then, my grandma sets off on her voyage through a vertex.

I hope I made the right choice. She was a good ally to have around. Harsh, but an ally all the same.

———

Mom tells me that Dad wants to talk to me alone. Thanks a lot, Penelope. He hasn't left the bedroom since Penelope's departure, and I find him sitting on the edge of my parents' bed. I plop down next to him with plenty of space between us in case he decides he's so angry at Penelope that I'd make a good venting bag.

My parents' bedroom is definitely a mix of Mom's and Dad's tastes, including an heirloom quilt bedspread with a huge American red, white, and blue star pattern across the center. His old cigar box on his bureau. Pictures of Benji and me on the wall in various stages of puberty. A gross one with me in braces from sixth grade grins at me.

"Mom said you wanted to see me?" I prompt. The sooner we get it over with, the better.

"I need to explain something to you. Only your mother knows this story. I don't want Benji to know."

Already I'm interested because it's information Benji doesn't have. Whatever he's going to tell me, it's not good. Dad's cracking every finger one at a time nonstop. I worry that he might break one.

"Penelope acted like I don't care about my family. I need you to understand something about me." He pauses and takes a deep breath like I always do. "During my time in active service, I made a decision that cost the lives of four in my unit."

He doesn't look at me. He holds onto his knees. I notice that despite his graying hair, his face suddenly looks like that of a scared ten-year-old.

"We were surrounded," he continues, his voice wavering. "I made the call."

An uncomfortable heaviness builds in my stomach. I have the urge to rub his back like Mom does, but I can't do it. *What did he do? Pull out a machine gun and let loose?*

"I chose to retreat." After rubbing his eyes and blinking back tears, he continues. "If we had stayed..." He stands and paces near the boarded-up window. "Do you understand what I'm saying?"

I nod. "You regret the decision—"

"I have to give the government time to fight. Penelope has no idea how much I want to protect you. That I am protecting you."

He waits. My heart races like a team of horses fleeing a fire.

"I'm not ready to leave yet, either." I know it's what he wants to hear. I don't know if it's what I want to say. *Why don't I want to fight for myself?*

"That's my girl," he says, reaching over and patting my knee for my loyalty. I feel proud and guilty and pathetic all at once.

———

To stay or to go, to burn or to jump, to obey or to rebel—it's like cats are clawing at my insides, one hot scar for every wasted minute. I can't decide, I just can't. And the more I can't decide, the more my body feels like it's on fire. One of Dante's circles of hell should be indecision because it secretly burns the hottest.

My prescription bottle beckons me from my dresser.

It would be so easy. The urge to swallow them all overwhelms me like a tide of fear and relief rolled into one wave. As I reach for the bottle, I feel like I'm drowning, yet it's easier to breathe. I roll the orange plastic container between my palms. The pills inside click together like tap dancers. I miss Rita. Penelope's gone. *Nothing is the same. Nothing will ever be the same.*

I don't know what to do. I stare at my escape. All of my problems would go away without needing to choose a side. Freedom in a bottle. But the logical side of me fights the emotional side in a battle for my future. *Isn't death just another choice?* I put the bottle down. I need to process all of these feelings in a rational way outside my body. Arianna mentioned that I should use my journal to help with anxiety, instead of storing information.

I pull my journal from the bookshelf and write.

All of my horrible feelings come spilling out in a cathartic scribbling that leaves me dumbfounded. Time loses all meaning. I don't know what to do to escape the changing world around me. I can't deal with such deep, profound decisions. No one should. After an endless session of frantic writing, I read over the pages of drivel, pages about utter nonsense. As I'm about to tear the pages out and chuck the whole disaster, one line I wrote catches my eye:

*When the truth is shrouded in fear
and clouded by dreams,*

*when fact and fantasy become secret lovers,
Maybe there are no real heroes anymore.*

I read that line over and over again. It's beautiful and haunting and I cannot believe I wrote it. My new mantra of frustration. Of indecision. Of hopelessness.

Nearby, the prescription bottle still sings its mellow song of relief. I spill the contents into my hand. Ten left before my next refill. *Is it enough? If I swallow all of them, will the onslaught of thoughts and questions end? Or will I wake up in a worse situation?*

Ah, there's that good old Shakespearean rub Hamlet talked about.

I repeat my line. Somehow it articulates my foggy emotions. It makes me sad. It makes me let go.

I cannot control the world. I cannot control my family or my friends. I am only one person. But I can control me.

I put the remaining pills back into the bottle and take only one. For now.

CHAPTER 18

QUESTION: Do you have cell phones? The internet?

ANSWER: We have advanced technology for communication, but it has evolved from the cell phone and internet to a holocom interface with genetic recognition.

The internet has gotten weirder if that's possible. It's morphed into an electronic graveyard where people are mounting tributes to themselves on social networks before they leave through a vertex. Dominick said it's a just-in-case memorial, where their electronic selves can live on regardless of where the vertexes lead. A false sense of the infinite.

Let's be real. If the comet hits, the internet will disappear like everything else. It's the skin of our civilization, carved in electricity instead of rock, able to withstand nothing, and completely pointless without a body. And if the comet does not destroy us, don't they realize that no online company is going to store the electronic remains of all these people indefinitely? They will hit some secret red delete button, and all traces of their inactive online accounts will vanish forever.

I look up Rita's account anyway. She listed her departure date, favorite foods, television shows, best friends. A picture of the two of us posing outside a Billie Eilish concert. I take screenshots of everything, print them out, and keep hard copies. As if paper can withstand an apocalypse.

———

Christmastime usually brings stress and activity into the house. Mom typically cleans like a lot in November, then the day after Thanksgiving, she puts up the tree and decorates everything in red, gold, and green, including the outside of the house and the front lawn.

Not this year.

You would think that for our last possible Christmas ever, she would go all out. Nope. In fact, the house is looking messier and messier, and she hasn't been on my case about doing chores or about the piles of laundry growing on my bedroom floor. Maybe she's been distracted by Benji's wedding, or she's upset about Penelope leaving. All I know is that Mom might be joining the depression squad. Clean for an apocalypse? Nope. What's the point?

A week before Christmas, she finally puts up our artificial tree. I help her decorate it while Dad's at work. She plays carols and prances around like a happy reindeer. Her joy disturbs me even more than Dad's drinking.

When we're finished, I stand back to admire the lights.

"I'm never taking it down," she mutters aloud.

I face her. "Never?"

"Nope." She smiles wide.

I think she really means it. A forever Christmas tree. *Until.*

Every time I walk past and see the twinkling tree, it creeps me out. Like someone mourning in a sequined dress at a funeral. An ornamental oxymoron.

———

The United Nations predicts that today we will learn whether or not part 2 of the CORE plan, *Hera II* completing its gravity trick, was successful. An early Christmas gift.

We wait in front of the television screen.

"If it doesn't work," Mom says to me from the couch, "they still have another backup plan." She pats my knee.

Like I don't already know that. Sounds like she's scared and trying to be brave.

The television breaks from regularly scheduled programming for an important announcement.

"Here it is," Dad says.

I hold my breath.

News reporters scramble to inform us that "the mass gravity transfer has been aborted." They repeat, "The mass gravity transfer has been aborted."

The message crawls across the bottom of the screen.

"Oh, no," Mom says, then covers her mouth.

They failed. Something about not being able to get close enough. Gases and ice coming off the comet kept messing with sensors and navigation.

A comet is still heading to destroy us.

"Like you said, they still have a backup plan," I say, trying to stay positive.

"I was hoping it wouldn't come to that," Mom says.

Dad's quiet. About time.

Part 2 of CORE is finally revealed. A second, manned ship, *Hercules*, will be loaded with the largest nuclear bombs ever detonated. More than three hundred megatons. I'll have to ask Dominick what that means later. They had to get special permission from the UN to allow it. According to NASA, sending a manned ship with a single bomb will help with accuracy, something to do with light-speed communication being limited by distance, the major reason they believe part 2 failed.

It sounds like A.) this won't be ready until the last minute and B.) if we do survive, this will cause nuclear fallout, and we'll die anyway. I scribble facts into my journal to avoid visualizing the consequences. Scientists finally explain it has something called a directional neutron blast, so apparently this will keep any residual effect from reaching us.

Right. Sure. 'Cause whenever we've used nuclear weapons in the past it's always turned out just fine.

NASA and the PDCO is very specific that this is not intended to blow up the comet but to move its path from colliding with Earth. *Of course, it could backfire.* Hercules *could accidentally blow the comet and itself up, and the pieces and radiation could rain down and fillet us anyway.* Now I know why they kept this part a secret.

On Christmas Eve it snows, blanketing the town in crisp white wonder. Thanks, universe, for giving us a white Christmas before possible obliteration. It's so nice to be granted happiness before debilitating despair.

Despite the recent CORE news, Dominick and I have plans to celebrate together tonight since my family always gets together on Christmas Day. On the phone he says that he has a surprise for me.

"Dress warm," he says. Sounds ominous.

I pack a backpack with a present for him, snacks, and my pills. When the doorbell rings, I zip up my fleece-lined hooded jean jacket and put red fleece gloves on my hands. My neck remains scarf free as usual.

Using the back door, I escape and meet Dominick at the front porch stairs. He smiles and kisses me immediately. How I ever thought I could be without him is beyond me. Snowflakes stick to my eyelashes. Thank God for my hood; my curly hair would soak up the moisture in seconds.

His car is nowhere in sight.

"Where's your car?" I ask.

"Conserving gas," he says. "Don't worry—we're not going far."

I plant my feet firmly in place and pull on his arm. "Where are we going?"

"Stop asking questions. Try to go with the flow for once."

"I don't do that," I say. "I'm anti-spontaneous and proud of it."

He rolls his eyes and walks away from me. Then he spins around and yells, "You coming or what?"

I take a deep breath and follow his lead.

We travel around the corner and over several blocks, past the historic Millicent Library in the center of Fairhaven that by day looks like a storybook castle, but by night looks more like a sinister torture tower. At least the snow is beginning to cast a magical spell over everything, covering the neighborhood with a white film. As we approach the Atlantic coastline, the cold air pulls at my nose, cheeks, and ears. My eyes water in the wind. The snow falls heavier, like feathery grains of flour piling underfoot.

"Promise you won't freak out," he warns.

To be honest, that immediately makes me start freaking out. The dead trees cast grisly shadows in the moonlight.

"What're we doing?" I ask, more insistent this time.

He touches my shoulder. "Do you trust me?"

I stare at him and smile. "No."

We laugh, and then I give in. "Fine, I guess I trust you."

"Then run." He grabs my hand, and my body jerks forward. I run to keep pace as he darts into a huge yard that overlooks the ocean. When he races up the back stairs and across a huge deck of a random house, I pull my hand free.

"What—" I try to argue, but he cuts me off by placing his finger on my bottom lip.

"I'll explain. Come inside first." He slides the glass door open. *It's not his home. It's not the home of anyone he knows.* No one we know could afford a place so big on the water. *This is illegal.*

He smiles. The world's ending. *Carpe diem.*

I walk inside.

Candles illuminate a path from the dark kitchen to the dark living room. Once there, a fire burns bright, carrying heat to my stiff bones.

"I've been staking out the place for the past two weeks," Dominick explains. "They've gone. I checked online. No squatters around, either."

"What is all this?" I ask, pointing to the candles and the fire.

"Your Christmas present. I wanted to give you—well, us—a special memory. All the hotels are full or closed and money's tight."

I feel silly having him do so much work and put a massive spotlight on me, yet I can't help but smile like a spoiled child.

"Are you telling me you committed breaking and entering for me?" I tease. "How romantic."

He turns his face and stuffs his hands in his pockets. He thinks I don't like it.

"Hey," I turn his chin to force him to look at me. "I love it. It's perfect."

"Oh, good," he grins. "I did have to break a window, though," he admits. "There's no power or heat, so I set up the fireplace."

I plop down in front of the dancing flames. *He left the fire burning while he came to get me? The whole place could've burned to the ground.* Crackling sparks and burning wood warm my face. I unzip my coat.

Dominick sits down next to me. "They left some salvageable food behind, too. It's in the kitchen." He pauses. "I brought some of it home, too."

His eyes look lost when he talks about his family. I wonder how many other abandoned houses he's been breaking into to feed his family.

"Changing the subject," I announce. "I have a present for you."

"How?" Dominick asks. "Most stores have been looted."

"I saw them on clearance a few months ago."

I pull a large holiday gift bag from my backpack. Dominick digs his hands inside and lifts out a shoebox. After opening the lid, he laughs. "Red Converse?"

"You said you're more like David Tennant. I could've gone with a bow tie."

"No, these are awesome."

"They were all out of sonic screwdrivers."

He leans over and kisses me. We don't stop.

Christmas morning I wake up in an abandoned master suite, Dominick snoring softly beside me in bed. Daylight floods the room. I miss having windows at home. Without waking Dominick, I slide out of bed and stand awash in the bright morning light. I soak in the breathtaking view. The backyard leads to a rocky ledge, the dark gray-blue Atlantic rolling toward the house from the other side. The blinding sun sparkles across the ocean. I wonder if that's how bright the comet will be. Except instead of starting a new day, it will end them all.

Sometime yesterday, I made the decision to shut off my cell phone and stay the night. My parents are going to kill me, but I don't care. Last night was about me and Dominick. They can say whatever they want, but they can't take back one of the best nights of my life.

"Come back to bed," Dominick calls. I turn and smile and jump back into bed. We roll into a warm ball of sheet and blanket, the covers undulating like a wave as we crash and break against each other.

Afterward, we eat cold strawberry Pop-Tarts in bed and let the crumbs fall where they may.

We spend the rest of the morning pretending the house is ours. We find a pair of matching navy robes with the white initials LM stitched on the shorter one and RM on the longer one. Wonder what their names were. Lauren & Roger? Lorraine & Richard? Dominick gives me a tour of the whole house now that sunlight pours in from the windows. The house has five bedrooms, all with attached bathrooms. Pictures of the family who lived here line the walls. A couple in their sixties. Two adult sons. I count about six grandchildren in various photos. Seeing their faces creeps me out. It's like they've died, and they're watching us use their stuff.

Dominick wears the enormous bathrobe and searches through a bureau in the spare bedroom. He picks up a watch from inside a drawer. I expect him to pocket it, but he puts it back. I could get used to a life in a big house with him. Last night was the first time since August that I didn't think about the holograms or the vertexes or the comet or the world ending. I wasn't even worried about getting arrested for breaking and entering. He gave me that. I could picture us staying in the house until the inevitable happens. Why not? We could live here together, die here together.

Morbid much? What's happening to me?

We return to the master bedroom to get dressed and pack.

"Ready to face the music?" Dominick says, breaking my train of thought.

"Ready as I'll ever be, I guess. What did you tell your mother?"

I disrobe and start getting dressed. Even though he's seen me naked, I still turn away to put on my bra and sweater.

"The truth."

I can't see his face so I assume he's joking. "No you didn't." I slide on my jeans. "Your mother would've freaked."

"Actually, I did tell her. Alex, we need to talk."

I spin around. His face matches the tone of his voice. *Not good. Did I do something wrong? Is he breaking up with me? After a night like that?*

"I didn't want it to ruin our night together." He twists his sweatshirt in his hands.

He is breaking up with me.

"My mother has decided to leave with Austin through a vertex. I have to go with them."

"What?" My eyes fill up and blur. First Rita, now Dominick. The world stops spinning. "Why? When? Today?" I cannot control the tears and blubbering sounds that emerge from my throat.

"We're leaving on New Year's Day," Dominick states. "I asked my mother to at least wait until then to give you some time." He wipes away my tears. "You know I have to be there for them. We are running low on food, and with *Hera II* failing…"

I understand, but I don't want to.

Dominick grabs my hand and places it on his chest. "I love you. I want you to come with us." He tries to capture my gaze. "Please say yes."

It's right there, on the tip of my tongue. But I can't promise him that. It's too soon to decide my fate, leave my world. My family's still waiting to see if the third part of the CORE project works. But I'm not ready to let him go, either.

"Dominick…" I can't say the words. I push my palm against his chest, holding him at a distance. I don't know how to do this.

He breaks my barrier and kisses me hard. It's not a goodbye kiss. It's a pledge. I kiss back.

How can I choose?

I look into his eyes and remember last night. "Yes."

———

Dominick tries to walk me all the way home, but I refuse to subject him to the wrath of my parents. I should be more worried about their reaction myself. I even took a pill before we left the seaside house to prepare. Instead, all I can think about is almost losing Dominick for the second time in months.

That was before we got serious. I let my guard down. Now I'm too steeped in love to see a path without him. But I also don't want to make a life decision I'll regret.

He kisses me goodbye on the corner. "New Year's Day."

I nod. I can tell by his eyes he's relieved. If only I had a way to stall for more decision- making time. As if time helps when both choices suck.

As soon as I step on my back porch, the door flies open. I'm ready for a fight.

"Oh, thank God." Mom runs and embraces me. Not what I was expecting.

"Where were you?" Dad stands right behind her with a vicious gleam in his eyes. Exactly what I was expecting.

"I spent the night with Dominick." Figure if Dominick can go with the truth, so can I.

"You what?" Dad yells.

I take off my gloves. "I spent the night with Dominick."

"So you turn eighteen and you think that's acceptable?" Dad says. "Making your mother worry all night. Calling the hospitals, police stations."

Mom releases me and strokes my face gently, crying. "I thought you left."

It takes me a minute. "Through a vertex?"

"Yes." She hugs me again. "I kept checking online to see if your name was added to the departed."

Dad says nothing. I know what he's thinking. He's thinking we had sex and he doesn't want to go there. Oh, we went there.

"Dominick's leaving with his family," I say for clarity.

Silence. That did it. What can they say? He's leaving the freaking planet. And apparently, so am I. Saying the word "leaving" aloud splits me in half. How am I supposed to leave without my family? I'm not as strong as Rita.

"You could've at least called," Dad says.

"I didn't want you to say no." I wipe my nose on my jacket. "I needed time with him."

Mom hugs me again. Dad looks annoyed. "When are they going?" she asks.

"Next week." I almost tell them he wants me to leave with him—and I said yes. But that's enough truth for one day. I don't know how I'm going to break it to them, but something inside me knows it's time to pack.

CHAPTER 19

DAY 147: DECEMBER–902 HOURS TO DECIDE

QUESTION: What are your laws?

ANSWER: That question is too long to answer. Our basic precept is that violent or negative behavior cannot infringe upon the rights of others.

Christmas day, and the media discusses the gas crisis sweeping the nation. Fifteen dollars a gallon. Lines around blocks at stations. President Lee has encouraged everyone to conserve gas by carpooling, walking, riding bikes. *Bikes? During winter in New England? Yeah, okay.*

While the world argues over gas conservation, I cannot stop checking the vertex countdown app on my phone. We are now down to triple digits. Rita, Penelope, soon Dominick, and I guess me. Without my family. *How am I supposed to tell them?*

Benji and Marcus visit for Christmas. They come bearing gifts, which is weird since we didn't give them anything for their wedding. Most stores have been either looted or closed, so Mom made a rule that Christmas this year would be gift free. I guess Benji didn't get the memo or chose not to follow it. Mom doesn't seem to mind. She fawns over the gift bags like a cat on catnip.

Way to make me look bad again, Benji. Marriage hasn't changed you one bit. Looking around at my family members, all I can think about is Dominick and our night at the house on the ocean. That's the life I want. Not this one.

But have I really become that girl, that weak girl who leaves when her boyfriend leaves? Am I the daughter who stays when her parents stay? Am I making an independent choice? Does it matter? Are any choices independent?

"Alex," Mom interrupts my thoughts. "Hot chocolate?"

"Sure." I take a steaming mug from her. Hot chocolate, pre-apocalypse. Thanks, Mom.

Across the room, Dad grins as he sips. Instant hot chocolate mix was his latest acquisition. He waited weeks for a shipment to come in so he could put aside a few boxes for us. The five of us sip from colorful mugs in front of our forever Christmas tree as Dad tells random stories. I tune him out and focus on the carols playing in the background. I've heard his tales time and time again. He's retelling them for Marcus, and Marcus is giving him his utmost attention. Now I understand why Benji and Marcus get along. They both know how to play Dad.

Benji and Marcus get center stage when they hand out the gift bags. Turns out that Marcus's mother knitted each of us a scarf. Mom oohs and aahs and wraps her neck several times in wool jewel tones. I feel my neck closing in just watching her. Dad places his black one around the back of his neck and folds it once in the front like a Boy Scout. Inside my gift bag is a beautiful, bobble-knit red scarf. My favorite color. I'll never wear it.

"Thank you," I say to Marcus as I lay the scarf in my lap.

"Ooh, let's see it. Put it on," Mom says.

I want to throw it in her face. *Hello? Daughter who doesn't wear things around her neck. Did you forget?*

"Maybe later," I stall.

Benji flips. "Why do you have to be so difficult all the time?"

Difficult? He was there. He knows. He had to bite Dad to get him off me.

Marcus puts his hand out in front of Benji. "It's fine."

"No, it isn't. She can never let anything go, and everyone has to placate her all the time."

I open my mouth to protest, but what he says rings true. It's how I used to feel around Dominick. Like a burden. Benji, always making me feel like crap, acting like my anxiety is a choice. I always thought Dad was the problem, but maybe my problem has been both of them.

"Leave her alone," Dad says. "She said thank you."

Everyone freezes. *Did Dad stand up for me and not Benji? Has the world ended early?*

"Well," Mom steps in. "I think it's time to spike up the drinks." She runs around the room and pours Bailey's into everyone's hot chocolate. Everyone but mine.

Great, Mom. Give alcohol to volatile people. Fabulous idea.

"Let's toast," she adds, holding up her mug. "To lost family. To lost friends." She looks at me. "To Christmas. Let's make it a good one."

"Exactly," says Benji.

"Exactly," says Dad.

I roll my eyes. Benji sips his drink. Marcus watches him.

"So how are things at the vertex site?" Dad asks Benji.

"Busy. People are trying to fight through lines, pay for access. I heard rich people are paying for VIP treatment to fly out to special vertexes in reclusive locations to bypass the crowds. Whatever. It won't matter soon, anyway. Even money's becoming irrelevant when there's nothing left to buy with it."

Dad nods. "People don't want luxury goods right now. They want food, basic supplies, fuel, shelter. Family. Important stuff. Using money becomes like trading paper for oxygen."

"Benji and I have been discussing whether or not it's time to leave," Marcus says. "Like he said, it's getting crowded at the vertexes."

I sit up in the chair.

Dad keeps it together, moves in closer to Marcus's face, and says, "Family stays together."

Crap. He's back on that again. That's not what he said to me after Penelope left.

Marcus is taken aback. Benji steps in, "Maybe you should start thinking about leaving, Dad. We could all go together."

Now Dad looks scared. "The comet is still a month away. We still have time. Give CORE a chance."

Mom sips from her hot chocolate.

"Time's running out," Benji says.

I think about Dominick, his family's mutual decision to leave, and I respect their camaraderie. It's what Dad wants but can't have 'cause he's too stubborn to change his mind.

Dominick calls the next morning, and I answer the phone grinning like I won a prize. I'm ready to jump into the abyss for him. Just thinking about it like that, however, makes my stomach sink.

"Hey, sexy," I say, trying to be cute.

"Alex, I'm on my way to pick you up."

I sit up from the sofa, still in my pajamas—sweats and a crappy T-shirt. "For what? You ready for another break-in?"

"This is serious. I'll be there in ten minutes."

My stomach sinks further. "What's wrong? We aren't leaving early, are we?"

"No, there's another massive looting going on."

I laugh nervously into the phone. "And you want us to join in? Need to get a new flat-screen TV before you leave the planet?"

He doesn't laugh back. "Alexandra, your father—"

He doesn't need to say more. I drop the phone and run to my room for clothes. Dad's the manager at the supermarket today.

What if he tries to be the hero? Tries to fight? I take a pill to calm my looping, spastic brainwaves. I call Dad's phone as I wait for Dominick. No answer. Mom's out visiting with a friend. I can't call her until I know something. I call Benji's phone to see if he knows anything. No answer. My hands can barely hold my phone steady since they are shaking so much. *Why don't people ever answer their phones when something's important?*

Dominick beeps the horn instead of coming inside. I run out the back door and hop into his car.

"What's going on?" I ask.

"I only know what my neighbor said. A large shipment of food is scheduled to arrive at the supermarket, and a group plans to riot."

Dominick's car races through the streets, and I can only stare out the window and hope that we make it in time.

We don't.

The supermarket parking lot is sheer chaos. I can't see Dad anywhere in the crowd. After abandoning the car, Dominick and I weave our way to the front where the police have set up a barrier of uniformed bodies and metal barricades. As I make my way through the commotion, people bump and push and yell. From a distance, it looks like a bad concert scene. Up close, it becomes something primordial. I've never seen people so out of control in one location. Occasionally, I've witnessed someone turn red in the face and word vomit their anger and all its glory and ugliness at another person. But this is different.

This is the face of a mob.

Mostly young men and women in their twenties and thirties. Some older. All different shades of skin color, hair styles. Yet in the pushing and shoving, the ranting and raving, their faces blur until all I see is one furrowed, pained, spiteful brow of revenge, a face stuck in time. Slow motion rage and desperation. Spitting and shrieking—anger fit to erupt ash and spew evil to conquer evil.

This is the face of freedom, the face of oppression, the face of the devil, the face of humanity, all in one. It's not a good versus evil fight. It's people on people, screaming for survival. I somehow become wrapped up in it, somehow remain separate. I cannot escape the dichotomy.

No wonder Dad's been slipping, dealing with this every day. He said food was running out, but I didn't understand how bad it was. He was right. I didn't listen to his worries. He has been protecting us all along.

I move close to the nearest officer and yell over the din, "I'm looking for my father, Ben Lucas."

The officer doesn't respond. I don't think he can hear me. Or doesn't want to hear me.

Dominick touches my arm and yells into my ear, "This was a bad idea."

I turn my attention back to the police officer. "Sir? Hello? My father, he works inside. I need to know if he's okay." I reach out to tap his shoulder since he doesn't seem to notice me.

"Stay behind the line!" His body shakes as he bellows the command. He looks Benji's age behind the riot helmet.

The crowd behind us reacts and pushes forward. Dominick loses his balance. His body is thrust at the police officer.

The officer pushes him back over the line and hits him once with his baton. Blood trickles in a line down Dominick's forehead.

I feel the anger of the mob reach my veins. I can't stop myself. "No, someone pushed him! Stop!"

I jump between Dominick and the officer, pushing a little to create space. The officer shifts either to push me back or use the baton. It all happens so fast I can't be sure. All I know is that I hear Dad's voice over the crowd.

"Alexandra? That's my daughter!"

Thank God. My heart skips at the sight of him running out of the store behind the line of officers. Within seconds, however, my skin senses the tension in the air like thick, hostile humidity.

The officer pauses long enough for Dad to get closer. Just when I think that things might be okay, that things are over, things become unhinged.

The face of the mob sees my father, many heads acting as one. He's wearing his supermarket shirt and BENJAMIN LUCAS, MANAGER name tag. He symbolizes their struggle, their hunger, their confusion. My dad is their enemy.

The mob attacks. Bats, fire extinguishers, crow bars, knives, bricks, broken bottles, fists, boots, elbows, anything and everything, in a mix of force and vengeance and righteousness and sinew.

In a flash, I am run down, my palms slapping frigid pavement and sending shock waves up both arms. People step on my legs and arms, oblivious that I'm beneath them on the ground as they rush past. The pain is sharp, stunning, stifling. I roll into fetal position and tuck my head to shield myself. Somehow Dominick and I have ended up at the line of scrimmage.

I can't see anything but moving boots and sneakers. I can't risk lifting my head to find Dominick or my dad. I squeeze my eyes shut and pray to a God I'm not sure even exists.

"Please, please, please. Help."

The popping sounds of gunfire. Then a loud, airy noise followed by a hollow thunk. Seconds later, my eyes and throat burn like the rage around me, and my nostrils and mouth start dripping with snot and saliva. I choke on my own spit. The fire in my throat makes my windpipe close. I hold my neck and gasp. Dad is in danger, and when I try to help him, try to reach out to him, I cannot breathe. It's the attic all over again. Only this time, it's not his fault. Not his fault.

My world collapses.

CHAPTER 20

QUESTION: Do you have sicknesses? Diseases?

ANSWER: We have advanced medical knowledge of the human genome and brain that we no longer have sickness, advanced aging, or disease. When new outbreaks emerge, we can easily cure them.

I wake to harsh lights and a female voice mumbling near me. Whatever she's saying, it sounds like a muffled plea. The voice reminds me of the angry lady from the hospital and vertex site, begging for someone to listen to her poetic rants, but as my mind drifts into full awareness, I recognize the shape of my mother.

"Where am I?" The heaviness in my temples and ears dulls my thoughts. My throat and eyes feel dry and sore.

"You're at the hospital."

Then I remember.

"Where's Dad? Oh God, where's Dominick?" My heart freezes, waiting for information.

"Alexandra, relax. They're okay."

It seems like she's talking in slow motion. As my mind clears, I see nurses in scrubs walking in the distance. *Why am I in a hallway on a cot?* I sit up, toss a sheet off my lap, and try to stand. I'm not wearing a hospital gown. The pants I threw on before Dominick picked me up still cover my body, but they're filthy and one of the legs has a ripped hole.

Dominick and Dad are nowhere in sight. I need to see them to believe they're okay.

"Where are they, then? Dad? Dominick?" I yell down the corridor. A few nurses head toward me, but Mom shoos them away.

"Dominick's fine," she explains. "He's got bruises and a broken arm, but he's fine. They're also monitoring him for a concussion. Dad's being prepped for surgery."

"Surgery?" My mouth goes dry. "I thought you said he was okay."

"He is, but he broke his leg, dislocated his shoulder, and has some internal bleeding."

My head gets woozy, and the floor slants awkwardly. Mom catches me and leads me back to the cot. Her words sting my already tired eyes, and I think I'm crying, but it's hard to tell.

"Why am I in the hallway?" I ask through the haze.

"The hospital is overcrowded and understaffed, and your condition is not as severe as other patients."

Not as severe. That means Dominick's and Dad's conditions are severe.

I start to hyperventilate, my chest caving in and out in rapid succession. My skin is on fire, and sweat pours down my back. I fall off the side of the cot and onto the checkered floor. I can't find my pills to anchor my body to my mind. *How can this not be what death feels like?*

Two nurses scramble over to me. The pinch of a needle, and then nothing.

I wake up feeling physically numb and emotionally drained. Whatever they gave me, I'd love it in a pill form. As I glance down, I see that I've become worthy of a hospital gown. Mom says my injuries are minor cuts and heavy bruising, but since I collapsed, they want to check me for a possible concussion or something worse. Dad's still in surgery, and there's been no update on his condition. Benji and Marcus are waiting near the surgical unit for more news.

After I plead with my nurse, she allows Mom to push me in a wheelchair to Dominick's room. I try to convince her I can walk, but she says it's standard procedure.

Dominick's in a hospital room built for two but currently houses six patients. His glasses are missing, and one of his eyes is swollen shut. A large bandage covers the side of his head, and his left arm is in a sling, which sucks since he's left-handed. His mother and Austin sit near his bed watching television. Austin waves to me. Dominick's mother gives me a grim stare. I guess it's always the girlfriend's fault.

I watch Dominick sleep.

My family and I watch television together to pass the time. It's ironic that we've been clinging on to every possible minute left on the planet, and now we cannot stand each second as we wait for word of Dad's condition.

I click through channels and notice something odd about the news. The media has changed focus. Every newscast is reporting

feel-good stories about the nation and the world, optimistic anec-
dotes about CORE scientists working hard to defeat the comet with
Hercules, heroic tales of those journeying through the vertexes, and
hopeful speeches from world leaders that we will overcome.

What's missing is the violence, the looting, the breakdown, the
truth. I know the violence must be happening across the globe, but
it's absent in every segment. I'm guessing the media content has
been censored to stop the spread of mayhem. People need to hold
on to the notion that the world has rules. Anarchy cannot be televised and promoted.

I search the internet using my phone. Some sites are spreading
optimism, but on other sites, especially on social media, people
are scared and posting videos of spreading mayhem. The contrast
between the news and personal videos disturbs me on a deep level.
How can they expect people to look out the window and see violence with their own eyes and still blindly believe the media's message of hope? *How can we edit the truth and it not have consequences?*

All I know is that when the media starts focusing solely on the
good, it means we're really screwed.

———

Hours later, Mom sits with me, Benji, and Marcus in my hospital
room with five other patients and their families.

"You're lucky you weren't arrested," Benji says.

"Thanks," I mutter. I didn't even know that was a possibility.

"Why would she be arrested?" Marcus asks. "She wasn't doing
anything wrong."

Thanks, Mr. Blu.

"Wrong place, wrong time. Police usually arrest everyone and sort it out later. They were outnumbered, and she was unconscious. They may come back to ask her questions."

"Great. Thanks for that," I spit back at Benji.

"Thanks for what?"

"Making me worry about the police coming here."

"Welcome."

Marcus rolls his eyes and smiles at me. I'm liking him more and more. I wish he was my brother instead of my brother-in-law. I don't understand how Marcus can stand Benji sometimes. Now I know why he made such a great teacher.

"So who's gonna tell Dad about the store?" Benji asks the three of us.

"What about the store?" I ask.

Mom places her hand on my back. "The supermarket was burned to the ground. Arson."

It's gone? Dad cannot lose his job. He loves his job.

"No one was hurt in the fire, though," Marcus adds.

"I'm not breaking the news to him," Benji says.

"I will," Mom volunteers. "When the time is right."

A knock on the door ends the conversation. Two men wearing scrubs enter the room. Mom takes a deep breath and doesn't exhale. She holds onto my bed rail so tightly her knuckles change color.

They brief us on Dad's condition. Aside from the broken leg and dislocated shoulder, he suffered from a stab wound to the chest that punctured and collapsed his lung. They stabilized the lung and put him on a ventilator, but he lost a lot of oxygen and still has low levels. They aren't sure if there will be any brain damage. He's still unconscious.

It's a waiting game.

My family wheels me to his room. His skin is the color of paste, and from what I can see of his lips behind the ventilator, they have a bluish tinge to them. Like permanent Zombie Night. Mom kisses his forehead and strokes the side of his face, whispering things I cannot hear into his ear. She doesn't cry. I sit by his side and listen to the machine breathe for him as silent tears fall over my cheeks. Benji and Marcus stay in the corner as if he's contagious. I only have one thought.

I cannot leave him like this. I cannot leave him like this.

———

When Dominick wakes up and sees me, his mouth smiles, and his one good eye tears up. "You look terrible," I say, crying and laughing.

"You look gorgeous yourself," he says back and hugs me with his right arm. I flinch as a pain in my left side shoots forward.

"Sorry," he apologizes.

"It's okay." I lift up the side of my shirt and see a huge bruise. "Ouch."

"Looks worse than it feels," I lie.

"Why are you in a wheelchair? Is something wrong with your legs?"

"No, no. I just fainted. It's protocol."

He doesn't look convinced.

Dominick's mother asks my mom, "How's your husband?"

"No change." After a few strained minutes of minor conversation, Mom proposes, "What do you say we leave these two alone for a bit? Good time to search for a decent cup of coffee."

Yes. Please say yes.

"Sounds good to me," Dominick's mother agrees. "Let's go, Austin."

"Aw, but I was watching that." He points at the television screen to a Pokémon cartoon.

"I'll let you pick a snack from whatever they have left around here." Then I hear her whisper to my mom, "I bet some people are coming to the hospital just for the food." She turns her attention to Dominick. "We'll be back in a little while. Do you need anything?"

"No, I'm fine," he says.

She kisses him on the forehead, and the three of them exit quietly. We still aren't exactly alone since there are five other patients in the room, but four of them are asleep, and one old man stares out the window.

Dominick touches my shoulder. "I'm sorry. I shouldn't have brought you there. I'm such an idiot."

His words stun me. I had no idea he'd blame himself.

"Dominick, it's not your fault. Not at all. We didn't know what was going to happen. You were trying to help."

"By walking right into a violent situation? We could've been killed. You…" His good eye fills with tears.

"I'm fine. We're fine." I kiss his forehead, his cheek, his lips. He half kisses back. The last time I saw him this low was after his father's funeral.

"I'm so glad you're going with us," he whispers.

I kiss him to avoid having to say anything, and his eyes close, the drugs pulling him under.

I can't leave him like this. I can't leave him like this.

The problem is that the "him" my brain is referring to isn't Dominick.

"Maybe," I whisper back.

CHAPTER 21

QUESTION: What is the weather like on your planet?
ANSWER: Much like earth's. But we have the ability to control and manage the weather to meet our agricultural needs.

Dominick and I were released from the hospital, me two days before him. Dad has only gotten worse. Still unconscious. High fever. Infection at the surgery site. Understaffed must also mean incompetent. One small piece of good news: the hospital refilled my prescription.

Today is New Year's Eve. Dominick and his family leave tomorrow. His mom waited as promised, and the fact that her son was attacked only reaffirms her wish to leave ASAP. Dominick still thinks I'm going with him.

I meet Dominick at the house near the ocean for one more night. We need one last night alone so I can say goodbye.

———

"I will go. Eventually. But not yet."

Dominick flips out. "Are you serious? You can't wait for him. You don't have time. The vertexes are becoming a bottleneck nightmare. The holograms gave us six months to leave for a reason. It comes down to math."

"Dominick, I know. I will come. I promise."

He paces in front of the fireplace. The glow from the fire highlights his face, displaying both his anger and his recent facial injuries. It's heartbreaking to see him hurt physically while also hurting him emotionally.

"How can I believe you? Seriously. Once I go, I can't come back. It's a one-way exit. If you don't end up going…" His voice cracks.

"I know. I will go." I hold his good hand, try to make him look at me. "I won't leave you again. That was a mistake I won't ever make again. You have to have faith in me."

He grunts and tears spring from his eyes. "If the other side is like what the holograms are saying, I want to experience that world with you. I need you safe. The world is falling apart. Look around. All this time, your father didn't really care about your safety, and here you are worrying about him?"

"This isn't about worry. He would wait for me. I have to give him one last chance to change his mind. I won't be able to live with myself if I don't try. Can you convince your mom to stay longer? Or can you stay longer?"

"You know I can't do that." He turns away.

"Because of your father, right?" I clarify. "Well, this is because of mine."

"But you don't even like your dad," he says. "Not really."

Low blow. I don't know what else to say to him to make him under-stand. He's too worried about me, and I'm too worried about my dad.

We spend most of our last romantic night together not talking. He pokes at the fire. I eat a small bag of trail mix. It's what they call a stalemate. At some point, I crawl into bed under the heavy blankets to help my body let go of the weight of the world.

In the morning I find Dominick lying awake next to me. We reach out to one another across our divided loyalties. The whole time I hope beyond all reason and fantasy that it's not the last time.

"Can you do one thing?" Dominick asks as we get dressed.

"What?" I'm worried what his request might be.

"Come with us to the vertex today. I want you to be the last thing I see in this world."

A lump develops in my throat at the power and love in his words. But the lump constricts as the memory of the last time I went near a vertex replays in my mind. I know Dominick would never do what Dan the Drunk Dude did. At least, I think Dominick would never do that. *But desperate men take desperate measures.*

"Sure." My voice squeaks, and I clear my throat. "Of course."

Dominick's mother hugs me when we arrive at their apartment. She's never hugged me before, so I'm not sure what has changed. Dominick whispers something to her, and her face drops. I think it's about me not going. I'm surprised that she cares. She hardly knows me.

Together we pack up the few belongings they each want to bring with them. Dominick drives his car with his mother in the passen-ger seat, and Austin and I ride in the back.

The ride is both endless and finite. I can't wait to get out of traffic, and I hope we never escape. I don't want him to leave without me. I don't want to stay without him. I cannot let him go, but I don't have a choice. He's chosen his path, and I've chosen mine.

The radio announces that *Hercules* is on schedule to rendezvous with the comet in two weeks. Dominick glances at me in the driver's mirror, and I beg him with my eyes to wait two more weeks. If his mother and brother weren't here, I'd beg with other body parts.

The normal fifty-minute ride to Quincy takes five hours. When we finally reach the crowded vertex, a blur of heads fills the area like a screen of giant pixel dots. They never showed this scene on the news. At the sight of all the people, my brain flashes a memory of the vicious mob scene, and my body flinches. It's different from a panic attack. It's like the pores of my skin have gone into high alert.

The four of us walk through the slush on the ground and join the line. Dominick hands me his car keys. "I won't be needing these anymore."

Normally, I'd refuse such a gift. I hold his hand.

We stand in silence as the line inches forward. The tension in my body relaxes as it realizes the crowd is following social rules. As we wait in the line, protesters walk past and chant random phrases like, "Don't be a lemming" and "Jesus is the only savior." I want to join in with the protest and stop Dominick from leaving. I say nothing. What's left to say?

My body goes numb, and I don't think it's the cold. Around us people get impatient. One family quits the line; a teenager curses under his breath. The religious chanting continues.

More waiting. Dominick hugs me. I take in his heat, his touch, his physical presence. The crowd doesn't matter. Nothing matters. It's only the two of us, barely talking, our breath escaping and mingling together in a mere wisp of cold air and then dissipating. Like us.

An hour later, we reach the front. I begin convulsing in massive waves of grief. It's like Dominick's walking to his death and I am forced to watch.

"I can't. I can't," I whimper.

He puts his forehead on my forehead. "Alexandra," he whispers and wipes my tears. He never calls me that. "I love you. Promise me. Promise me."

"I promise. I promise. I love you. I love you."

I kiss him one last time as if our lives depend on it.

His mother checks in with the guards, and they add their three names to the list. I spot Benji on duty off to the side, avoiding eye contact with me. I'm probably embarrassing him again with my behavior. I don't care what he thinks anymore.

As Dominick's about to step through the vertex, he turns around and waves goodbye to me. The last sliver of him I see before he vanishes forever into an ocean of electric blue is one of his red sneakers disappearing into nothingness. The hologram bows in acceptance.

By the time I get into Dominick's car, I can't see straight. The TARDIS air freshener dangles in front of me, and I rip it down and throw it into the back seat. Over and over I slam my fists into the steering wheel. The horn beeps and beeps, and people stare at me. I hate life. I hate everything that made this happen and took him away from me.

I change my mind. I want to go. I want to run back and jump in and make everything the way it was. Pull him back out and make him stay with me until I'm ready.

But I can't. I can't.

I can't stop the pain with any amount of medication. I keep

pounding and pounding on the steering wheel and hoping that something will change and fix it and make it all better. It can't be real. It has to be some bizarre nightmare. Somebody wake me up. Please.

Wake me up!

———

I open my eyes and find myself slumped over in Dominick's car still parked near the vertex site. It's dark outside the windows and much of the crowd has gone.

I visit the vertex again, alone. I need time to look into the eye of the hologram and the center of the vertex without the pressure of people I care about standing next to me. I want an unbiased view. Benji should be gone by now, thank God.

At the vertex, I watch as a young family takes one last look at each other. They enter one at a time, in a chain, holding hands. Father, mother, sister, brother. And I see it in each of their faces. They don't know if it's the right decision, but they don't know that it's wrong, either. They have hope. They have each other. There's strength in making a choice. Strength in choosing a side.

What have I chosen? What side am I on? What do I believe in?

Both Rita and Dominick walked through the swirling haze, one for freedom from religion, one for a promise made to his deceased parent. Hundreds of years and parsecs between us, and I can still feel them here with me. I wonder what they are doing right now, somewhere out there, on another planet, in another time.

Rita could run into Dan the Drunk Dude. I can only imagine what he's up to by now. He has to be sober. Imagine that hangover. *I'm where?*

Maybe Dominick will meet Dan. Maybe he'll deck him for me.

My two best friends will each have to figure out how to start over. What to do with their lives in a world that doesn't require work or money. *That is, if they're still alive. That is, if the holograms are telling the truth.*

The hologram stares ahead, unblinking. I am surrounded by ghosts of the past and possibility. And I don't know where I fit in the present.

As I walk back to the car, I notice the same unruly lady as before lying on the ground near the road. She must hang out at the vertex. She looks worse than ever if that's possible. As I get closer to her, I see that she's foaming at the mouth and shaking. I yell for help then kneel at her side.

Her whole body begins spasming and her head bangs against the concrete. I know what to do. I've seen the school nurse handle seizures before.

Clearing the area is my first task, but the ground near her has nothing except melting snow. I roll her to one side. When the jerking of her body stops, I allow her to lie flat again.

She looks up at me in a moment of clarity. I can see it in her blue eyes—something clicks. She grabs my arm, squeezes, and sputters a series of non-words. I scream for help, and I hear running footsteps coming to aid us.

With the rest of her energy, she hands me a sweaty piece of crumpled paper. Scrawled in neat penmanship, it reads:

When the truth is shrouded in fear
and clouded by dreams,

when fact and fantasy become secret lovers,
maybe there are no real heroes anymore.
Maybe that's when heroes are born.

I recognize the phrase right away. I wrote the same message that day in my journal, the day I thought about taking all my pills to escape. It looks like my handwriting. The end of the sentence is different, though. It's been edited to be more positive. I had written "maybe there are no real heroes anymore." I don't understand. How did she get it? I didn't post it online or anything. It's been sitting in my journal. *Did she rip it out somehow? When all our food was stolen?*

"Where did you get this?" I ask her, holding up the note. "Did you go into my house?"

Soldiers stationed at the vertex come to assist with an ambulance. She loses consciousness and stops breathing. I wonder if she has a family, and if they will go through a vertex somewhere and live in another time and space while her body remains lost in this fading world.

As soon as I get home, I pull my journal from my bookshelf. It doesn't look like it's been tampered with. I compare my version to lady's note. It's verbatim except for the ending.

Did I tap into some cosmic phrase? Some sort of alien telepathy from first exposure to the vertex?

I search online for an author or reference to it. Nothing comes up. I wish I knew the lady's name so I could search for her at the hospital. I want answers to how she read my mind.

PART 3
MESSAGE THREE

This is the way the world ends
Not with a bang but a whimper.

—*T. S. ELIOT*

CHAPTER 22

QUESTION: Does your planet have oceans and other bodies of water? Mountains and deserts?

ANSWER: Yes, much like earth's. Except our oceans look crimson from a distance, and our mountains are bigger. We do not have deserts since we can control the climate.

One week later, my phone rings at four in the morning. As I reach for it, half awake, I expect Dominick's voice to be on the other end of the line. At the sight of my mom's name, I lose my breath realizing once again that Dominick's gone and that she might be calling to tell me Dad's gone, too.

On the contrary, Mom's voice screams into the receiver, "He's talking. Not clearly, but he's awake."

Using my phone as a light, I stumble in the darkness to wake up Benji and Marcus, who have been staying with me in the dark house. Without changing clothes, we race outside, choosing to take Dominick's car since it has the most gas left. Benji grabs the keys from me since I'm crying so much. I don't even fight him on it. I'm starting to wonder if people have a finite number of tears. I feel like I'm reaching my limit.

I never thought I'd be so happy to hear Dad's voice again. Then again, I never thought Benji would be driving around in Dominick's car while Dominick's in another universe.

At the hospital, Mom sits at Dad's bedside. *I am afraid to look. Afraid to celebrate too soon. Afraid of hope.*

Dad stares back at me. The ventilator's gone. His coloring's still off, though.

"Alex?" His voice barely registers in my ears.

"Dad." My voice hurts my throat.

He seems to be searching his own brain. "Dominick?"

Whoa. He used Dominick's full name.

"Dominick's fine," I say, then choke on the reality of what I said. Fat tears roll down my cheeks, and I manage to add, "Dominick's gone through a vertex."

"He saved you," Dad whispers.

My skin is on fire, and sweat pours down my back as I remember that day. He must be confused. "Dad, no. We were all attacked."

"No, you went down. I couldn't—" He takes in a labored breath. "The tear gas. He jumped on top of you. Protected you." Tears escape Dad's eyes, and I wipe them for him.

Dominick saved me? "He didn't tell me that."

"I need to thank him. Tell him I'm sorry."

"It's okay, Dad," I say and begin to sob uncontrollably. It's really not okay because Dominick's gone, and I should have gone with him. And I'm grateful and pissed off that he saved my life and never told me before he left the planet. He was willing to sacrifice his life for me, and in the end, I couldn't even say yes.

We gather in the hospital hallway to let Dad sleep. As people pass us in a stream of unending misery and various states of unrest, I know I need a team of my own to make it through this. What happens with the comet isn't my concern anymore. My focus is on leaving, not staying and hoping for survival. I promised Dominick.

"We should convince Dad to leave," I announce to Mom and Benji.

"About time you say something that makes sense," Benji says.

Mom looks out the window of the hospital floor and says, "He's too weak. We have to give him more time to get stronger before we can move him."

Wait, was that a yes? "So you will convince him to go?"

"He'll go if I say it's time," she states.

"Since when?" Benji asks. "He doesn't listen to anybody."

"He'll go if I say it's time."

I realize she's right. He will.

"Yeah, okay." Benji walks off. "I'll believe it when I see it."

His lack of faith makes me all the more determined to help Mom convince Dad and show Benji that we're stronger than we seem.

On January 10th, the governments releases the second round of prisoners to exit the planet via vertex. Dad's in and out of consciousness, so Mom and I haven't had the chance to speak to him about leaving. Doctors say his condition is slowly improving, although they are still not sure about possible brain damage. They say moving him now would likely kill him.

So we wait.

———

Days later, while Mom sleeps nearby, I watch television in Dad's hospital room, thinking about Dominick and wondering what he's doing right now. If he's still alive. Come to think of it, if he's in some faraway future and I'm living in the past, then for him I am long dead. The thought unsettles me on such a deep level that I take a pill to stop the roller coaster of sci-fi paradoxical thinking my brain cannot escape.

At midnight, a news flash from Boston appears on the television. The holograms have a new message. I turn up the volume and watch a gray-clad holographic human deliver its new speech to a crowd:

"If you are still listening to this message, you have been unwilling to admit to the urgency of your situation. In eighteen calendar days, a comet will strike your planet and destroy your people. This is your known destruction; there is no way to prevent it.

"You are in grave danger. Put aside your pride and possessions for your lives. Simply walk through the vertex. We are willing to help you. You can survive. It is your individual choice.

"This is the last automatic message. You only have four hundred thirty-two hours left to decide. The vertexes will remain open until then.

"Consider. Save your people. Save yourself before it is too late."

I watch Dad's unconscious body and will him to get better.

———

What would it be like to leave Earth forever? I mean, really. I imagine the brilliant sunrises of Earth and the calming sunsets, the thoughtful moon and the hopeful stars, the lapping of the ocean and the magic of snow. Can I live without these things? Will I be the same if my world changes?

I tried to follow Buddhism a few years ago to see if would quell my anxiety. Basically, Buddha accepts that everything changes. Everything. And if we can accept that, we will find inner peace.

Change can suck it. I'm tired of the unpredictable. I need something to hold on to. I need something to stay exactly the way it should.

———

It's January 15th. *Hercules* should reach the comet today. Everyone in the hospital waits, staring at televisions, computers, tablets, and cell phone screens for the play by play. It's like a cosmic sporting event. Who knew that in a world disaster, rather than fighting for ourselves, the majority of us would simply stare helplessly at technology waiting for someone else to rescue us?

I try to focus on the screen, waiting to hear news, but my mind keeps wondering about Dad's current condition so I can ask him to leave. I'm worried Benji will be right, and I'm waiting for nothing. Either Dad will never wake up again, or he will wake up and refuse to go.

"Did we miss anything?" Marcus asks as he and Benji join me and Mom in the hospital room to watch the state of humanity unfold before our eyes.

"Any minute now," Mom says. "I don't think I can take the pressure."

"You sound like me," I mutter.

"No one was meant to take this kind of pressure," Marcus says. "I just hope it works."

"No trial runs," Benji says. "One miscalculation and it blows the comet to pieces."

"What's wrong with that?" Mom asks.

"The pieces would still kill us," I say.

The television breaks from regularly scheduled programming for an important announcement. The Secretary of Defense fills the screen, clears his throat, and says in an unwavering voice, "Unfortunately, our last effort with the United Nations to divert the comet with the CORE project have failed. The president will be making a public address shortly. We have a scientist from NASA here to answer questions."

We watch in horror as the scientist scrambles to show diagrams of what he thinks happened. Some navigational math error. Despite the nuclear blasts' enormous energy, it had no effect on the comet's trajectory. The scientist on screen is shaking, apologizing, not understanding what went wrong. The consolation prize: no nuclear fallout as far as they can tell.

It's over. Within seconds, the media frenzy kicks in. They seem almost happy it missed. More dramatic footage. More rapid-fire reporting, microphones shoved in people's faces. "How do you feel knowing NASA failed?"

How do they think people feel? It's not like winning the Superbowl. They don't want to go to Walt Disney World. The world is ending. Drop the freakin' mic.

Mom, Benji, and Marcus are all on their feet. Mom has her hands over her face. Benji starts moving back and forth from the bed to the windows. People move when they panic. Marcus starts to cry. I rub his back.

Panic: from Pan in Greek mythology, a satyr who was known to create irrational, sudden fear in people for fun. Something that happens to everyone except me, apparently, when an Earth-crushing, hot mass barreling toward the planet is imminent.

What the hell is wrong with me? Why am I not panicking? I think I'm broken.

When the time is right for the feeling of panic, I feel the way I always do. There's a comfort in this. Panic cannot get bigger. It caps off. I feel the same tightness in my chest, the same pulse in my ears, the same inability to catch my breath. And for the first time in a long time, I'm not battling it alone.

I fit in. I don't look weird or out of control to others. Instead, I can stay remarkably calm and provide comfort. I've practiced. This is my normal.

Maybe deep down, I wanted CORE to fail so we would finally have an absolute reason to join the others. If CORE had succeeded, we'd have stayed, and Dominick and Rita would've been lost forever. *I mean, how would we have gotten them back?* The thought that I would want the planet to blow up makes me start to gag on my feelings. *Just call me Nihilistic Girl.*

A flashing news ticker across the TV screen reminds us of our fate: "CORE fails to divert comet. President Lee to address the nation momentarily."

I wonder if the president had two separate speeches prepared, one for victory and one for failure. We're getting the Plan B speech. The apocalypse speech. Must have been difficult to write. I wonder if they've always had the speech available, saved in a vault for the end of days.

On screen, President Lee sits in the oval office wearing a navy blue suit with a crisp white shirt. I wonder how they decided that should be the outfit to tell us we are all going to die. *Why not black for our funeral? Or red for our fiery destruction?* The American flag and the President's flag curtain a dark window behind her. Underneath the window lies a table with framed pictures of the presidential family.

She begins her speech after a quick voice-over introduction:

"Unfortunately, as you know by now, our efforts, along with the United Nations and the wonderful scientists across the world, have failed to divert the comet. At this time, we cannot control or predict the outcome and aftermath of the comet's inevitable impact.

"We suggest that citizens decide for themselves whether they will exit through a vertex or stay and hope to rebuild the world. Our nation began as a pilgrimage centuries ago and so, perhaps, it is only fitting that it ends with another voyage to an unknown land.

"As president, I will not leave. I will stand with my fellow Americans who stay behind to rebuild whatever is left of this great nation. The Secretary of State and his family have chosen to leave through a vertex and will serve as the voice of the U.S. for those who choose to depart.

"Whether you stay or go, we are still one. America will live on. Though we face an adversary greater than any before, though it comes to wreck our world, it will not, cannot, crush the American spirit."

She stands and spreads out the presidential flag to reveal its national symbol for the camera. "The bald eagle, as seen on the flag, has for many years symbolized our nation. The eagle is not only a sign of freedom. An eagle with spread wings is a protector, represented by the American shield it wears proudly on its chest.

"In one talon it holds thirteen arrows; in the other talon it holds an olive branch, symbolizing peace. Notice that the eagle's head faces toward peace. Given two choices, the eagle seeks peace and grace above all else.

"Last, in its beak the eagle holds a ribbon with the motto *E pluribus unum,* meaning 'Out of many, one.' We are still a united nation of states unified as one with an undying, unyielding spirit. Carry that spirit with you wherever you go. We may be many families and friends and faces, but we are one country. We are one world. We are one human race.

"This is not the end, my friends. It is never the end. This is only a goodbye.

"So for perhaps the last time, I stand before you and say, 'Good night. And may God bless America.'"

She salutes the camera.

Benji and Marcus salute back. Mom joins them, crying, but I can't. I try to swallow and breathe. Tears finally start to run down my face. *It's really happening. The end of the world.*

Benji elbows me to participate. I still can't salute. The National Anthem plays in the background. The three of them start singing along. Other patients and families in the room join in an off-tune choir of the famous song, getting choked up at various lyrics.

It's all too patriotic for me. My death will not be patriotic. I'm an eighteen-year-old girl who had plans to be a lawyer and now has to either leave the planet or face a comet. It's not an American tragedy. It isn't even a world tragedy. Death is a solo experience.

When the television returns to frantic media coverage, Benji shuts it off and says, "We need to leave. Now."

Marcus agrees with him.

"What about Dad?" I ask.

"He'd want us to go. He'd want us to be safe. He wanted to give the government a chance, and we did, and they screwed it up. Now he'd want us safe."

Mom nods wearily. I stare at Dad's body breathing gently up and down. I know what Benji said is exactly what Dad would say, and yet I can't do it. "No. I'm not leaving. Not yet."

He shakes his head. "You're an idiot."

"Benji," Mom intervenes.

I can feel my blood boil. "I want to give Dad a fighting chance. He would do it for us. I know he would. There's still, like, two weeks before the comet strikes."

"But we don't have that long. There's gonna be chaos at the vertex sites. Mass exodus. Don't you get it?"

Mom stays quiet, rubbing Dad's cheek. It looks to me like she's saying goodbye.

When no one speaks, Benji yells, "Are you for real? We need to leave! Mom?"

She replies, "You and Marcus can go with Alex. I'll stay with my husband."

I can't leave her alone at my dad's side. "No, I'm staying with you, Mom."

She rubs my shoulder in solidarity. A staring contest ensues between Benji and Mom. I'm not sure who's winning until Benji hugs her.

She sobs and whispers, "I love you. Good luck." Then she hugs Marcus.

Benji gives me a half-assed hug and whispers in my ear, "Let him go."

And I whisper back, "Take care."

CHAPTER 23

QUESTION: What is the name of your planet?

ANSWER: We cannot answer that in order to protect historical integrity.

We've all watched enough apocalyptic movies and read enough stories to know what it's supposed to feel like. The real thing is supposed to be visual, fast, big. Earthquakes. Giant waves. Fire and brimstone. Social chaos. Maybe that's the problem. It isn't some Orwellian nightmare or some Hollywood blockbuster.

This is slow, painfully slow. Invisible, internal.

And then maybe fire and brimstone and chaos.

In these moments, everything other than death becomes personal and timeless and equal.

Benjamin and Marcus Lucas-Blu have been added to the online registry of the departed. People across the globe are leaving in droves. Some people, like me and Mom, are staying, but most are doing it for religious, political, xenophobic, or anti-establishment reasons.

Since it's January 20th, the government is true to its word and releases the last round of prisoners for vertex departure. Of course, there aren't enough guards available to transport them since many of them already left the planet, so several overcrowded buses end up in chaos with prisoners attacking guards before reaching a vertex site. A Massachusetts guard describes one heroic situation, however, where a female prisoner stopped a bus riot and rallied the other prisoners to leave through the Quincy vertex with her. The guard says the prisoner, who couldn't be identified, told her "today was her lucky day." The news plays a grainy video of the prisoners entering the vertex, flagging one of them as a hero in these trying times. From a distance, the prisoner looks vaguely familiar, like she used to live in my neighborhood or something. According to my journal, getting released in the last round means she had a sentence of fifteen years or more. Wonder what she did.

Because of the logistics and the high threat levels, the wardens decide to forgo the remaining eligible releases and go into lockdown. Again, with the lack of staff, prison riots break out all over the country, the gates are forced opened, and massive escapes ensue. So now I am stuck on a planet with hardened, violent criminals who were supposed to be locked up for life possibly running loose and looking for one last freebie kill before departing.

Mom and I camp out in Dad's hospital room. Each day the hospital staff diminishes twofold. All stable enough patients have been discharged, and other patients have been shipped here to merge and shut down other area hospitals. A female doctor takes over Dad's case since his other doctors left. She is the only neurologist left in the hospital.

Are we the stupid ones? The ones who care, sacrifice, and wait? Does that make us weak? Or does that make us strong? I look at Mom sleeping and wonder if she's really staying for him or because of me?

Regardless of the pills I swallow, I cannot find sleep. My medication isn't strong enough for this kind of stress. How can I find a moment of peace in a world of turmoil? How do I accept the chaos?

Later that week, I turn on the television, and it takes me a minute to flip through the channels and see the change. The media is no longer airing feel-good stories. The few channels still airing are focusing on prayer. Yep. Prayer. Different religions, different words, sometimes massive moments of silence, all with the same purpose. Prayer as an answer. Prayer as a savior. Prayer as action. Religiosity blossoms as death approaches. I always figured religions would turn on each other in the end. Instead, they've come together in a weird unity of peace to create some sort of great global spiritual.

God help us. The world must really be ending when religions unite.

And then—the electricity goes out for good. Using my phone, I find out it's statewide and spreading. Once my cell phone battery dies, I'll be closed off from any more media coverage, the countdown app, and the online hologram questions and answers. A cold sensation creeps down my spine.

The hospital emergency generators kick into high gear to keep equipment working. Mom and I play rummy by the window light to pass the time.

I'm mildly distracted until she states, "January 29th."

"What's January 29th?" I ask, playing three kings.

"It's when we leave."

She holds up her pinkie finger. I swallow down the words she isn't saying. *With or without him.*

We seal the pact.

———

On the night of January 27th, Dad fully wakes up. Mom and I cry in relief and hug him together. We don't mention the pact, that he almost missed the deadline. I wonder what would've happened if he had woken up after we left the hospital. No telephones. No way to communicate with us to come back for him. The thought stays with me, and I take a pill to swallow the guilt.

It doesn't take long for Dad to agree to leave the planet. I mean, CORE failed. It's leave or fry. The few doctors left on staff release him to our care. He needs a wheelchair and an oxygen tank since he cannot walk and has residual breathing issues. I explain to Mom that the holograms said they have advanced medical knowledge in their world. As long as we can get him to the other side alive, they can fix him better than ever.

Dad's voice is soft and hoarse. He asks to go home first before we leave. Mom and I struggle to lift him into the car, and he screams in pain every time we move him. Benji should've stayed to help us. If I ever see him again, I'm gonna knock him out for leaving us.

As Mom drives down our street, an eerie, abandoned road stretches before us. There are no cars in our neighborhood. None. Not in the street, not at the curb or in driveways. There's an unnatural stillness in the environment, like time has stopped and we're the only ones moving. We are the last remaining inhabitants on our block. It's like a zombie apocalypse without the zombies.

We spend one last night in our house. We have a real last supper together and eat a large portion of the remaining food that doesn't need heating. I have peanut butter crackers, applesauce, and water. Mom has to help Dad eat by mashing the crackers in the applesauce and lifting the food to his mouth. His coordination is completely off, and he's having trouble swallowing. I hate seeing him so vulnerable. We eat by candlelight surrounded by pitch darkness since the windows in the house are still boarded up. The Christmas tree sits dark in the corner of the living room, a reminder of the way things used to be. The house feels like it died. It's not home anymore.

After dinner, I sit in my dark bedroom, sleepless and eager to reunite with Dominick, Rita, and the others. In the beam of a flashlight, I paint my fingernails a shimmering purple-mauve color called Meet Me on the Star Ferry. It was either that or a metallic rose confetti color called Two Wrongs Don't Make a Meteorite. I went for the hopeful choice for once in my life.

In the morning I pack a backpack. What do I bring to a new world? I grab my journal, a pen, the printouts of Rita's and Dominick's online existence, snacks for the road, the Star Trek shirt Dominick bought me, a copy of Harry Potter and the Sorcerer's Stone, and my dead cell phone. I just want to get out of here. I finally want to leave this world and embrace another.

I wonder what it will feel like to step through a vertex. *Will it hurt? Will it take forever? Will I be able to breathe?*

I swallow a pill because that thought makes me too afraid to leap.

CHAPTER 24

Gridlock. I now completely understand that word.

If I did my math right, we left the house approximately one hundred twelve hours before the comet strike. You would think we could reach a vertex site that's only fifty minutes away in time. But the traffic snakes up Route 24 for miles and miles. We aren't moving. I waited too long to leave. I should have gone with Dominick. Or Benji and Marcus. Or Penelope. I stood in front of that same vertex time after time. I had the chance to live.

On the first day, traffic moves slightly and we have hope. On the second day, traffic comes to a complete stop. By the third day, people ram cars into each other in frustration. There are abandoned cars littering the highway because people have decided walking or riding bikes through plowed snow is faster. Driving has become impossible.

Dad's in a wheelchair. We will have to take turns pushing him through slush and ice for an obscene number of miles.

"Leave me here," he whispers.

"That's not an option," Mom whispers back.

The three of us begin the trek of our lives. We run out of food in our backpacks. My stomach kills. My fingers and toes ache from the cold through my boots and gloves. The idea of frostbite enters my mind, but it's the least of my problems. I didn't think the crowds would be so massive. How could there still be so many people left in Massachusetts? Why did we all stay so long?

By the fourth night, day one hundred eighty-four, January 31st, with maybe two to three hours remaining until midnight, I realize that Benji and Dominick were right. Damn it.

Up in the night sky, a spark grows bigger and brighter.

I'm going to die.

We're all going to die.

CHAPTER 25

We get close enough to the vertex to see it glowing on the night horizon with a tight swarm of people and traffic clamoring around it. People race past us. Pushing, shoving, beeping, yelling. Like a giant net of humans trapping us from moving forward. Some give up and sit on the side of the road, staring up at the sky. Waiting.

Tears fall.

We can't make it through the crowd in time. Wheelchair or not.

When faced with absolute death, I expected to give up at some point. To face my last moments on the planet with no regrets. I expected to give in to death. To slip into the silence in peace. If the planet goes down, we all go, like Dad said once.

But I know I could've saved myself. Saved my parents. Dominick will hate me for not coming. I hope he finds someone to love there. Maybe he and Rita will get together. Might as well. At least they won't be alone.

Up ahead, a teenage boy with gauges in his ears and a guitar sits on the side of the road singing "Hallelujah." His fingers must be freezing. An older woman, possibly his mother since she puts her arm around his shoulder, joins in. I don't know how they can sing. I can't even speak.

I don't want to die. *I don't want to die.*

I don't know if I believe in heaven.

The night sky is ablaze, like the stars have caught fire. A deep rumble, worse than thunder, opens above us.

No one runs and hides. It's inevitable, and we know it. We move forward like rats in a maze fighting for the last bit of cheese, hoping that somehow the sea of people will part and we will still make it in time to run through the vertex. Mom and I keep inching the wheelchair forward even though it's clearly over.

Dad whispers, "I'm sorry."

Mom touches his head. He reaches his hand for hers and she holds it. We stop pushing. We know.

"I love you both. Dearly," Mom says and reaches out for me. "At least we are together."

Dad looks at us with tears in his eyes. "I love you. You are my world."

"I love you," I say to them. What else is left to say?

A brilliant, icy mass blazes forth with a split tail of blue gas and white stardust cascading in its wake. The night sky ignites in a blinding firestorm, a rocky ledge piercing the atmosphere. The stars seem to wink out as the light grows brighter. It's awful and beautiful and my legs tremble at the weight of it. I close my eyes to wait for impact. *Bright blue island sky. White rope hammock tied to palm trees. A book waiting for me.*

Will it hurt? Or will it be so big, so horrible, that I simply cease to exist? Annihilation. No history. None of us. None of it mattered.

And then—

CHAPTER 26

The singing stops. I open my eyes and look around. Everyone stares up at the ominous sky. We cover our ears as a sound wave hits.

The fiery comet streaks in a wide arc across the darkness, a terrifying rainbow that swallows the stars. Night becomes day. It crashes into the earth and smashes into a trillion pieces of light. Iridescent orbs dance and disperse throughout the air, seeming to pass through us, then silently dissipate into thin air.

We wait for the wave of destruction to follow. The stars return and shine over us as always. *Am I Dead? Is this heaven?*

Around me, people stand motionless, waiting for an aftershock, an aftermath, just—an after.

Nothing.

A voice in the crowd yells, "It missed!"

Everyone cheers.

People hug. Dance.

We survived.

We survived.

But how? We didn't change the comet's path. It crashed—I saw it with my own eyes. *So how are we still here?*

Everyone looks toward the nearest vertex. We wait for the hologram's next speech. To acknowledge its error. To apologize. To send our people back.

But the hologram bows and vanishes into the vertex.

Everyone looks around. Everyone stares at their neighbor. We lived.

WE LIVED.

The Earth is fine.

Was always fine.

And then—I see the horrid realization slowly spread to everyone around me.

We all saw it. It didn't miss.

The particles went right through us. The comet was a fake.

The comet was a hologram.

CHAPTER 27

People start screaming and wailing worse than when they thought we were dying. The crowd steps back from the open vertex as it begins to change color and fade. They cannot put enough distance between them and it. Some start throwing anything they can grab at it as they scream and retreat.

The others are gone. Taken.

To salvation? Execution? Or worse?

Dominick. Rita. Benji. Marcus. Penelope. Dan the Drunk Dude. Rogers, the astronaut. The Secretary of State. At least a third of the Earth's population. Maybe more. Maybe a lot more.

What. The. Fuck.

———

We often think of ourselves as smart. Invincible. But we're not. We're all fragile creatures at the mercy of the universe. But we are given choices, and there are moments in our existence where neither decision is right nor wrong. But by virtue of making a choice, it becomes right. It has to be right.

I fumble inside my coat pocket and find a slip of paper.

When the truth is shrouded in fear
and clouded by dreams,

when fact and fantasy become secret lovers,
~~maybe there are no real heroes anymore~~.
Maybe that's when heroes are born.

I look at the waning vertex and remember the last time I was here, Dominick's red Converse slipping through the cracks of time. Maybe it's my overstimulated brain, or maybe it's from watching too many *Doctor Who* episodes with him, but something suddenly clicks.

I blink.

There's no other way that lady could've gotten my words and altered them.

Unless, somehow.

In my future.

I give them to her.

Maybe that's when heroes are born.

And even though I don't fully understand, I know what I have to do. What I will do.

The anger and truth of the situation fuels me and erases the anxiety. For the first time in my life, the decision comes automatically. No time to overanalyze. No time to wonder what Dad or Mom will think. No time to reconsider.

I turn to my parents and state again, "I love you."

They look at me in resolution that we are still a family, alive. But Dad's face drops quickly. He grabs my arm, hard. He knows what I'm about to do. He knows this is a goodbye. For a second I think he's going to stop me.

Then he lets me go.

I set off for the vertex, racing as it starts to flicker into obscurity.

I think of Dominick and Rita and Benji and Marcus and Penelope and everyone else who entered the vertexes across the world. If they are still alive, they'll think they've been saved. They'll be grateful. They won't know we survived. That Earth survived. That it was all a trap.

Panic invades everyone at the site, people stumbling and shoving in the opposite direction—fleeing the vertex. But I've been trained for this. Panic and I are old enemies. I can face it while others are forced to turn away. I run forward. My hood falls back, exposing my ears to the frigid air as my curly hair trails behind me in the wind. I hear Mom screaming my name to stop. But I can't. I need them to know the truth. They deserve the truth. If I die trying, so be it. I promised him.

The crowd flees past me as I jet forward like a salmon swimming upstream. It reminds me of when the hologram first appeared, and people from the train fled as police shot at it. But Dominick isn't here to protect me this time, and I can't lie down and take it anymore. I can no longer be a victim in an attic, no longer another victim in a riot. I wear the bracelet from Rita, the ring from Dominick. This is my team. This is my strength to hold on to despite the incredible fear inside me.

My forearms block and push and shove to create a path through the moving bodies. People scream around me, crying for lost loved ones, pushing to get away from the collapsing vertex. My heart urges me forward, adrenaline coursing through my veins to make it there in time. I squeeze between two abandoned cars, hurdle over toppled barricades, and run and run as my chest explodes in the cold night air.

I dive into the blue swirling unknown before I can reconsider.

The glowing oval blinks closed behind me and disappears from my world. I am trapped inside theirs.

ACKNOWLEDGMENTS

Writing this book has been a labor of love and marks the beginning of a lifetime dream for me. It was not the journey I expected. It's like I stepped through a vertex into the brave new world of publishing, clueless of what would be on the other side. I have so many people and organizations who helped make this version possible.

First, I'd like to thank the wonderful people who physically made this version a reality. To my agent, Ali Herring, for being a huge fan of this series way back in 2016. Ali, you are a godsend! To my new publisher and the creative team at Sourcebooks Fire, especially to Dominique Raccah, CEO and believer in books, thank you for giving my series another chance. To my editor, Annette Pollert-Morgan, thank you for listening to my concerns and helping me see my series in a new and improved light. To Lynne Hartzer, for dusting off the text with me and making it shine again. To TJ da Roza, my first editor at JFP, your genuine enthusiasm for the series made me fight to keep it alive. To the Philip K. Dick Award Committee and the PEN New England Susan P. Bloom Children's Book Discovery Award Committee, for seeing a spark in my pages and making it brighter. To my critique group, Michelle, Peter, and Nichole, thank you for reading my wacky ideas, always taking them seriously, and giving me honest feedback. I couldn't do this without you.

To Eladio, my husband and best friend, for always giving me the space and emotional support I need to dream and think and write without judgment. To Kylee and Chloe, I am so proud to watch you both revel in the arts. Thank you for inspiring me. To my mom, who died in 2020, thank you for being so damn proud of me the first time around. I know you are cheering this time, too!

To all the friends, colleagues, teachers, librarians, students, bloggers, and readers out there, thank you for celebrating with me. I cannot express how much I appreciate all the love and support you gave this series over the years to help it grow. I cannot thank you enough for reading my book and sharing it with others.

They chose survival...but at what cost?
Don't miss

THE FALLOUT

CHAPTER 1

DAY 1

The holograms should've warned us to take a deep breath. Close our eyes. Then again, the holograms should've done a lot of things. Like told the truth.

Traveling through a vertex is like being dragged underwater through blinding ice. The mask of the universe suffocates me, ignoring that I'm a human being who needs oxygen and heat to survive.

I have one thought as I'm pulled through a blanket of frozen light: *This. Is. Death.*

My body fights with my mind as my muscles and lungs scream, *Go back. Please, please go back.*

But I can't go back. I made my choice. I chose friends.

I chose truth. I chose death.

———

Before my chest explodes, before my anxiety has time to kick into overdrive, I am pushed through the vertex onto my hands and knees. Harsh magenta light surrounds me as I gasp for air, my chest filling and collapsing with each deep breath.

I am still alive.

I am still alive.

My heartbeat pounds behind my eardrums, reverberating inside my skull and blocking out all other sound. Despite the utter disorientation, my mind dizzy with the lack of oxygen, I scan the surroundings for any sign of attack as the purple-pink glow around me fades in intensity.

I am in a huge, windowless space that resembles a concrete warehouse the size of Dad's grocery store before the looters on Earth burnt it down. Before my world fell apart. Up ahead, crowds of people from Earth who made it through before the comet disintegrated wait in lines for their turn to enter through unmarked passageways. Holograms identical to the ones that betrayed us stand guard. It reminds me of a massive airport security checkpoint. Destination unknown.

I glance behind me at the empty white space. The metallic blue vertex I traveled through from Massachusetts disappears in the fading magenta light. I have no passage back to my world. *To my parents.*

I gulp air, slowly grasping what I have done, what I have lost. The room spins as my body begins to sweat. *No, no, don't think about it now. Don't fall apart. You can't fall apart. Stay pissed off. Think about the others. They need to know the truth. They need to know it was a colossal trap.*

One of the holograms steps forward and hovers over me. I squint as ambient light filters through its gray uniform.

———

"Hello. Please state your full name and age."

If only the hologram had balls, I'd punch them into its throat.

I find my footing and stand. I open my mouth ready to answer, *Alexandra Lucas, age eighteen.* On second thought, if they can lie, so can I. The less I reveal, the better. Knowledge is power, after all. The first two names I come up with are from *Doctor Who* and *Star Trek.*

"River... er... River Picard. Eighteen."

The hologram gestures forward with its arm. "Welcome to 2359, River Picard. Please wait in line for Decontamination, Evaluation, and Integration into our world." It bows and adds, "May your contribution lead to freedom."

More politeness. A cover for world domination.

As I join the last of the people in line, I watch families and friends hug, relief and gratitude spilling from their naive, worried faces. All oblivious, scared, grateful victims. I bite my tongue to keep from screaming, *Run! Fight! It's all a cosmic scam!* Looking at the holographic guards, I know it's not the time. I need to pretend I don't know the comet was a fake until I uncover why humans from the future sent holograms to trap us here. I need to understand their motive to know my next move. I need to wait. I need to find my friends and family first.

Waiting is the absolute worst.

Standing last in a crowd of loud lines, I examine my body to see if my clothes are ruined, my skin shrunken or decayed, my hair burnt off from traveling through the vertex. Same fleece-lined hooded coat, short black boots, jeans. My curly, long hair not singed away. The silver heart ring from Dominick and the charm bracelet from Rita, reminders of my eighteenth birthday only months ago. My fingernails painted with the color Meet Me on the Star Ferry, chipped by me peeling them as usual. When I chose that color, I imagined reuniting with Dominick on another planet, that it would be romantic even if the Earth had been destroyed in an apocalypse. How sick is that?

My backpack still sits on my shoulders, heavy but intact. The only pieces of my life on Earth carried on my back. Everything I've ever known feels deleted. I'm a conch without a real shell. Vulnerable to the elements. Vulnerable to everything.

Focus. Embrace the rage. I blink away the gathering tears and try to wear anger as an armor instead. A reminder of what they did to us. An ally. If I survived the vertex, then the others probably did too. My boyfriend, Dominick and my best friend, Rita. My brother, Benji, and his new husband, Marcus. Penelope, my grandmother. And everyone else who left before me. They don't know what really happened, and I need to warn them before it's too late.

A sinking feeling in my gut tells me it already is.

At the front of each line, a hologram waves the next person forward into a tall, enclosed rectangular black structure. After a few seconds, the person exits in a daze and enters an adjacent room. I stuff my hands in my pockets like Dominick does when he's nervous, hoping to stop the shaking. *That's where the cloning happens, I bet.*

A white-haired woman wearing purple glasses and a teenager with acne scars and slight facial hair on his chin abandon their spot in line and walk toward me.

"Excuse me, young lady," the older woman says. "Were you the last one through the vertex in Quincy, Massachusetts?"

The noise around us dims. All heads turn from the back of the lines, waiting for my response as if I hold the secret to Area 51.

My voice sticks in my throat. "I think so."

Faces contort with mixed emotions. People cover their mouths in a collective gasp, and the echoing word "no" floats through the room.

I change my answer. "Maybe not."

"We're looking for my daughter." The older woman's voice wavers, and her hands begin to shake. "She's a police officer. Said she'd be right behind us."

The teen turns his back on us, but I see his shoulders tremble with grief. I think I just inadvertently delivered the news that his mother is dead, lost in the catastrophic comet collision with Earth. The one that never happened.

Before I respond, another woman around my mother's age with an infant balanced on her hip touches my arm, full panic in her bulging eyes. "Did you see my husband? Tall, dark hair, chubby, with a big tattoo of an owl on his neck?"

They look to me for answers. I should tell them they're all okay. The Earth is fine. We're the ones who are screwed. But I don't know what's really going on and letting out the truth too soon might give the future humans who brought us here more ammunition. *What if they decide to kill everyone I tell, and the rest of the population stays trapped in ignorance?*

"I'm not sure," I stall. The truth bubbles and burns inside of me like lava in a volcano that's not allowed to erupt.

"Thank you," says the older woman with the purple glasses, tearing up at the last moment. She turns to her grandson. "We'll be okay, Nolan. We have each other."

He throws a black hood over his head to hide his face.

The wife with the missing tattooed husband hugs her baby to her shoulder, caressing its wobbly head. Her chin trembles uncontrollably. She returns to her spot in line but keeps staring back at the area where the vertex disappeared, probably hoping by some miracle another one opens, and her husband runs to find her.

I clamp an invisible vise on my tongue while my heart screams to tell them. Staying silent transforms the truth into something far worse. Like the enemy has inserted its secret inside of me, and I am forced to carry it for them.

Time passes in line as people grieve the loss of loved ones who didn't make it through a vertex. I was the proverbial nail in the coffin, the period on the sentence. I witness and absorb their pain. This is what the future humans did to us. *I need to remember. I need to always remember.*

A hologram waves Nolan and his grandmother forward one at a time into the rectangular black box. I see him pull his hand away from his grandmother, and she covers her mouth and finally breaks down.

One by one they disappear into the next room after they leave the box. If I could plug my body into a socket, the energy running through my veins could probably light New York City.

Soon, all that's left in line is me and one bald, bearded man with dark skin and a nice suit. The last two people waiting for the universe to chew them up and spit them out.

He glances over his shoulder at me. "Tough situation in line. Being the last one saved. You handled it well."

———

That's the most ironic statement a stranger has ever said to me. I don't handle anything well.

"Whole thing is surreal, isn't it?" he says.

I nod. Holding up a heavy lie makes small talk impossible. I'm like Atlas from the Greek myth, carrying the fate of people on my shoulders. Except I'm only a mortal, liable to meltdown and collapse.

He sticks out his right hand and loosens his tie with his left. "Dr. Aiyegbeni, Boston Children's Hospital. My patients call me Doctor A."

I shake his hand. "River Picard. High school senior."

"Waited until the last minute too, huh? Shows something about us. We don't give up easily."

I pick at my nail polish and shrug.

"Or we were in complete denial about leaving." He strokes his salt-and-pepper beard and laughs with a deep chuckle that shakes his upper body. "Are you meeting family here?"

"Yeah." Hot regret builds with each ticking moment. "You?"

"No. I dedicated my life to medicine instead." His shoulders shift in his suit, and I sense regret. "Thank God, we made it through."

I rip off a chunk of polish from my thumbnail.

The hologram at the front of our line waves Doctor A. forward. "Say *PSF OPEN*," it commands.

Doctor A. straightens his suit. "Nice to meet you, River. Good luck here."

"Same to you."

He picks up a duffel bag from the stone floor and marches past the hologram. He even nods politely to it as if it cares. *Oh, Doctor A., how far we've fallen. Already treating our captors with respect. Inadvertent Stockholm syndrome.*

"PSF OPEN," he says.

One side of the rectangular encasement clicks open, and he enters. *I imagine an alien crawling underneath his skin to set up shop, his face twisting in agony when it burrows into his spinal column.*

After several seconds, Doctor A. steps back out looking dumbfounded, then shuffles into the next room. He doesn't make eye contact.

The hologram waves me forward. "What does this thing do?" I ask.

"The PSF is used for decontamination. You must be processed. Decontamination, Evaluation, and Integration."

Decontamination. That word pulls me out of one worry and into another. Memories of hazmat suits and a stinging shower flood my brain. I hug myself for support.

"Do you require assistance?"

"No, I'm fine. I just need a second."

My nostrils burn with the ghost scent of the chemical soap used at the hospital after the first vertex sightings. *Deep breath, hold it, release.* Out of habit I spin my backpack around to get my medication, but the hologram is staring at me. Instead, I strip my coat off my arms to escape the heat. *More deep breaths, in and out. Focus.*

"It has been approximately eighteen seconds. Do you require more time?"

My hatred for holograms grows deeper as my anxiety fades. "No, I'm fine." Maybe if I keep saying that to myself, I'll believe it. "Do I have to go through decontamination?"

"Yes. You cannot integrate with our environment carrying malignant bacteria and harmful viruses from the past. The PSF will scan through your clothing and supplies and eradicate any problematic findings."

PSF. Eradicate. Sounds painful. I exhale. "What's a PSF? Will it hurt?"

"A PSF is a photosonic filter. There is no pain involved. Your body temperature may rise slightly. It is temporary. The sonic vibrations also help relax the somatic system."

It points its translucent arm to guide me into the black box.

Sonic vibrations. Somatic system. My brain is teeming with questions, but I approach the structure anyway. It reminds me of a stand-up tanning booth. Or a black TARDIS. I'll go with that.

"Say PSF OPEN."

I have no choice. It's the only way to find the others and tell them the truth. "PSF OPEN."

One side of the encasement clicks open. I walk inside the tall rectangle with my backpack on my shoulders and my coat twisted in my hands. As soon as the door clicks shut, my heart flickers into mini-spasms. It's not like a tanning booth or a TARDIS. It's like an upright coffin.

Is there enough air in here to breathe? What if this is part of the future humans' evil plan? I'm a freaking idiot—I walked right into another trap. Some futurized gas chamber. What if it's not gas? What if they fill it with water and I drown? Or even worse, what if it's a giant microwave, and I'm dinner?

I bang on the blackened walls and scream, "Open it! Let me out!"

It's too late. A soft hum fills the machine. White light floods under my boots. The light and sound waves penetrate through my clothing, traveling from the soles of my feet, up my ankles, over my calves, to my knees, waist, arms, shoulders, and scalp and then back down again. It repeats the process, and I stop fighting it. The steady hum and gentle vibrations massage my skin, and the light radiates heat to my nervous heart.

It ends too soon. I could live in here. The door clicks open.

"Say *PSF EXIT*, not *OPEN* to leave a photosonic filter mid-process."

"I'll remember that," I say, too exhausted and relaxed to argue. *I'm an idiot; the PSF didn't hurt anyone else—why did I think it was a death contraption?* Thankfully, I was last in line, so no one witnessed my freakout. Public humiliation is my fastest path to a panic attack.

As I move into the next room to join the others, I notice my fingernails have been stripped of all Star Ferry nail polish. Cleaned. Convenient. Creepy. *I couldn't even tell it was happening.*

———

In the evaluation area, the chaos starts slowly, like water coming to a boil on a low flame. It takes a few minutes for the panic to spread. Body language shifts. Faces drop, and the respectful attitudes morph into loud, open questions and outrage.

Doctor A. spots me. "What's going on?"

I shrug. "Can't see over the crowd."

On tiptoe, I strain to get a better view. Even though there's nowhere to go, my mind starts mapping imaginary escape routes. I've had my share of angry crowds to last several lifetimes. Along the far wall, people are being scanned by a color-changing light coming from the walls, floor, and ceiling—without a black box this time. Looks harmless enough. After the people are scanned, they are led to the right side of the room to wait for the rest.

The woman who asked about her missing tattooed husband is scanned next, along with her baby. Right when I think she's passed the exam, a nearby gray hologram snatches her baby from the light scan.

Are they selecting us one person at a time for experimentation? Human guinea pigs? I'll unleash the truth before I let them take me.

"Give me my baby!" the mother screams. She attempts to punch at the chest of the nearby hologram, her fist passing through its translucent body.

Like trying to fight with sunlight.

Another hologram holds her back as the others carry her baby away.

They can touch us, and we can't touch them. How will we ever rebel against the untouchable?

I rush over to the nearest hologram.

"What does that light do? Where are they taking that baby?"

"It is an HME. Holographic medical evaluation. The child must require further medical assistance."

"So, you take a baby away from its mother?"

"Family interferes with proper treatment. The child will be released once they are deemed healthy."

I consider this. "So, what if I have some disease or something?

Do I not get to join your world?" *Do they incinerate me with the trash? Do they toss me down a garbage chute vertex and spit me out into space?*

"You will receive the proper treatment for your medical needs before integration into our world."

You will. No choice. Sounds like a mix of ableism and assault to me.

I watch as the mother screams and pleads and kicks to change the situation. The holograms don't flinch. Instead, blue electric currents swell up from the floor and zap her legs to silence her. Her body collapses and convulses in spasms.

"The BME has been automatically activated," nearby holograms announce in unison. "Please remain calm and orderly as we deal with the infraction."

A clear, crystalline structure encases her body, subduing her in place on the ground. Everyone backs away. Self-preservation.

This is no utopia. It never was.

The holograms signal for us to continue the evaluation process as if nothing happened. We must walk past the frozen mother to face the HME light scan. I walk with my eyes to the ground, waiting for a random bout of lightning to zap me. Even though my hands are shaking and all I want to do is run screaming, I continue forward. I have to.

ABOUT THE AUTHOR

Kristy Acevedo loves to write stories that make people think and give people hope. She is a public high school English teacher, gardener, and *Star Trek* fan. When she was a child, her "big sister" from the Big Brothers Big Sisters Program fostered her love of books by bringing her to the public library every Wednesday for seven years. She lives in Massachusetts with her husband, two daughters, and two cats. Learn more at kristyacevedo.com.

FIREreads

 #getbooklit

Your hub for the hottest young adult books!

Visit us online and sign up for our
newsletter at FIREreads.com

 @sourcebooksfire

 sourcebooksfire

 firereads.tumblr.com